UNFORGETTABLE

S.B. ALEXANDER

COPYRIGHT

Cover Design by S.B. Alexander
Photography: Wander Aguiar
Cover Model: Connor Cushing
Cover copyright © 2023 by S.B. Alexander
Visit: https://sbalexander.com

First Edition: August 2019.
Unforgettable

E-book ISBN-13: 978-1-7329767–6-4
Print ISBN-13: 978-1-7329767–7-1

ALSO BY S.B. ALEXANDER

THE MAXWELL SERIES

Upper Young Adult/New Adult Contemporary Romance

Dare to Kiss

Dare to Dream

Dare to Love

Dare to Dance

Dare to Live

Dare to Breathe

Dare to Embrace

THE VAMPIRE NAVY SEAL: SAM & LAYLA

Paranormal Romance

The Hunted

The Predator

The Union

The Dawning

The Prodigies

The Prophecy

The Rebirth

THE MAXWELL FAMILY SAGA SERIES

Young Adult Sweet Contemporary Romance

My Heart to Touch

My Heart to Hold

My Heart to Give

My Heart to Keep

Maiken & Quinn Collection

STANDALONES

New Adult Contemporary Romance

Crazy For You

Unforgettable

Breaking Rules

Rescuing Riley

Holding On To Forever

THE HART SERIES

Romantic Suspense

Hart of Darkness

Hart of Vengeance

Hart of Redemption*

THE VAMPIRE SEAL SERIES: Jo & Webb

Young Adult Paranormal Romance

On the Edge of Humanity

On the Edge of Eternity

On the Edge of Destiny

On the Edge of Misery

On the Edge of Infinity

Visit https://sbalexander.com/all-books/ to learn more about S.B. Alexander books and future releases. Please note release dates are subject to change based on reader demand and the author's schedule. Subscribing to the author's newsletter or following her on Facebook is the best way to stay updated with planned new releases.

To purchase books direct from S.B. Alexander, please visit https://sbalexanderbooks.com.

1

RYKER

The media room was dark, cold, and downright comforting—an atmosphere I'd come to enjoy over the warmth of the sun or the brightness of light. The music pounded out of the speakers overhead.

Boom! Boom! Boom!

The bass kept beat in time with the rhythm of my pulse as I knocked back another beer.

I couldn't get enough alcohol in my system to erase my nightmares in recent days. I tried like a motherfucker to forget everything that had happened, but nothing worked. My dick couldn't even get hard, and that was equally maddening.

Usually sex helped to take away my troubles. Being buried inside a woman was always my answer. *Not anymore.*

Lucas snapped his fingers. "Dude, the doorbell."

I didn't know how the hell he could hear anything over the music. I swore my best bud wasn't human sometimes.

I blinked away my misery, and like a robot, I stood up. "Robot" seemed to be a good word to describe me lately.

Wobbling, I dropped my beer bottle. It bounced off the wooden coffee table with a resounding thud before spilling onto the shag carpeting.

Like I give a fuck.

Lucas grabbed my bicep, or maybe someone else did. After all, a party was going on around me. In addition to the music, booze permeated the air, and I even sniffed weed. I stuck to the booze rather than drugs. Booze made my mind murky, but drugs fried a person's brain cells.

I growled, listing to one side.

"Couch," Lucas shouted in my ear.

I winced. "Shut the fuck up." Between his deep baritone voice and the bass pumping out of the kickass speakers, my head was about to explode.

"Are you sober, man?" I slurred the words.

Lucas was hardly sober when he wasn't on the football field or in class. Normally, I was the one not getting drunk, but since the plane crash, all bets were off. I had to take away the pain that gripped me by the balls and squeezed so fucking hard that I lost my breath.

As Lucas helped me sit, the room spun, and within a second, I heaved all over the ugly blue rug. If I ever got sober or got out of my funk, I would rip that rug to shreds with my bare hands. Actually, that didn't sound too bad now that I was wiping the puke from my mouth.

"Man, you're a mess. I'll be right back." He snapped his fingers. "Stay with him."

The minute my head rested against the leather couch, nausea rose again. I closed my eyes, but the spinning only intensified.

The cushion dipped beside me, and it felt as if I were on a boat in high seas. "Ryker." The feminine voice sounded like an angel's.

Oh shit. I was dying.

Her small hands landed on my unshaven jaw.

I swatted at her.

"Hey," she protested in the same sweet voice.

Normally, I was a cocky bastard, but lately I was an ornery fuck on and off the football field. I didn't want to be coddled or hear that old cliché that time healed all wounds, something I'd heard a time or two. In fact, my coach, who was worried about me, had said I needed time. I suspected if I didn't straighten up, he would bench me.

Don't give a fuck.

I didn't even care that classes were starting up in another week or that my first football game was next weekend. Sure, I went to practice every morning and every afternoon. The time leading up to a game was balls to the wall. I worked out in the weight room, pushing myself as hard as I could, sweating out the liquor from the night before. I ran drills like I was on speed. I barked at my teammates for no reason. Dickwad was a nickname that was slowly sticking.

But without football, I would be no one. Honestly, the game, the plays, and the crowd lit me up. They always had.

Coach wanted me to take some time and mourn, but I couldn't. Keeping my mind drenched in liquor or running and sweating on a football field was my way of coping. I still hadn't a shed a tear. The day I did was the day someone would have to call in a cleanup crew because the tears wouldn't stop.

"Ryker," she said again. "Let me help you."

Oh, man. The girl was still there.

Other voices in the room buzzed like angry bees.

I willed her and the others to go away.

As if my wish was granted, Lucas yelled, "Everyone out." His voice was commanding and, if I didn't know him, I would have thought it was fucking scary. In fact, his nickname was Hellion on the field.

I opened my eyes, trying to clear my vision, but the room spun like a washing machine on a high spin cycle. Then I laughed and hiccupped at the same time and laughed harder when I turned my head. The girl at my side had the deepest green eyes that sucked me in and made my cock jerk.

Hallelujah!

As that word rang free, so did the song "Follow the Yellow Brick Road." I had a thing for *The Wizard of Oz*. As a kid, I had been obsessed with the movie. While my other friends were into DC comics or Avengers, I was the pussy who wanted anything related to Dorothy. I had a thing for her. I dared not share that with anyone.

I leaned in and narrowed my eyes. Black rimmed her irises, which had specks of gold in them. Emeralds came to mind. Or maybe I was hallucinating.

Footsteps rustled, sounding like a herd of cattle running in fear of getting slaughtered.

"The room reeks of puke," Lucas said.

Suddenly, the music stopped, but not the damn song going through my head: "Follow the Yellow Brick Road."

"Red," Lucas barked. "Out."

I wrapped my hand around Red's wrist. "Not her."

"Your lawyer is here," Lucas announced. "I'm going to make coffee."

Red tried to get away. "I should go." She seemed afraid of me.

Well, I guess she should be. I was well over six feet tall, broad in the chest, with arms built to throw a football, and my hands were bigger than her two put together. Actually, she reminded me of a pixie, tiny and cute.

Lucas touched Red's shoulder. "Haven, if you're going to stay, can you watch him for a minute?"

Her eyes went wide, and her expression dripped of fear.

Don't be frightened, little one. Those words sat on my tongue, but my lips were frozen or numb. I couldn't tell.

Regardless, I repeated the name Haven in my head a few times… Or was it Heaven?

Heavy footsteps pounded on the stairs.

"Can I have my hand back?" she asked politely.

I hesitated just to see what she would do. I was a fucker. I liked to play. I studied her like I was in biology lab, working on dissecting a squid.

She stuck out her bottom lip, and my dick instantly began to harden.

Hallelujah!

That pouty expression she was sporting was making Mr. Dickwad happy.

Interesting. I hadn't had a hard dick since before the accident two weeks ago. I'd always thought that the booze had affected me. Maybe there was hope.

I laughed out loud.

As if my laugh scared her, Haven bounced off as though I had some contagious disease.

Way to go, Ryker. You know how to scare off a woman. Just as well. I didn't need to ruin her life anyway.

Leaning my head against the back of the couch, I closed my eyes, giving in to that merry-go-round feeling. I swallowed several times to tamp down more nausea that wanted out.

Breathe, man.

I inhaled, and the second round of puke crept up my esophagus. To spit out the bile or swallow? That was the question. The shag rug was already ruined. So it didn't matter if I soiled it again.

But I didn't get a chance to puke before the scent of lilacs tickled my nose, pushing down all that acid that was burning a hole in my throat.

"Ryker."

I blinked my eyes open at the same time the beautiful redhead placed a cold washcloth on my forehead.

Heaven.

I licked my dry lips, zeroing in on her wide green eyes.

She gave me one of those sad looks, as if to say it was okay and she knew my pain. But no one knew my fucking pain. No one knew how it felt to lose both of my parents, my sister, and my brother in one day.

Haven patted my face as gently as she could, no doubt afraid I was going to bite off her head or maybe puke on her low-cut T-shirt.

I stared at her tits as though they were my next meal. My hands had a mind of their own. The next thing I knew, I was gripping the tiniest waist I'd ever touched. The women I usually dated or fucked weren't tiny, and that was on purpose.

I liked my women with wide hips and an ass I could grab on to. Lucas always asked me what the draw was. My answer had been and was "Big women own their shit." At least the girls I'd dated had. "They've got meat. They know how to fuck, and they're confident in their own skin."

Society was so screwed up, and the media drove the helm by showing skinny girls in ads and commercials. No one said a lady had to be a size two to be pretty or attractive.

My mom was a big woman, and she had been comfortable in her own skin. My old man hadn't had any complaints either.

I moved a red curl away from Haven's face. "Sunshine, is it dark outside?"

She flinched, almost falling back on the coffee table. I tried to catch her, or I thought I did, but she righted herself, giggling, a sound that was refreshing and soothing.

"I really don't bite." *I do bite. I like to bite.*

I loved to fucking play when it came to sex until the girl was screaming and wriggling and to the point where she was begging me to get her off. I took foreplay as serious as I took a game of football.

"Giggle again." I slurred the words.

She angled her head.

I saw two of her and frowned.

She giggled.

I grinned like a lovesick bastard. "Is your name really Haven?"

She was standing in between my legs and primed to drop to her knees to suck my dick.

You're an asshole. You would definitely scare her off with your dick.

"Yeah." That one word from her lips sounded musical.

"Do we know each other?" I'd never seen her before. Then again, I hadn't seen many people since the accident. But she didn't register as someone I'd seen even before then.

She flicked her head once, knitting her brows, which blended in with the color of her hair.

I touched her lips with the pad of my thumb. She visibly shivered.

Without much thought, I lifted her up and onto my lap.

She sucked in air.

"Has anyone ever told you that you smell like lilacs?"

Shaking her head, she tensed.

"Cat got your tongue?"

On my last word, her tongue snaked out, and if that wasn't the most ball-busting move I'd ever seen, I didn't know what was. Suddenly, I was the horniest quarterback south of the Mississippi.

Her eyes grew as big and wide as the lake in town, and that lake was bigger than the state of Rhode Island. Then she lowered her gaze to my crotch. She fixated on my groin as my dick swelled at a rapid rate between her legs. I would probably bust her in two as small as she was.

She flattened her equally tiny hands on my chest and licked her lips as though she wanted me but didn't want me.

I traced the curve of her perfect-sized breasts that seemed a little large for her small stature. I continued down one side of the V in her T-shirt then switched to the other side.

Goose bumps popped to attention on her chest.

So I did it again. I loved when a woman's body reacted to my touch. With my free hand, I took one of hers and guided it down to my dick.

I never said I was a gentleman. When I wanted something, I took it, particularly when a woman wanted me, and it was clear from the lust in Haven's eyes that she wanted every inch of me.

She froze, fear overpowering the lust in her eyes.

I fixated on her firm, round breasts that I was salivating to taste. Hell, I wanted to taste more than her breasts.

She gave me a shy look as she rested her hand on my dick.

There you go. Now that was heaven.

I closed my eyes briefly, savoring the feel of her squeezing my rock-hard cock.

I gripped her hips and guided her to move her body. I needed friction. Actually, I needed to fuck her. I was a second away from flipping her on her back when a door slammed nearby.

Haven's body went rigid.

I couldn't give a fuck if Lucas saw us.

She scurried to her feet. "I have to go."

And I have to jack off now.

I sat for the longest time after she left, unable to move, knowing I should get my ass upstairs. But getting up as drunk as I was would be a hurdle I wasn't ready to take on.

A slap to my arm jarred me awake. I found Lucas grinning at me with his bulky arms crossed over his chest. The wide receiver's arms were magical on the field.

"What did you do to Haven?" he asked.

"Does it look like I did anything?"

He held out his hand. "You know who she is, right?"

"Can't say I do."

"I'll tell you when you're sober. Right now, get your ass upstairs, drink coffee, and deal with your lawyer."

That was the last thing I wanted to do.

2

HAVEN

Run, Forrest, run! I couldn't get that saying out of my head as I ran out of Ryker's house as though the place were on fire. I swore it had to be because my body was burning up. I felt ready to explode if I didn't get some relief for the pulsating between my legs.

I sprinted one block back to campus and to my dorm. The humidity was unbearable for eleven at night, making my skin wetter and hotter as I huffed and puffed until I was splayed out on my bed with my fingers seated in my panties.

I was a decent girl and got good grades. I did what I was told by my father and tried hard not to talk back to my stepmother who was, in a word, a bitch.

Oh, I wanted to tell her more times than I cared to remember to shove everything and anything up her tight, scrawny ass whenever I was around her. Luckily for me, I'd attended boarding school and hadn't had to deal with her too much, although now that I was back in the great state of Texas, attending college not far from my father's estate, I had to deal with her a little more than I cared to.

I envisioned Ryker's dick as I circled my clit furiously. That pulsing need was so high that I swore I would pass out from my erratic breathing.

Come on, Haven. You're almost there.

I closed my eyes, remembering the feel of his hard pecs and oh-so-hard dick, and I imagined him inside me until a door slammed. My fingers froze, but my pulse didn't. I suspected my roommate, Vicki, although she was supposed to meet me at the party.

Knuckles wrapped on my door. "Haven, are you in there?" Vicki's high-pitched voice came through loud and clear.

I let out a frustrated laugh, removing my hand from between my legs, and lifted up on my elbows. The lust coursing through me vanished. "It's open."

Her brown eyes surveyed my small room, which consisted of a twin bed, a desk, a chair, and a closet—the same setup as hers, only hers was located on the other side of our common room. Unlike boarding school, the dorms at Lakemont University were set up like mini apartments with two bedrooms and a living area in between, although we had to share the one bathroom on our floor with the other girls living there.

"Why were you laughing?"

I crossed my legs underneath me. "You'll never believe what happened to me." I'd only met Vicki when we moved into the dorms, and I had immediately felt like she was the sister I never had.

Like me, she was feisty and bold and had a potty mouth, qualities I never displayed in public. If I did, my father, a Texas senator, would push out a cow. I couldn't do anything to make the headlines or come off as anything other than prim and proper. Otherwise, he would hide me away for the next four years like he had when he'd sent me off to boarding school.

Vicki got comfortable on my bed, tucking her streaked brown-and-blond hair behind her ear. "You got laid?"

I snorted. "I would've if we hadn't been interrupted."

Her eyes grew wide as she waited with bated breath. "Who? Was it Lucas? I wouldn't mind getting him between the sheets."

Lucas was a hottie for sure. He had a head full of wild blond curls that I was sure women wanted to massage their fingers in, tawny-colored eyes, and a body built like a stone wall. Aside from his body, his other attributes didn't give me that mouthwatering feeling I'd had with Ryker.

"Not Lucas but his quarterback."

"Ryker James?" Her high-pitched voice went up two notches.

I bobbed my head, smiling as though I'd won the football bowl game and brought home the trophy. "His dick is huge."

Her brown eyes nearly popped out of their sockets. "So you did fuck him."

"God no. I wanted to, though. The man is all muscle, but he was drunk as a skunk." As horny as I was, I at least wanted him to remember me.

"Tell me every detail," she said.

"Other than grabbing his dick, there's not much to tell. Lucas kicked everyone out. Something about Ryker's lawyer, who showed up."

She checked the clock on my desk. "At almost midnight?"

I shrugged. "Maybe he's going to jail."

"Because he hit that tree? Surely not. It was a tree."

I laughed. "Maybe the tree is pressing charges." Okay, I was outright giddy and stupid at the moment, and I really needed to finish what I'd started before she walked in.

She joined me, and we both giggled uncontrollably. I felt as though I were the one who was drunk.

I caught my breath. "In all seriousness, maybe the chancellor is pressing charges. You know, destruction of property."

She dragged a finger underneath her eye. "Nah. He's a football god. He brings in money for the university. The school isn't going to do anything to mess that up."

I agreed, but Ryker had more to deal with than football. The guy had recently lost his entire family in the blink of an eye.

"The funeral for his family is next Sunday," Vicki said. "We should go."

I nodded. "I think the whole school will be there, especially since classes begin the Monday after the funeral."

Students were slowly filling the dorms, buying books, and getting ready to settle in. Lakemont allowed students to move in up to a week in advance of classes, and I took advantage of that time only because I couldn't stand to be in the same house as my stepmother. Vicki, on the other hand, wanted to get a head start since her family had driven her down from Maine. Plus, she hadn't wanted to miss her sorority open house.

"So we got off track. How did your sorority gig go?"

"Just a lot of excited girls who either looked scared or are salivating to get in. We're meeting again Wednesday if you want to check it out with me."

I shook my head. "No way. I don't want to be tied down or following rules this year. I had my fair share of that in boarding school. This is my time to explore and have fun."

"But you can have fun in a sorority," she protested.

"I beg to differ." I waved my hand around the room. "I like the cave I'm in. And I can have fun without some high and mighty sorority in charge. No offense."

"But you can meet more guys at a sorority party," she said, not sounding that convincing. "Please just come to a meeting with me."

I sighed. She was my roommate, and I wanted to support her. Besides, it wasn't like I was signing up.

My phone buzzed on the bed between us. My father's name brightened the screen.

"What the heck does he want at this time of night?" Something bad must've happened. I knew it wasn't my mother. She'd passed away years ago from ovarian cancer. Maybe something had happened to my stepmom. But he knew how I felt about her.

My phone continued to buzz.

I sighed. "I better answer this. He's relentless when he wants something."

Vicki bounced off the bed. "Come get me if you need me to give him a talking to."

That would actually be a funny thing to see. Vicki was a political science major, and her goal was to work in Washington DC one day. Yet if she met my father, she might decide to change her major.

I wanted nothing to do with the limelight or politics. My major was English with a minor in secondary teaching.

I tapped the screen on my phone to answer. "Yes, Father."

"Young lady, do I have to remind you of our deal?" his voice roared in my ear.

I scrunched my nose. "I don't know what you're talking about." I really didn't. Aside from Ryker's party, I hadn't been anywhere else except to the bookstore and out to dinner, which hadn't brought out the reporters or cameras.

"I have a picture of you dry humping Ryker James. Again, have you forgotten the rules?"

I should've been screaming about his rules, but I couldn't get past dry humping Ryker James. *What the hell?* No one other than him and me was in that room.

Unless… *Oh my God.* After I'd gotten a towel out of the bathroom, some girl with blue eyes and bleached-blond hair had been waiting to go in. I'd lost all sense of my surroundings when Ryker had grabbed my hips and set me on his lap.

"Do I have to put a security detail on you, Haven? I can't have this kind of crap when elections are coming up."

It was always about him and elections, or him and his crazy wife, or him and his golf game. He didn't have time for me unless he wanted to point his finger and tell me what I could or couldn't do. I swore I'd ruined his life by being born.

"Dad, if you so much as have your goons follow me or stick me somewhere like you did when you sent me to boarding school, I'll leak something to the press you won't like."

He lowered his voice. "You wouldn't dare?"

"Do you want to test me?" I was my father's daughter, but I hated that side of me.

Still, we both didn't like scandals, and what I had on him would surely give the media something to dissect and talk about way past the election even though what I had on him was my word against his.

If I were being honest, I wouldn't throw my father under the bus no matter how much I butted heads with him, but he didn't need to know that. Besides, I was tired of living by his rules. Although if I wanted him to foot the bill for my college tuition and expenses, I didn't have much of a choice.

"We agreed, Haven. No media attention. No sororities. Two things. And for Pete's sake, stay away from Ryker James."

"He wasn't part of the deal. And how did you get that picture?" Then something occurred to me. "You have someone watching me. Don't you?"

"Haven." His tone softened. "I have to make sure—"

"Save it, Father Dearest. I don't care about your stupid election. I've barely moved in, and you're already on my ass. You haven't even given me a chance to breathe." Fury blasted through me, and I clenched my teeth so hard, I swore I cracked one. "And I will not stay away from Ryker James." My voice grew louder and deeper. No way was he going to decide who I dated. Not that Ryker and I were an item, nor would he remember me anyway.

"Haven Hale, you will stay away from Ryker James. He's not right for you."

I belted out a laugh. "Oh, so now you care who I date?"

"I do when it involves someone who sleeps around and can't stay sober for one measly minute."

"His family just died. Give him a break. You weren't any different when Mom died." My father had done nothing but drink until he'd passed out.

"I didn't throw parties and fuck every girl that walked. Do you want to be a headline and another notch in his belt?"

Bastard.

He knew I didn't want to be in the papers, or on the news, or have reporters in my face. But I would entertain screwing Ryker just to piss off my father. I might even join a sorority to add to his misery.

"Look, young lady, the James boy is headline news." His voice boomed again. "Don't you throw your idle threat at me again because you know I have the upper hand. Date any other guy, but not him. He's too volatile, and I don't need the headaches." Then the phone went dead.

I grabbed my pillow, covered my mouth, and screamed. My mind was running amok with ideas on how to get under my father's skin without sabotaging my freedom.

Vicki poked her head in. "Is everything okay?"

I threw the pillow across the room. "Someone took a picture of me sitting on Ryker's lap." Heat pinched my face as I realized my father had seen me grabbing Ryker's dick.

She busted out laughing. I couldn't blame her since she didn't know the deal I had made with my father. Nevertheless, I laughed too. I could get as mad as an angry bull, but it wouldn't change my father.

"Maybe I will join the sorority," I said on a sigh. That would get my father riled up.

Vicki plopped down on my bed. "A few minutes ago, you weren't interested. Look, I'm sorry, but I heard bits and pieces from your convo. Care to tell me more?"

"It's an election year, and I have to be a good girl and not bring any unwanted attention towards my father, and staying away from sororities was part of the deal. But as mad as I am, I might just join."

"What will he do if you violate his rules?"

"Hide me away until after the election."

Her mouth parted slightly. "For real?"

I bobbed my head. "My dad can be a royal asshole."

"Do you know who took the pic?" she asked.

"Nope. But I intend to find out."

3

RYKER

A distant buzzing droned from somewhere. I rolled over and grappled for my phone on the nightstand, but it wasn't there.

The buzzing stopped.

Thank fuck.

I rolled back over, stretching out my arm, and my hand landed on something soft.

Huh? I lifted my eyelids, which felt heavier than hundred-pound barbells. The body next to me slowly came into focus—nice, round ass; curves steeper than a black-diamond ski slope; and blond hair piled on top of her head.

She moaned, turning to face me. "Morning, sexy. How did you sleep?"

I wracked my brain as I tried to figure out how the woman got in my bed. My cock wasn't having a problem, though. He was ready to say, "Sit on me," which was surprising, although morning wood shouldn't have shocked me.

The girl smiled, snaking her hand under the covers until she was gripping my junk. "You're awake. It's about time. You were having problems last night."

I should have been mortified that I hadn't been able to get it up with a beautiful girl like her. After all, she was my type—plump in all the right places with humungous breasts that needed two hands for one tit.

My eyes rolled back in my head as she continued to pump me good and strong. I needed a release more than I needed my next breath.

"That's it," I groaned. I lay on my back, giving her full access to do as she pleased. But I didn't want her hand. "Suck me off."

She was between my legs in a second. Then she flicked her tongue over the tip of my cock, and I groaned again, and again even louder when she took me in her mouth, balls deep.

Fuck me.

When she began sucking, I saw stars. I fucked her mouth like I hadn't fucked anyone before. It had been too long since a woman had given me a blow job. Too damn long.

I gripped the sheets as her head bobbed up and down, sucking, licking, and pumping me like a madwoman. Just as I was at my peak, she stopped.

I lifted my head to find she was about to sit on my dick.

Hell no!

"Blow job or get out," I barked in a cracked tone. I wasn't ready to find a condom, and I sure as shit wasn't going bareback in anyone, especially a girl I didn't know. I might be a screwup as of late, but I wasn't ready to ruin my life with the chance of a kid. I had too much going for me. Or maybe I didn't anymore. Maybe I wouldn't be able to play football because of alcohol, fuck-ups, and little desire to get my head on straight to play the game.

The blonde massaged her breasts and squeezed her nipples hard. "Are you sure? I can fuck you like no other girl."

Says you and every other girl on campus.

In my book, a lay was a lay. I'd never found a girl that blew my mind in the bedroom to the point where I couldn't stop thinking about her after sex.

Regardless, I didn't want to piss off Blondie too much since I wanted her mouth back on my dick. "I'm sure you can. But right now, your mouth is all I need."

She sat back, opening her legs and showing me how wet she was. Normally, I would've dived head first, but I wasn't in the mood to please the stranger. I needed to either jerk off or blow my load in her mouth.

She started to play with herself.

My cock jerked as I watched her lick her lips while she circled her clit. Maybe I was crazy, but that just pissed me off. *What happened to giving me a blow job?*

Well, I could finish myself off in the shower.

That buzzing noise started up again.

Blondie closed her legs. "Your doorbell," she said with a huff.

My head was still foggy as I padded across the room and grabbed my sweatpants. "Get dressed."

She sat on the edge of the bed, pouting. "Can I at least finish what I started?" She played with her nipples.

After slipping on my sweats, I tied the drawstring. "Blondie, you had your chance."

She sighed as she looked around the room for her clothes. "My name is Beverly."

The doorbell rang again.

The clock on my dresser blinked 12:00.

Crap, it's noon already? Where the heck is Lucas? He was always up before me. I racked my brain, muddling through last night's events, and tried hard to figure out what day it was.

The doorbell kept ringing as though someone were holding the buzzer down. I was going to kill that person unless it was Coach Chapman. He would turn his hammer on me.

I chuckled out loud. Coach Chapman reminded me of Thor. At least his fists did when he rammed them down hard on a table, trying to elicit my attention or the team's.

"I need you to leave." My boner was completely gone now. I walked out of my room without another glance at Blondie.

I navigated the stairs, not in the mood to deal with whoever was standing on my porch. I knew one thing was certain—it couldn't be the cops. I didn't have any other close family members who could be dead. However, my aunt Kari was due in from England for the funeral. She'd been calling me nonstop to give me updates about her arrival, which wasn't for… Hell, I didn't even know. I'd lost track of days.

As I descended the last step and walked into the foyer, my blood gelled as I scrambled to think whether I'd missed football practice. Maybe that was the reason Lucas wasn't around. I discarded that thought. For sure, Lucas would've dragged my ass out of bed early that morning.

I opened the door swiftly, and a red-haired pixie fell backward onto my bare feet. She was definitely not my aunt Kari.

Red scrambled to stand then swiped her hands down her jean shorts. At the same time, I was blatantly allowing my gaze to roam up and down her petite frame. Her tits were round and perfect. Her tanned legs were toned. Her lips were plump. *Mmm.* I liked plump lips. But she had no meat on her body.

"May I help you?" I asked. *Maybe I can help you get your lips around my dick.* At that thought, he jerked in my sweats.

She brushed her fingers through her hair, her eyes going straight to my crotch. "You can start by not sizing me up like I'm your breakfast."

Tell me not to do something, and I'll do it.

So once again, my gaze took a road trip over her body, slow and sure. "I haven't eaten yet. Are you hungry?" I waggled my eyebrows, hoping she would get my underlying meaning.

She pushed past me and stomped into my house like she owned it. "We need to talk."

The air around her filtered into my nose—lilacs. As if her scent was all I needed, bits and pieces of the night before registered in my murky brain.

Heaven.

"Talk or fuck? Because you were checking me out too," I said, not that my erection wasn't evident.

She gave me a cheeky smile. "I don't do one-night stands."

I grinned. "It's daylight. How about a one-day stand?"

The sun poured in through the open door and the windows in the living room and dining room on either side of us as we stood in the foyer.

She shoved her middle finger in the air. "How many fingers do I have up?"

I closed the door and stalked toward her until she was pinned up against the banister. "Be careful, dollface. That gesture means something completely different to me."

She rolled her green eyes as her chest rose and fell. "You're an ass. And I'm not dollface."

I lowered my head until our lips were a half-inch apart. "What would you like to be called, then?"

"Ew, your breath is disgusting." She flattened her small hands against my bare chest and froze, staring at my pecs.

Not caring about my morning breath, I inhaled her lilac scent, which was doing crazy things to my body.

She worried her bottom lip. "Um. Can you step away?"

"Are you sure you want me to?" *Because I want to fuck your brains out.*

I didn't know what in the hot Texas sun was happening. More memories of her on my lap bombarded me. This chick had some kind of juju that jumped off her and into me.

She finally ducked under my arm. "I need you to focus." She wound her way down the hall and into the kitchen as though she owned the house. "You need a maid and a monstrous fan to blow out the stench in here."

The only aroma I had in my nostrils was her.

I followed her as a door upstairs opened and closed. "I need a blow job."

She snorted. "Ask one of the many women you sleep with."

I didn't recall her being so feisty when she was sitting on me. But I wasn't complaining. I dug strong women. I also loved a challenge, and Red was throwing out challenge after challenge.

When she settled at the granite island, a squeaky voice behind me laughed. "He's rather delicious." Beverly, who I'd forgotten was there, waltzed in, wearing a pair of shorts that could've passed for a thong.

Crazy me envisioned both Beverly and Red in my bed. I shook off the images.

Red narrowed her eyes at Beverly. "You're the girl I'm looking for."

I swung my gaze between them. Maybe Red batted for the other team and was there to give Beverly a tongue-lashing for cheating on her.

Again, images of a threesome slapped me one way then the other.

"I'm into girls," Beverly said. "But sadly, you're not my type."

There went that idea.

I started a pot of coffee, but maybe I should just get a beer—the hair of the dog and all.

Footsteps slapped on the floor as Lucas appeared in the doorway, wearing boxer briefs and not caring that two women were in the kitchen.

Both girls threw their attention to him. Their eyes widened, and their lips parted.

I chuckled. Lucas was a looker. As he stood there with sleepy eyes; wild, curly hair; and a bulge in his boxer briefs, I was sure the girls were clenching their thighs together.

I went about making coffee. Caffeine was as much a necessity as booze.

"What's all this noise?" Lucas rubbed his eyes and farted.

I busted out laughing.

The girls scrunched their noses.

"It already stinks like a dumpster in here," Red said. "Now your shit."

"Have you never farted?" I asked innocently.

Red snarled at me.

Lucas came over to the sink. "What's happening?" The whites around his brown eyes were red.

"No idea, dude. What day is it?"

"Saturday," Beverly and Red said in unison.

I filled the coffeepot with water, sighing. Coach Chapman had given us the day off.

"Did you take pictures of me dry humping Ryker last night?" Red asked Beverly.

My hand froze on the faucet. If I hadn't been coherent, I was now. "Pictures?" I didn't do pictures.

Lucas took over making the coffee.

I ponied up to the granite island, my attention on Red. "Explain." I shouldn't have been so freaked out. I'd been getting drunk night after night since the cops showed up at my door to tell me that the small private jet my family had taken to Tahoe for the weekend had crashed. Since then, I hadn't cared about much, except hoping I could drink myself into a coma and not wake up.

Red pursed her thick lips, looking darn cute. "Do you remember me grabbing your dick last night?"

I shivered. Oh, I was remembering a lot about the night before. She'd been the first girl since that fatal night to get my libido working again.

You got an erection with Beverly.

No. I woke up with morning wood.

You keep telling yourself that. Your dick is fine.

"Why would he remember you?" Beverly piped in. "He certainly remembers my mouth on his penis a few minutes ago, though."

Lucas choked as he set the coffeepot on the machine.

"Are you saying someone took pictures of you sitting on me?" I asked Red. We hadn't been naked and hadn't done anything worthy of a headline that would get me in trouble with Coach Chapman.

The coffee machine began to gurgle before the caffeine aroma floated in the air.

Lucas sat on one of the stools next to me. "What's all the fuss about? You guys didn't do anything that was earth shattering." He stabbed his thumb at me. "Now this guy ramming into a tree with his car while he was drunk? That's something he needs to worry about."

Lucas was right. But Coach Chapman might not see it that way.

I remembered the coach's speech verbatim. *"While you're on this team, you'll conduct yourself in a professional manner on and off the field. And I don't want to see stupid shit in the media. The only headlines I want are winning games."*

"Dry humping," as Red had put it, might not be considered stupid shit to Coach. But as long as the photo didn't get into the hands of the media, I was good.

Then something occurred to me. "Why are you so concerned, Red?" Most girls I knew salivated to get a piece of me.

She whipped her head in my direction. "It's Haven."

That's right. I preferred Heaven, though.

I raised my hands. "Chill."

Her nostrils flared as she set her gaze on Beverly. "If you so much as take any more pictures of me or follow me, I will hunt you down and make sure you're splattered all over the news."

Lucas and I exchanged a wide-eyed look.

Beverly jabbed a red nail into Haven's chest. "I didn't take the picture."

"You fit the description," Haven fired back.

"So do eighty percent of the girls on campus," Beverly said in a tone that could cut ice.

"Ladies," Lucas said in a soft tone. He was always one to referee. "No need to fight."

Haven clutched the strap of her purse like it was her lifeline. "My threat stands," she said to Beverly. Then she stomped out of the kitchen.

I rushed to catch up with her. "Haven, you didn't answer my question. Why are you so upset?"

She stuck out her chin. "You should be as upset as me. Your reputation was poor to begin with, but now you have no idea what you're in for."

The crease in between my brows was so deep, it hurt. With the exception of ramming into a tree on campus with my car, my reputation was great. I won games, and I got any chick I wanted. "What are you talking about?"

She glided out the front door and tossed a satisfied look over her shoulder. "Shape up, Ryker James, or the only championship you'll be bringing home will be a token from your AA meetings."

I stood in the doorway, dumbfounded, wanting to fire off a condescending remark, but the soft hands that came around my waist jolted me out of my stupor.

"Ryker, can we finish what we started?" Beverly asked.

I peeled her hands off me. "That ship has sailed." I guided her out of the house. "See you around." Then I closed the door, locked it, and went back into the kitchen.

Lucas was sipping coffee with a grin the size of Texas stretched across his face.

"What?" I poured coffee into a mug then sat down across from him.

"I can see Haven has you all riled up, as in you want her," Lucas said. "But dude, I would stay away from her."

I chugged the strong black coffee. "My memory is returning from last night. You said you would tell me who she was when I was sober. Well, I'm listening."

A phone rang. I searched the kitchen, as did Lucas.

"It's your phone," he said. "Mine is upstairs in my room."

I found my phone on the desk beside the fridge and answered it. "Yeah."

"You sober today?" Franklin, my lawyer, asked.

I sighed. "So far. But the day is still young. And you shouldn't show up at midnight on Friday during a party to talk business while I was drunk."

"If you made it to your appointments, I wouldn't have to track you down," he barked. "Get your ass in my office this afternoon."

I was tempted to be a jerk and ask, "Or else what?" But the funeral was coming up, and emotions were delicate, even for Franklin. He and my old man had been best buds in college. So I knew he was hurting too even though he didn't show it. Regardless, he wanted to discuss the ramifications of the tree accident, which was one of the reasons he'd shown up last night.

"I'll be there in an hour," I said then hung up.

Lucas put his cup in the sink. "Go. We'll talk later."

Darn straight we would.

4

HAVEN

I finally let out a huge breath as I got into my car. The house stunk like a landfill on steroids, but it wasn't the stench or Ryker's bad breath that had left me gasping for air.

I flicked the air conditioner on high and adjusted the vents toward my face and neck. Yep, I was sweating and not from the hot Texas sun beating in through my windshield. Ryker was a class-A jerk, and a large part of me got off on his vulgar mouth, even more so when my eyes had landed on his growing erection.

Oh my word. I fanned myself with my hand.

Maybe my father was right, and I should stay away from Ryker. Yet every fiber in me was drawn to his hot body, and it didn't help that I was horny. It had been more than a year since I'd had sex.

I started the car and got on the road. I would've run back to campus like I had the night before and taken care of my libido, but Father Dearest had requested my presence at home that day. I'd asked him what he wanted, but he'd just replied, "We'll discuss it when you get here." Regardless, he didn't like anyone to be late for his meetings. He'd been trained in the military to always arrive fifteen minutes early.

I checked the time on my dashboard, calculating how long it would take me to get home. My father had an expansive ranch forty-five minutes north of Lakemont University. Considering that it was Saturday and traffic would be minimal on the freeway, I had about five minutes to spare.

My phone rang, shutting down the radio and automatically connecting.

"Haven." Vicki's voice came through loud and clear. "How did it go?"

I slowed at a stop sign and saw the freeway sign looming up ahead. "Not sure. The chick who I suspect outed me was there."

"Who is she?"

I pressed on the gas. "Crap. I didn't get her name." I'd been so focused on Ryker that I hadn't even asked who she was.

"Is she his girlfriend?"

"He doesn't have girlfriends." At least that was the rumor, and if my father was right about Ryker sleeping around, then the blonde was just another conquest. "I guess I'll have to ask Ryker." Which meant another visit. Maybe my subconscious purposely hadn't asked her name so I could see him again.

No way.

If I did return to his house, I would give the man what he wanted.

So what? You want him, and one time wouldn't hurt him or you.

She snickered. "Damn the bad luck." A beat of silence ticked. "Oh, wait. Come to think of it, he's giving a talk at the sorority meeting on Wednesday."

Ryker didn't strike me as a guy who gave speeches.

I zipped onto the freeway, merging with traffic. "What about?"

"According to the resident assistant of our dorm, the football team does a fundraiser every year for a local charity. And they make the rounds to get the word out. So you definitely should come with."

I might not be available if my father locks me up.

I hadn't given Vicki an answer when she'd asked the night before, but now I really wanted to go, more out of curiosity and the fact that I could corner Ryker in public. I didn't trust myself alone with him.

Watch it, missy. Someone could be snapping pictures of you and him again at the sorority event.

Well, I wouldn't be sitting on his lap, and surely just talking to the man couldn't piss off my father.

"Okay, I'm in."

The sound of her clapping boomed through the speakers. "Great. Good luck with your dad today. I'll be here if you need me."

Despite the warm feeling flooding my chest at how Vicki and I were becoming good friends, I didn't want to involve her in my personal dealings with my dad. No one needed to be subjected to my father and his scrutiny.

"I'll see you later." I hit the end button, and music filled the car. I sped down the highway, passing vehicles, listening to Jason Aldean. I had to clear my head before I got home. Or rather, I had to prepare myself for the meeting with my father, and God only knew what interaction I would have with my evil stepmom. I was sure she would have something to say about the picture of Ryker and me.

My mind drifted back to Ryker and the blonde who'd barely been dressed. *Why didn't I get her name?* It was so unlike me. My father had taught me at a young age to know a person's name because it was essential to know who I was dealing with.

Pfft. I'd failed big time on that lesson. The campus was big, but considering she was tied to Ryker, I could get more info on her. Besides, I could spot her in a crowd.

I eased up on the gas as I changed lanes and headed off the freeway. After another fifteen minutes, I was pulling into Hale Ranch. Father had had the name engraved prominently on a white wooden gate at the entrance.

I slowed to ten miles an hour, looking out at the horses grazing in the distance. One of my father's hobbies had been racing horses. He'd given up the hobby when my mom died seven years ago. She'd loved horses and the race circuit. The Kentucky Derby had been one of her favorite times of the year.

I wheeled down and around the large fountain in the circular drive then came to a stop just past the front door. I wasn't staying long. Otherwise, I would've parked in my normal spot in the back, where the ten-car garage was located.

I checked myself in the mirror to make sure I appeared put together. The last thing I wanted to hear from my stepmom was how bad I looked. Then again, I could be perfectly made up, hair in place, clothes pressed and crisp, and she would still drop some derogatory comment about how I dressed or that my makeup was too much or not enough.

Why are you trying to please her? That was a question I always asked myself. But I never had a good answer. Deep down, I wanted my father's approval, and if she approved of me, then maybe my father would pay more attention to me or at least show me he cared. The word "love" wasn't thrown around in my house, not from my dad anyway. My mom had always told me she loved me, but my father didn't seem to have a loving bone in his body. I wasn't sure if he even told his wife he loved her.

Marriage to him was a contract, although I remembered pieces of my childhood when my mom was alive, he'd doted on her. I hadn't seen him show that kind of love to his current wife, although I'd been away at boarding school since I was thirteen.

I got out of the car with my purse in hand then rolled back my shoulders. Before I ascended the stairs to the portico, the front door opened.

Arlene Long Hale, former Miss Nevada, bleach blond hair, Botox lips, fake breasts, and a scowl that would scare away a puppy. "Haven." Her voice was sweet and salty, heavier on the salt. "So good to see you."

Liar.

Be nice, Haven.

I swallowed all the cuss words streaming through my brain. "Arlene." I brushed past her and into the foyer, which reminded me of the mansion in *Gone with the Wind,* my mom's favorite movie. "Where's my dad?"

Baxter, her white Maltese, came trotting in, wagging his tail.

I went to pet him, but Arlene snagged the dog as though I were about to poison her baby. "Your father is out back, finishing up lunch. Roya will bring you some food."

"No, thanks. I'm not staying long." I didn't want to be there any longer than necessary.

I started for the veranda when she said, "Your father and I can't have any distractions with elections around the corner."

I stiffened, not turning to look at her. "Good to know I'm a distraction."

Her heels clicked on the shiny, white tiled floor until she was facing me. "What you were doing in that photo was inappropriate for a young lady."

And what I found my father doing behind your back was equally inappropriate. But I dared not voice that out loud unless my father pushed me to my limit. I might not out him to the press, but I had no problem hurting Arlene.

Keep walking.

My legs came unglued as I meandered through the house. My flats pounded on the floor as I passed the palatial rooms on both sides that faced the wall of windows overlooking a stone veranda.

My father read from his iPad with a glass of whiskey on the table. The French doors were open, allowing the hot summer breeze to flow in. My father preferred the heat and humidity to an air-conditioned space, which was odd since Arlene hated the Texas heat. But my father ruled with an iron fist, and as much as Arlene came off as a hardcore bitch, she didn't go against my father. What he wanted, he got.

I kissed my father on the cheek, set my purse down on the granite tabletop, then eased into one of the thick-cushioned chairs beside him.

He studied me as he exchanged his iPad for the whiskey. "You look good."

I arched an eyebrow, regarding my lookalike. We both had red hair, although my father's color was brighter than mine. He also had more freckles sprinkled across his nose and cheeks than me.

"I'm listening," I countered. He wanted something. He hardly complimented me.

His green gaze roamed over my face. "You do take after me."

I let out a small laugh. "You're just now coming to that conclusion?" As much as I hated some of his qualities, I wouldn't deny we were much alike. "So what do you want that you didn't want to tell me on the phone?" If I knew my father, he wanted to see my body language when he delivered whatever news he had on his mind.

"I want you to move back home," he said. "Arlene has your room ready."

I popped up. "No, thank you."

He caught my wrist. "Sit." His tone permitted no argument.

Smart man.

If he had told me that on the phone, I would've hung up on him. Regardless, I obeyed. I kept my posture straight, head up, and shoulders back. I schooled as much of my ire as I could. As much as fighting with him was fun at times, I wasn't in the mood.

"You don't trust me to keep my end of the bargain," I said more than asked.

He sipped his whiskey. "Frankly, I don't. Your behavior so far has been embarrassing."

"I beg to differ. Who do you have following me? Is she one of your conquests?"

He glanced over his shoulder at the open door. "I have my resources."

Oh, I was certain he did. "Blond, big boobs. Ring a bell? Just so you know, she's sleeping with Ryker."

He continued to sip his whiskey, not giving me any indication I was getting under his skin, which gave me reason to pause. I normally could get a reaction out of him, and at the moment, I was glad he'd requested my presence. Body language told the real story if the person wasn't good at keeping his cards close to his vest.

"She's Ryker's style," he said with a grin.

I wasn't sure what I'd been expecting as far as a reaction from him, but that grin said it all. Blondie was his spy.

"What's her name?" I asked.

He placed his glass on the table. "I don't keep up with who Ryker sleeps with."

The question then was how did he know Ryker's type? On second thought, I knew the answer. My father had security goons to find info on people.

At the moment, I had to find a way to convince Father to let me stay in the dorms, which was far more important than Ryker James.

"I'm not moving home. You didn't want me around when I was a teenager, so don't start now. Besides, the drive is too long with rush-hour traffic. I told you I would keep my end of the deal."

He scrubbed a hand over his chin. "Then you won't give me flap when I tell you to stay away from Ryker James."

A scream was ready to break free. "Why are you worried, Dad? You just said blondes are his type. Last I checked"—I grabbed a wad of my red hair—"I'm not blond."

He resumed drinking his whiskey. "Let's recap then. No media attention. No sororities. And no Ryker James. Any violation, and you'll force my hand."

"What is your hang-up with the guy?" I dug my nails into my thighs. "And don't tell me media attention. I know you. You're hiding something."

"Why can't my reason be that I care about my daughter?"

I would love to believe him. "Since my mom died, you've never even told me you loved me. So, sorry if I don't believe you care. And give the guy a break. He's going through some hard times." I rose. "Don't worry, I won't ruin your election. But I am going to go to parties. I'm going to date. So get used to that."

He stood, pursing his lips. "Then I have your word?"

I let out a heavy sigh. "I want nothing to do with Ryker James." My tone was convincing only because I wanted to leave, and maybe a small part of me didn't want the hassle that came with Ryker and the women he screwed.

Father's jaw loosened. "Good. I also need your help."

I laughed because he never, ever needed my help. He had aides to do his dirty work.

"I'll be in DC the week after next," he said. "And I made a commitment to speak at Woodcreek High's government class. I need you to take my place."

My face twisted. "Since when do I fill in for you? Get one of your aides to do that." It wasn't that I was afraid to speak on the topic. I knew the government. But asking for my help wasn't in his nature.

"Mr. Bridges is a good friend. He asked me for a favor. When I told him I had a change in my schedule at the last minute, he thought it would be a good idea to have you speak to his class."

I knew the teacher. He'd been over for dinner on two occasions when I'd been home from boarding school during the summer. He'd been impressed with my knowledge of not only the government but my ability to speak two foreign languages. I'd spent one summer in Spain and one summer in Greece. So I'd taught myself both. In fact, a friend from boarding school and I had learned together.

"If I do this, then you owe me." My father didn't do anything without bartering or bargaining. *Like father, like daughter.*

He draped his arm around me. "Don't give me any reason not to owe you."

Spoken like a strict father.

5

RYKER

Ikicked out my legs as I sat across the large mahogany desk that was OCD neat for a lawyer. Then again, Franklin Bumgardner had been put together since I could remember. He wore a blue Armani suit, diamond-studded cuff links on his pink-striped shirt, and a tie that had a fancy design with paisleys and polka dots.

Franklin scribbled on a legal-sized pad. "You look like shit."

I laughed. "How do you know? You've been writing since I walked in."

"I saw you, and you stink like cigars and booze."

That was the aroma parties were made of. Nevertheless, I smelled my underarms. My deodorant was working. It had to be my breath. Haven had scoffed at how bad it stank, but I had taken the time to brush my teeth before I came.

Haven. The chick had been stuck in my brain since she'd stormed out of my house.

I'd been turning over her sassy comment about how I needed to shape up. I wasn't ready to do anything but wallow in misery. Unless she'd experienced the death of a loved one, then she wouldn't know what I was going through.

"Whatever. Can we get on with why I'm here?" I didn't want to waste my Saturday sitting in a lawyer's office.

I had no idea what I was going to do when I walked out of there, but I sure as hell wasn't going to be all happy and shit like those people in the park outside his window who played fetch with their dogs or lounged on a blanket, eating lunch without a care in the world.

Franklin set his expensive Mont Blanc pen down and sat back in his leather chair, moving his jaw from side to side as he scrutinized me.

I hated when his black-as-night eyes screamed how disappointed he was in me, much like my old man's had. I'd known Franklin since I was a tyke. He and my dad had been best buds in college. They'd both studied law. However, my dad hadn't practiced even though he'd passed the bar. He'd had a vision of starting his own company with products designed for the oil industry. Texas was rife with oil refineries, so he'd thought he could make more selling a good product rather than chasing down thugs and witnesses since he'd been into criminal law.

Despite that, he'd hired Franklin to handle all the legal stuff that came with a company.

"So is partying how you mourn your family?" His scowl said I was a loser.

"Fuck you. If you must know, I'm still numb to it all. I don't see you crying your eyes out."

He steepled his fingers near his mouth. "I've got work to do."

I popped forward and rested my elbows on my knees. "So do I." *Beer to drink.* "I have football games to win."

"You think you can throw a football?"

Hot and sticky anger made me tense. Now that my old man wasn't giving me the third degree about football, Franklin was. While I occasionally didn't mind the kick in the ass every now and then, I wasn't in the mood to hear his condescending tone.

"Leave football to me. I'll leave the law to you. Now we can get on with things." My head was starting to pound.

He sighed, briefly closing his eyes. Then he lowered his hands to the desk, sitting up straighter. "I'm sorry, Ryker. I'm so fucking pissed that he's gone, that your family is gone." His eyes filled with tears.

I inhaled deeply, hoping that all the emotions I had buried deep inside didn't come spewing out. Because once they did, I wouldn't be able to play football or do anything else.

I threw my head in my hands and grabbed onto my hair. Pulling every strand out seemed like something that would take away the pain in my chest.

How do people deal with this shit? Losing anyone, let alone the four people who had meant the world to me, was beyond my comprehension.

I needed a drink.

I blew out a loud, audible breath as I eyed the tray on his credenza that banked the side wall.

Fuck it.

I hopped up and practically sprinted like a damn alcoholic who needed a quick fix.

"You think that's wise?" Franklin asked.

I uncapped the expensive single-malt scotch with one hand and flipped him off with my other. "I Ubered over here." No way was I driving. The alcohol from the last two nights was flowing freely through me. So given the bad luck I'd had, I was treading lightly. If I lost the opportunity to play football, then I would bury myself with my family.

He sighed. "Pour me one too."

Now we were getting somewhere. "Coming up."

After pouring two glasses of my father's favorite Glenlivet Scotch, I handed Franklin his and returned to my chair.

We toasted to my father, mother, sister, and brother.

Once the aged twenty-one-year scotch hit my taste buds, the tension eased even more.

Franklin's tight features loosened after a couple of swigs. "The chancellor sent over what you need to do to atone for your accident on campus."

I couldn't wait to hear what the crusty old man had to dish out. I was sure he wasn't banning me from football. The sport drew in lots of money, and without me, he might not have the draw of fans in the stadium. After all, football was a religion in the great state of Texas.

Franklin set his drink down, flipped open a folder, and scanned it. "After the funeral, you'll be assigned to a clean-up crew with the maintenance department. You'll do ten hours of penance, which is nothing if you ask me."

"Like I have time to keep campus clean. He realizes I have football and away games and parties to attend, not to mention the football fundraiser."

"You're the big man on campus, and he can't just let this slide. You know as well as I do if your old man was here, he would make you do much more than that. And let's not forget, the chancellor could make your life hell. He could've called the local police, and then you would've been slapped with drunk driving. Seriously, Ryker. I'm not going to tell you not to drink. If I were in your shoes, I would probably drink myself to death. But you've got a future in football. Don't fuck that up."

I had never been a good little boy. But when it came to football, I was the perfect player. I was the one spurring my team on. I was the one who played like my life depended on it. But that was all before I lost everything. Now my world had changed. I was in shock and denial —the first stage of grief. At least that was what Lucas had told me the other day.

Well, I would be in that first stage for a long time. No matter what, I couldn't see past the shock.

I downed the rest of the scotch. "I'm out of here." I was done talking about how not to be a fuck-up. I had a case of beer at home with my name on it.

"When is Kari coming in?" Eagerness threaded through Franklin's words.

I arched a brow. He'd always had a thing for my mom's younger sister, who had never married.

"She's flying in Monday," I said. "She's staying at my parents' ranch. Are you ever going to ask her out?"

Franklin was a handsome forty-five-year-old and had been divorced for five years. He had thick black hair with streaks of silver in it, black eyes, a strong jaw, and a close-shaven beard. Sometimes my parents' circle of friends had ribbed my dad by saying I resembled Franklin more than him. But my mom had put that teasing to rest. She'd gotten so tired of hearing everyone say, "Are you sure Ryker isn't the mailman's son, or even Franklin's?" She'd actually produced my birth certificate as proof. Besides, my old man had had dark hair too. His hadn't been as black as mine, but I'd gotten my color from my mom.

Franklin knocked back the rest of his scotch. "Long-distance relationships don't work."

"Wait. Are you saying you and my aunt had fun between the sheets?" I grinned. "Way to go, man."

His jaw hardened. "None of your business. Which reminds me. Stay away from Haven Hale."

"Come again?" I knew the Hale name. Everyone did if they lived in Texas. But surely, the Haven I'd met couldn't possibly be related to the man I was thinking of.

Franklin took a sip of his drink. "Haven Hale, the daughter of Texas Senator Eugene Hale?"

I squeezed my eyes closed for a second. "He has a daughter?"

So that's who she is. That's what Lucas was trying to tell me.

"Are you living under a rock?"

"I don't pay attention to politics. You know that. The politics I get into are on the football field." But I did know the Texas senator and my dad had practically been enemies.

James Enterprises had violated one discharge water permit due to a piece of equipment that had failed. The company had paid the fine and had the equipment fixed, and all that had been needed was the final release from the water board to start up operations.

Unfortunately, that seal of approval had been a slow train from

China. Two months of calls and visits to the water board headquarters had gone unnoticed. Franklin had been told that the water board had a backlog of cases with a short staff, which might've been true until Franklin found that Senator Eugene Hale had stopped all permits from being released. My dad had lost customers and tons of money, and he'd had to let employees go.

Franklin rose and poured himself more scotch. "I shouldn't bust your balls. Not many people know about her, or if they do, they don't bring her up. The out-of-sight and out-of-mind thing. Anyway, he hid her away. Her school years were spent in a boarding school in Michigan. I only know this because of the turmoil between your father and hers."

I squinted at the sunlight spilling in as my mind spun like a tornado with ideas on how I could piss off the senator.

Franklin returned with the bottle of scotch and filled my glass a quarter of the way. "I see your wheels turning. Don't bring his daughter into this fight. And let's not forget he can ruin your football career. He's a number-one alumni donor to the university."

The senator might donate money, but in no way could he sway Coach on who played the game and who didn't.

Crossing my ankles, I kicked up my feet on the edge of the desk. "He also hates me, which I don't give a rat's ass about. But please let me have some fun."

Franklin leaned against the edge, swatting at my feet. "Down, boy."

I took a gulp from my glass as I lowered my feet. "Are you talking about my feet or my dick?" Because I was thinking the latter when it came to Haven. Man, it would be so much fun to get my rocks off and piss off her old man at the same time.

"Ryker." Franklin warned. "Leave Haven alone." The dude was in my head. He should be. He knew me well.

I pouted as something occurred to me. "Why are you bringing up Haven, by the way?"

He loosened his tie. "Her father sent me the pic of her on your lap, and I did see her when she walked out of your place last night. Look, you don't need the media attention. And it's an election year, so the media might be in her face. Besides, you've got a ton of shit on your plate. Don't add more."

That last line meant "Don't give me more work to do."

"Haven could be a nice plaything," I mused.

Franklin rounded his desk. "Forget her."

Easier said than done.

6

———

HAVEN

The Delta Sigma Pi sorority house was swarming with girls of all shapes and sizes. Their voices ranged from squeaky to low baritones as well as other pitches in between. Perfumes mixed together, creating an aroma that made my eyes water. I didn't use a fragrance other than body wash, shampoo, and my unscented sensitive-skin deodorant.

I weaved through the crowd, following Vicki to the front of the room where the podium was set up. One thing I'd learned quickly at school assemblies was never to sit in the front. It called attention to me, and I tried to stay out of the spotlight.

I tugged on Vicki's thin blouse. "I don't like the front."

She frowned over her shoulder. "But we get the best view of the football team."

"Are you forgetting that I don't need the attention?" I'd told her about the conversation I'd had with my father. I didn't need to stand out in the crowd.

I kept silently repeating, *I want nothing to do with Ryker James.*

The minute I'd walked out of my father's house was the minute I knew those words would eat me alive, especially since I couldn't get the hot football god out of my darn head. Or rather I couldn't get his penis out of my head. It was thick, large, and I would bet definitely in charge when he was in the bedroom. A lusty chill made me quiver. My darn body would give me away the minute I laid eyes on him.

Maybe part of me was strongly attracted to him now that my dear old dad didn't want me anywhere near Ryker James. Rebelling was in my blood. But I had to be levelheaded. I didn't want to move home or, worse, have my father send me away to some out-of-state university. When he and I had discussed colleges, he'd suggested any except those in the state of Texas.

"It's best if you attend a small private college where you can get more attention from the teachers. The larger ones can't give you that." What he'd really meant was that either he or his wife didn't want me around.

But I'd won in the end. I'd convinced him that having me closer to him was one way to make sure I didn't bring media attention to the family.

Stupid me.

Still, Texas was my home. The weather was great, and I didn't want to live anywhere that had eight feet of snow like I'd endured at boarding school in Michigan. More importantly, Lakemont University had one of the best teacher programs around.

Despite that, my curiosity was piqued. I had to know what my father wasn't telling me about Ryker. Sure, the guy was popular for his performance on the field and, no doubt, in the bedroom if what the women on campus said was true. But I got the feeling something else bothered my father about Ryker. The only thing I could think of was the election. But that didn't make sense. How could Ryker affect my father's election?

Just ask Ryker.

I doubted the hunky jerk would tell me. All he cared about was screwing women and drinking.

Vicki snapped her fingers. "Did you hear me?"

I blinked. "Sorry."

"You look like your wheels are turning." She tapped my head. "Reminiscing about a guy with a big dick?"

I busted out laughing. "You're not helping."

"Screw what your father says. Find out if the rumors about Ryker in bed are true. Seriously, it's not like you two behind closed doors will be captured on a cell phone video."

"Pfft. You would be surprised at how creative reporters or even nosy people can get when they want a story or a bribe." I wouldn't put it past my father to do something as screwed up as take pictures of Ryker and me in bed. The thought of us tangoing between the sheets sent another lusty chill through me.

She scanned the room as though she were about to tell me a dirty secret. "I recently heard some girls in the dorm talking about Ryker. His nickname is the Foreplay King."

I snorted. "Please. He comes off as a *fuck 'em and leave 'em* kind of guy."

It was her turn to snort. "How do you know?"

"Fair enough. Can we stop talking about him?" Just the mention of his name was getting me all hot and bothered... or maybe irritated.

She tugged me to two empty chairs at the end of the first row by the arched windows.

Whew! At least I could jump out of the window if I had to.

A brown-haired, heavily made-up girl tapped on the mic on the podium. "Everyone find a seat."

I glanced around the room as I fidgeted. "I'm out of here as soon as this is over."

Vicki patted my leg. "Sure."

I arched a brow at my roomie, debating whether to sandblast her for treating me like I was lying. But I didn't want to make a scene. Instead, I checked my phone for nothing more than to keep busy. I wasn't one to sit around, especially when I hadn't been thrilled about attending this event, although if I were being honest, I did want to see Ryker.

The air in the room was charged with excitement, laughs, and whispers as girls took their seats.

I leaned into Vicki. "How many girls in here want in Ryker's pants?"

She gave me a sidelong glance then rolled her brown eyes. "All of them."

That was just another reason to stay away from Ryker. I didn't want to compete with other women. But just as that thought careened across my mind, I spotted Blondie, the girl I'd met at Ryker's place. The hackles on my neck went up. I would kill her if she was following me.

I nudged Vicki. "Don't look now, but that blonde who was at Ryker's house is standing off to our left."

Of course Vicki leaned forward to look. "The one dressed in a tight pink blouse, showing off her big breasts?"

"Yep." Upon further inspection, I noticed that Blondie cleaned up well. Her hair was styled on top of her head in some fancy twist. Her makeup was painted on perfectly, and she had meat on her bones. Then I zeroed in on the phone in her hand, and I tensed.

Vicki shook her head. "That's Beverly Sims. She just became president of this sorority. So she's the one your father knows?"

"I'm leaving." The last thing I needed was my father to see me at a sorority meeting, especially one that included Ryker James. That was a double whammy and sure to get me locked in my room at the ranch.

Vicki swung out her arm. "You'll be noticed for sure. Wait until the meeting is over. No one will be able to snap a pic with you in the front row."

I begged to differ since Beverly's phone was in her hand, ready to go.

You're here to listen. You're supporting a friend. Your father can't chastise you for that.

Beverly sashayed up to the podium, adjusted the microphone, and swept her blue gaze around the room. Her eyes landed nowhere near me.

I was sure she was looking for the football players. Then a wild thought flashed before me, and my radar shot up. Vicki could have lured me there because she was helping Beverly get dirt on me for my father.

Stop panicking.

"Hello, ladies," Beverly said. "Welcome. Tonight is our official kickoff. Over the next couple of weeks, we'll be in recruitment mode. So those who are serious, make sure we have your name on the list."

The women tittered and whispered.

"Once we're done here, the party begins downstairs. Now on to the official announcement from the football team, the one you ladies are dying to hear." Beverly stared toward the back of the room, as did most of the women, who turned to check behind them, including me.

I didn't see one sign of Ryker or his right-hand man, Lucas, or any big guys for that matter.

Maybe the night was looking up. I came. I saw. But I didn't conquer. That should make my father proud.

Stop worrying about Father Dearest. You're here to have a good time. You told him you were going to parties. It's not like you're signing up to rush for Delta Sigma Pi.

I crossed one bare leg over the other, smoothing my hand down my frayed jean shorts. While most of the women in the room were dressed in what I called clubbing clothes, I wore jean shorts, a camisole beneath a low-cut, see-through blouse, and leather sandals strapped around my ankles.

The natives were beginning to get restless until a door squeaked and men's voices peppered the air.

A girl in the back shouted, "In here."

What I wouldn't give to be in the last row at the moment. *Easy in. Easy out.*

"Up here, gentlemen." Beverly's voice boomed through the speakers.

I held in a laugh as I watched Ryker's face twist in either disgust or a look that said, "no way am I getting up there with that woman." Or maybe he was gawking at her voluptuous breasts.

"He doesn't like her," Vicki muttered.

"Don't let him fool you," I whispered. "He would probably screw a hole in a wall if he was desperate."

"That man would never be desperate with all the women waiting in line," a girl behind Vicki said.

I should tell her to mind her own business, but I couldn't argue with her point. She was spot-on. Nevertheless, the six-foot-four, black-haired, gray-eyed quarterback strutted up to the podium in holey jeans that hung low on his hips and a well-ironed, buttoned-up white shirt stretched across his broad chest. His swagger exuded a sense of purpose.

He certainly owned his shit, and I found my body reacting in a way that was going to surely get me into trouble. I moved my foot back and forth, silently repeating, *I want nothing to do with Ryker. I want nothing to do with Ryker.*

Maybe if I kept reciting that over and over, my subconscious would kick in and make it happen. The problem was that I knew what was below his belt. I knew how he felt in my hand, and Father's rules or not, I was doomed.

Ryker positioned himself next to Beverly, who had her hand on his bicep.

The urge to growl was strong. But he'd had her in his bed once, and I was sure he would again. After all, as my dad had said, she was Ryker's type.

I switched my attention to Lucas and three other large men who stood next to him.

Lucas was dressed like his buddy, also wearing jeans and a button-up shirt. In fact, the other three men, who were equally buff as Lucas and their quarterback, wore similar outfits. I wondered if that was the football team's uniform of the day when they were off the field.

When Lucas turned in my direction, he winked at me.

I scrunched my nose. What was that for? Did he know something I didn't?

Vicki leaned in. "Lucas just winked at me."

Get over yourself, Haven. You're not the only girl in the room.

I did a quick check of the other women behind me. All had dreamy smiles as they salivated for the big man at the podium.

"Ladies, how's everyone doing?" Ryker's voice came through raspy with a slight Southern drawl.

Yummy!

The girls squealed, and words flew around the room.

"Better when I come over to your place tonight," one girl shouted.

"Are you into threesomes?" another asked.

I wanted to shout that he was. After all, I vaguely recalled him saying something along those lines.

Ryker grinned wide, and I realized he was stone-cold sober. Yet the night was super young.

"Now, now. My buddies and I are here to make our fundraising announcement, which I'm sure you're going to go fucking crazy over."

"I want you, Ryker," a girl in the back screamed.

"Tell us already," a mousy voice said.

Beverly was trying hard to contain her smile. No doubt she'd known that the women were going to freak.

The voices in the room elevated.

Ryker lifted his arms halfway and pushed down on air with his hands as though he were dribbling two basketballs at once. "Easy, girls." Once the room was dead silent, he started again. "How do you feel about an auction?" He waved his hands at his buddies. "This year, you'll have a chance to buy a date with some of us from the football team."

The ladies began squealing and talking, and I would bet the pheromones bouncing around the room were at an all-time high.

I wanted to say that mine were, but the idea of paying for a date didn't thrill me, although I might drum up some cash if it were for a good cause. I could bid on Ryker.

"What charity are you supporting?" I asked even though no one could hear me.

"I hope I can snag a date with Lucas," Vicki said. "Maybe this is your chance to get Ryker. Your father couldn't diss you for supporting a charity."

Want to bet?

"Ladies," Ryker said.

The room quieted.

"What charity are you giving the proceeds to?" I asked again.

Ryker's stormy-gray eyes whipped my way. He studied me for a long second, angling his head one way and then the other as his gaze roamed all over me. And for some reason, I wanted to strip down right there and show him I had the goods even though I wasn't his type.

I prodded him with my eyes. "Cat got your tongue?"

His buds chuckled. Beverly snarled at me.

That's right, bitch. Say something now, and I'll snap a picture of you and send it to a news outlet with the headline "Bleach Blonde Sleeps Around." Okay, I was a bit crazy at the moment.

"Haven Hale," Ryker said as though he were mortified over my name.

Yeah, there was something between dear old dad and the hunky quarterback.

"Please stand," Ryker said to me without tearing away his gaze. "And join me up here."

I crossed my arms over my chest. "I'll pass."

One or two or maybe the entire crowd exclaimed, "Are you nuts? Get your ass up there, girl."

Vicki nudged me. "Go."

I sighed loudly. "If you have something to say, Ryker, say it. I'm not your dog to command."

Ryker looked at his buds. "Hey, boys. What if we make the fundraiser a little more interesting and add a girl to the auction?"

The men nodded their approval, grinning.

"Pick me too," other girls screamed.

Beverly touched Ryker's arm. "Surely you could pick someone else other than her."

I popped up. "My name is Haven Hale." My snarl was lethal as I glared daggers at Beverly.

"Are you related to Senator Hale?" asked a girl somewhere behind me.

For someone who wanted to blend in, I was doing a bang-up job.

I turned to address the crowd. "My father is Senator Hale. I'm not rushing for a sorority. Ryker James is a jerk. And I am not up for sale."

A few phones flashed, and I noticed one girl holding her phone up, hopefully videoing my outburst so my father could see that I hadn't violated any agreement.

I turned to Beverly. "Make sure that gets back to my father."

Ryker's eyes went wide.

"I'll meet you back at the dorm," I said to Vicki.

Then I carried myself out with grace as I'd been taught to do when I was in the public eye.

7

———

RYKER

As soon as I stepped away from the podium, a swarm of women crowded around me. I felt like one of the dudes from that show *The Bachelor*.

"Ladies," Beverly said into the mic. "Head downstairs. Music is on, drinks are flowing, and the guys will hang with us for a while." She pierced me with her blue gaze. "Right, boys?"

I hadn't planned on staying, but I just might if Haven was lurking somewhere nearby. Man, seeing her squirm and stomp out of the room like a four-year-old who hadn't gotten her way had put a smile on my face. I liked her spunk. I was also finding I liked messing with her, which was new for me when it came to the opposite sex. Normally, women were only in my bed, not in my head. And Haven in my head was better than thinking about the funeral, which was coming up on Sunday.

I eyed Lucas, Erik, Vincent, and Ajax. They all gave me a nod.

"We'll be right behind you," I said to the sea of women, who were chomping at the bit to sign up to be in the auction.

One look at Haven, and my mouth had gotten in the way of my brain. Man, those legs of hers had appeared silky, and her breasts... I hadn't been able to think straight. The woman was small, and now that I wasn't drunk or hadn't just woken up, I'd noticed her tits were bigger than I remembered.

Not only that, her old man had come to mind the minute I'd laid eyes on her, and that had fired me up. The more I thought about the senator and how he'd made my dad's life hell, the more I wanted to do the same to Senator Hale.

Beverly touched my arm, pushing her chest into me. "You really shouldn't consider the Hale girl."

I knitted my brows. "And why is that?"

The five of us guys waited eagerly to hear her answer.

"She won't bring in much money. No one in this state wants to piss off the senator."

I did.

"I beg to differ," Lucas said. "She would bring in more money than Ryker alone."

Beverly laughed. "I doubt that."

No question I would bring in some dough for the charity, and so would my brethren. But I had to side with Lucas. A senator's daughter would bring in a lot, especially one who was beautiful, fun as far as I could tell from my interaction with her so far, and she carried herself well except for the childish exit she'd shown us earlier. Plus, Haven didn't seem uptight like Beverly.

"So did you take the picture of Haven and me the other night?" Not that I cared as much as Haven, but it would be good to know who Beverly really was just in case she decided to throw me under the bus. Plus, I was curious what the senator was up to. Maybe he'd had someone at my party to get dirt on me. Maybe he was campaigning to have Coach remove me from football.

She deadpanned. "I've done no such thing." Then she wiggled her ass toward the exit, her heels clicking on the wood floor. "Don't be long, boys. We have many hors d'oeuvres to choose from tonight." She sounded like a well-trained madam.

Once the five of us guys were alone, Lucas pulled out his phone. "She's lying, or she knows something."

No shit.

"You need me to get the truth out of her?" Erik panted. "I'm ready to tap that. She'll talk."

I plastered on a half grin as I glanced at Erik. Our tight end was big and wide, and if he didn't have a woman in his bed every night, he had the shakes. He lived for football, booze, and sex—in that order. He was also a loyal team player and friend.

"Well, I for one would like to see the senator lose this year," Vincent said. "My parents hate the man." Vincent, our team kicker, who we called Vin, had a snarl on his angular jaw.

I didn't follow politics. In fact, I wanted to stay as far away from politicians as I could, but I knew why I hated the man.

Lucas walked over to the window with his phone to his ear. "I'm checking on one last thing for the fundraiser. I'll be right back." He was our organizer and party planner, and the role suited him.

"So what's up with you and the Hale girl?" Ajax, our running back, piped in, sounding a wee bit concerned. "I would stay away."

I chuckled at the military wannabe with a dark high-and-tight haircut. "Really? Have you seen her tits?"

Ajax slapped me on the shoulder. "Your women have meat in other areas."

"You want a piece," I said. "Don't you?"

He shook his head. "Not going there, dude. Politics and me don't get along."

"I feel ya," I said.

Lucas returned, running a hand through his tamed wild curls. "The other sorority on campus is available tomorrow night. So we should tackle that after practice."

I pulled out my flask from the back pocket of my jeans and took a swig.

Vincent, the leanest of the five of us, asked, "What time is the funeral on Sunday?"

I took another swig. The last thing I wanted to do was think about that. My aunt Kari, who had shown up two nights ago, had been a blubbering mess as we'd gone through photos for the funeral director. The bodies weren't in any shape for open coffins.

Suddenly, I wanted to puke. So I drank more.

Lucas slapped Vincent on the back of the head. "Did you have to go and open your flapper?"

Vincent regarded me with sad blue eyes. "Sorry, man. If you told me, I forgot. And my mom has been on me to find out. She wants to be there for you."

"Noon," Lucas said.

"I really don't know how you're upright, Ryker," Erik added.

Fuck if I did either. Just thinking about the plane crash and what that would've been like was enough to keep me drinking for a lifetime. The other morbid part of all this was that I was supposed to be on that plane. I'd had every intention to fly to Tahoe with my family for that weekend. My dad had had a meeting with a client in Reno and had wanted to make the trip a family getaway.

I shivered.

I'd had practice, which was the only reason I hadn't gone. Coach had a rule that no one missed practice before the first game unless there was a good excuse, like a sickness or, as in my case, a death in the family.

I took another swig of the expensive scotch. I'd swiped the bottle from Franklin's office. Actually, he'd given me the go-ahead to take the bottle. I hadn't argued.

"Let's kick back. Enjoy the festivities." My voice came out scratchy, so I cleared it. "I want to see if my dick works anyway." Change of plans. Instead of drowning in just booze, it was time to add a woman to the mix.

The four of my friends busted out laughing.

I glanced at my crotch. "I'm serious. Aside from the mornings, I can't seem to get him to work."

Vincent raised a reddish eyebrow. "Drinking isn't helping."

"Nah," Ajax chimed in. "It isn't the alcohol. He just needs someone to give him a run for his money. He's always had it too easy with women."

"What are you?" I asked. "A psychologist now?"

Lucas started for the door. "Come on, boys. We need to change the mood."

For sure. I capped my flask and headed downstairs.

A myriad of scents overpowered my nostrils. Perfume permeated from the females, who were gabbing and laughing, while music droned in the background. But no one smelled of lilacs. Nevertheless, I searched for the redhead, but I didn't get far before a handful of women crowded me and hands were all over me. I felt like a celebrity who had just gotten out of the limo on a red carpet.

I lifted my arms over my head. "Ladies, let me get a drink. Then we can hang out."

Erik stuck out his big paw and grabbed me. "He'll be right back." He tugged me from the hungry women and had to swat off more as we headed for the coolers that were situated near a table of food on the back wall. Erik snagged two beers and handed me one. We toasted, our bottles clanging together.

"Thanks for the rescue." I knocked back a huge gulp of the ice-cold liquid.

Lucas, Ajax, and Vincent had gotten hung up, talking to three pretty ladies near the door.

"I got your back," Erik said.

I knew the entire team did, which sent a warm feeling spreading throughout my chest. The football team was my family now. Sure, I had Aunt Kari and an uncle, who hadn't talked to my dad for years. My father and his brother had had a falling out many years ago. My grandparents were no longer living. So Aunt Kari, Franklin, and my friends were the closest I would get to a family.

"You may have to pick me up off the floor one day," I said more to myself. That was the truth.

Coldplay belted out of the speakers.

Erik bobbed his head of shaggy brown hair. "Anytime, man."

A beat of silence stretched between us as we drank our beers.

Half the ladies watched Erik and me. Some were debating if they should come over and talk to us. *Freshmen, I suspected.* They were always the shy ones until they got the lay of the land.

"You know," Erik said, "I count eleven guys and thirty or so girls. We could play choo-choo train. Line all the girls up while us boys sample a kiss from each of them. It will give us an idea which one we want to fuck tonight."

I practically spit out my beer. "Fuck yeah. That sounds like a great game. Where did you come up with that?"

He hiked a broad shoulder. "My old man told me he played that as a kid in his garage with girls in his neighborhood. Only there were more boys than girls. So the girls sampled the lineup."

I continued to look around, deciding if I wanted to sample any of the hors d'oeuvres, as Beverly had put it. But when my gaze landed on the door, my lips split into an cheeky grin.

Erik chuckled. "I guess you've chosen yours."

I didn't move as I watched Haven weave through the crowd. She was probably looking for that girl she'd been sitting next to.

"She has an aura about her that I can't put my finger on," I said. My dick knew it too.

"Man, she's a politician's daughter." Erik shook his head. "That's not a good quality for you."

He might be right, but she had something that was drawing me to her.

8

―――――

HAVEN

Every voice in my head told me to go back to the dorm. But like an idiot, my curiosity pushed me to go back inside the sorority house, pushed me to see Ryker, and pushed me to ask the question I needed an answer to.

I spotted Ryker before he had a chance to look my way. It was hard not to spot him or any of the guys with him. All of them stood above the rest of the crowd. Ryker, though, was by far the one that commanded attention. I loved the way his gray eyes were clear rather than cloudy and droopy like they had been the other night or even the other morning when he'd pinned me against the bannister.

I want nothing to do with Ryker.

Vicki was talking with Beverly. The hairs on my neck rose. Maybe my theory that Vicki had partnered with Beverly and my father was true.

Stop being paranoid. Vicki is your roommate.

I wouldn't put it past my father to have set her up specifically to watch me.

Vicki wants to get into this sorority. That is all.

A girl with short brown hair came up to me. "Haven. Right?"

"Who's asking?" My tone came out rude.

The girl seemed like she belonged in high school. Then again, I was only nineteen and could pass for a senior in high school too. I suspected she was a freshman like me.

She held out her hand. "I'm April. I live in your dorm."

We shook. No sense in being impolite to someone I didn't know. That wasn't my nature anyway unless someone got under my skin, which Ryker was doing by standing feet away.

"Haven," I replied even though she knew me. After tonight, everyone would know that Senator Hale's daughter attended Lakemont University. *So much for keeping a low profile.*

"So why did Ryker pick you out of the crowd?" She angled her head, batting long black lashes. I would guess she was wearing the fake synthetic kind that many women had done by a professional.

I was into makeup and self-care, like regular manicures and pedicures, but lashes weren't my thing.

"Not sure," I said. That was another question I wanted to ask Ryker and one of the reasons I'd decided to turn around and come back into the sorority house.

April brought the wine glass in her hands up to her red lips. "So you really think he's a jerk?"

I chanced a look at the quarterback, and when I did, my heart rate took off.

Those swirling, stormy gray eyes were piercing through me as though he were ready to lay me out flat and do something to me that I was certain I would beg him to do again and again.

April looked with me.

Ryker lifted his beer bottle. The guy next to him said something to him, and Ryker grinned, biting his lip.

I was about to answer April when the guy next to Ryker pushed through the crowd, heading right toward us.

"He's hot," April said.

The guy had a wide chest, big arms, unruly brown hair, and seductive brown eyes. Yeah, I had to agree.

"Ladies, I'm Erik." He regarded me. "Big guy over there"—he stabbed a thumb toward Ryker—"wants a word with you."

I rolled my eyes. "If he does, then he can walk his tight butt over here just like you did."

Erik gave me a cheeky smile. "Maybe you are the right girl for him."

"What's that supposed to mean?"

"I'm April," the girl next to me said to Erik.

Erik sized her up. "I see you're all sunshine and flowers."

I held back another eye roll. "Cheesy line." Although April was wearing a flowered dress.

April giggled.

I guess his line worked. The two started talking, and Erik held out his arm to steal April away.

Instead of beelining it for Ryker, I started toward Vicki, who was now talking to another blond girl.

"Haven," Vicki cooed. "I'm so glad you came back."

The blond girl narrowed her beady dark eyes at me as though I were the enemy. Maybe I was since Ryker had made a spectacle of me. Then she left.

"It seems the women in here already hate me," I said to Vicki.

Her hair was twisted up off her shoulders, and she dragged a hand over the side of her head, moving a wispy strand out of the way. "You know, Ryker is staring at you."

I had my back to him, and I could almost feel his heated gaze. "So what did Beverly have to say?"

"She was going through some of the events for recruiting us freshmen. She's a nice person."

"She works for my father." Irritation rode my tone. Then something occurred to me. "The night of Ryker's party, you had a sorority meeting. I'm assuming Beverly was there." If she was, then she couldn't have been in two places at once.

Vicki frowned. "She left early. She got a call and then apologized to us because she had to take care of something."

Bingo.

Vicki's eyes widened as though a light bulb came on. "Maybe she isn't so nice."

I didn't get a chance to respond because large hands gripped my waist from behind. The song ended, as did the voices.

Lips were on my ear. "You didn't answer me." Ryker's voice was husky as hell.

"Take your hands off me." My voice barely came out even.

He tugged me to him tightly. "Ladies of the house, listen up," he announced in a loud voice.

Every hard inch of him pressed into my backside, and a heat like no other rushed to pinch my face.

"Haven has agreed to participate in our auction. So tell all your guy friends or even your gal friends if they swing that way. I'm sure she'll go for a pretty penny considering who her father is."

My whole body tensed, anger overpowering the lust coursing through me.

Ryker held me to him as he twirled us around as though we were slow dancing. "That's right. Take lots of pictures. Show your friends what's up for grabs." He was truly and utterly the biggest jerk in the state of Texas.

I tried to pry his arm from me, but he only pressed his body into mine. "Don't fight this, dollface. You've got the goods that men want."

"And so does every girl in here," I snapped back. "Now let go of me, or your balls will feel my wrath."

"I rather enjoyed your hand on my dick the other night," he whispered in my ear. "Care to replay that night back at my house?"

"In your dreams." That was a lame line. But I had no other words because I did want to feel him again—without clothes, though.

Yes, please.

Vicki leaned into me. "People are snapping pics."

I swallowed my ire and dug deep for my sweet Southern voice. "Ryker, baby, can you please let go?" *Then shove me against the wall and have your way with me.*

He loosened his hold slightly. "I like the word 'baby' off those lips of yours. Feel that?" His erection poked into me.

Holy hell. I'm doomed, not only by him, but my father is going to have a cow.

My face burned like a wildfire.

Lucas came up beside Vicki. "Dude, we're heading back." He flashed his tawny-colored eyes at me as though he were trying to say he was sorry.

"We're having a fundraising meeting next week," Ryker said in my ear. His damn voice was giving me goose bumps. "Lucas will send you the details." Then he let go of me.

I had every intention of telling him to stick that fundraiser where the sun didn't shine, but he left without so much as a look over his shoulder.

Suddenly, I felt used and needed a shower, or maybe fresh air to get my lungs working again.

Vicki fanned herself with her hand. "Man, that was hot."

I glanced around the room, finding all the women with jealous looks on their faces.

So much for not drawing attention to me.

I went in search of a beer or hard liquor, whatever I could get my hands on first—anything to calm my nerves, anger, and lust, although the latter wouldn't go away until Ryker James had his way with me.

9

———

RYKER

I covered my face in my hands as I sat in the front row of the church. I felt dizzy, nauseated, and so fucking angry. I didn't know how I'd gotten from the house to the church. My body was about to give out.

I didn't want to look at the pictures on the four coffins in front of me. I didn't want to listen to the speeches that a few of our close family friends were about to deliver. I didn't want to hear anything except my sister Leigh's voice, or my mom's, or any of them.

"Ryker, you got to be kidding me." That had been Leigh's line many times. "You can't go out with girls who only want you for your body."

I would laugh and ruffle her hair with my hand, something I'd done many times since she was a kid.

Franklin was on my left, bouncing his knee. My aunt Kari was on my right, rubbing my back, which did nothing to take away the pain I was feeling.

Since I'd left the sorority party four days ago, I'd been a hermit. As the funeral drew near, I couldn't function. I couldn't even go to practice like I'd thought I could. I had thought running, working out, and throwing the ball would help, but I'd barely been able to get out of bed. Plus, I didn't want to see the sorrow on the faces of my teammates.

"Take the week off," Coach Chapman had ordered. "Actually, take as much time as you need."

I would need a lifetime before my head was screwed on properly again. Still, I hated that I hadn't played in our first game of the season, which had been the day before. It was probably best for the team, although the loss yesterday wasn't a great way to start the season.

"Why don't you sit back?" Aunt Kari asked softly.

I shook my head, lowered my hands, and eyed the woman who resembled my mom only younger. "I can't. I'm not sure I can even sit through this whole service." I'd thought about bagging the funeral, but then I would be a schmuck. I would be dishonoring my family, and my old man would be so disappointed.

"Ryker," Franklin whispered as the sounds of rustling behind me scraped along my nerves. "Are you going to be able to speak?"

I straightened, staring at my brother's picture. His gray eyes stared back. The boy had only been fourteen, into football, baseball, and basketball. He'd loved video games and learning how to play golf with my dad. He'd even loved to cook, something my mom had taught him.

"Probably not." I had a speech ready, but I couldn't get up there and talk or say one word.

"I'll let the pastor know, then," Franklin said.

"Have you even cried yet?" Aunt Kari asked. "You need to let out all the pent-up emotion."

Easier said than done. "I'm dealing." If she or Franklin brought up that liquor wasn't a way to cope, I would go off like a madman.

Franklin shifted in his seat. "This place is packed."

I was afraid to look. I knew the football team would be there. I knew Coach Chapman would be too. I also suspected several of my friends from high school had shown up. I'd gone to school in this town, and my family and I knew lots of folks. When I'd been offered a free ride to one of the big universities in California, I'd turned them down.

Whether or not I had a full ride, I'd chosen Lakemont University, mainly to stay close to my family.

Lucas had also factored into my decision. We'd promised each other since high school that we would play football together. The university in Cali that had offered me a free ride had turned him down. Money was tight for him and his family, and the tuition at Lakemont was reasonable for in-state students.

Some of my friends had thought I was crazy not to accept a full ride to a NCAA Division I school. But as much as I wanted to play football, I also wanted to be around my family, and I could do both right there in Lakemont.

A hand gripped my shoulder from behind. "How you holding up, man?" Lucas asked.

I turned slightly, my gaze darting around the room. *Wow!* Standing room only.

Suddenly, I couldn't breathe. I jumped up and ran around the altar to the restroom. My family and I had never been devout churchgoers, but Mom and Dad had attended this church occasionally.

Once inside the restroom, I splashed water on my face.

The door squeaked open before Lucas appeared. He was dressed in a sharp black suit like me, with a white shirt and black tie. His wild curls were slicked back.

I ran my hands through my hair, blowing out a huge breath. "I can't do this. I've got to get out of here." I loosened my tie, ready to tear it off. The fucking thing felt like it was choking me.

Lucas handed me his flask. "Drink. I shouldn't be giving this to you, but you need to calm your nerves."

I poured whiskey into my mouth. The smooth liquid slid down my throat and kept going, warming my chest. My pulse was all over the place. My stomach felt like someone had used me as a punching bag, and my legs felt wobbly. The small amount of whiskey did nothing to ease any of that.

Lucas grabbed the flask before I emptied out his stash. I'd left mine at home for good reason.

He took a swig. "We should go back out there." He pocketed the flask inside his suit pocket.

I clutched my chest. "You've got to stay at my side." He was like a brother to me, and honestly, he was the only one close to me that I could trust.

He glanced at me in the mirror. "I'll be there when you fall."

Tears threatened. "When I fall?"

"It's going to happen," he said seriously. "And that's okay. Come on. I hear the preacher talking."

All I heard was a droning sound, like bees were buzzing in my ears. Nevertheless, I followed him out, my breathing labored. I swore I was about to pass out. That fall he'd just spoken of was about to happen.

I shuffled behind Lucas at a slow pace, and as I looked out at the crowd, my gaze fell on *her*. Haven's red hair was pulled up off her shoulders, exposing her long neck. Those emerald eyes were glued to me. Suddenly, "Follow the Yellow Brick Road" started in my head.

What the hell is happening to me?

Haven blinked slowly, sadness washing over her. Or maybe it was pity. Either way, that noose around my neck loosened for a mere second until my eyes landed on the man beside her. Then I was clenching my fists.

The senator had no business being there. I whipped my head to Franklin.

The preacher stopped talking, diverting his attention to me.

Franklin rushed up to the gray-haired preacher and said something to him. Then his long legs carried him over to me.

Lucas and Franklin escorted me back toward the bathroom, but instead of the restroom, Franklin went into the preacher's office.

As soon as the three of us were inside, Franklin closed the door.

I paced like a madman. "What is Senator Hale doing here?"

Franklin unbuttoned his suit jacket. "The whole town is here. So let's not cause trouble today."

"He doesn't belong here," I said with a growl.

Franklin could never find evidence that the senator had been responsible for making sure James Enterprises didn't operate. All Franklin had was an employee's word that had worked at the water board.

Lucas clutched my arm. "Relax. Franklin's right. Everyone, including the senator, is paying their respects." Lucas handed me his flask again.

This time, I did drain all the alcohol in the hopes that the effects of the liquor would calm me.

Franklin raised an eyebrow.

I shrugged. I didn't give a damn about etiquette or how it would look if I stumbled out of the pastor's office, although the small amount of whiskey wouldn't affect me in the least.

I wiped the back of my mouth with my hand. "If he so much as makes one comment that I don't like, then you'll have to hold me back."

Both of them nodded.

I took in a few big gulps of air then stalked out, returning to my seat, not looking at the senator or his beautiful daughter.

Franklin and Lucas followed.

I nodded to the preacher.

He started in on his sermon about loved ones, death, and grieving. I tuned him in and out as my aunt held my hand. Before long, five people paraded up to the altar, one after the other, to talk about Leigh, Randal, Jr., and my mom and dad. Each one talked about a memory or experience with one of them. It wasn't until Leigh's best friend, Jessica Davis, mentioned my name that I zeroed in on what she was saying.

"Ryker, you were Leigh's hero," Jessica said as tears streamed down her face. "She wanted to be everything you are—strong, determined, dedicated, loving—and you are what she deemed as special. The love for your family. The love you gave them."

Don't cry, dude. Don't do it.

Aunt Kari squeezed my hand. "It's okay. Let it out."

No fucking way was I about to be the biggest crybaby anyone had ever seen. *Be a man, my dad would say. Tough it out. Show people that you can handle anything. Because when they see you sweat, when they see you break down, they'll pounce on your weakness.*

But I didn't feel strong at the moment. I didn't have a determined bone in my body.

Jessica moved her dark hair off her shoulder, sniffling and smiling at me. "Leigh's wish for you is to find someone who will give you that deep love that you have in your heart."

Holy fuck! My head was dizzy. I felt as though Jessica were Leigh. My sister had said that very line to me a time or two. My response had always been that I would find someone when the time was right. But football was my love. Football was my future. Hell, it was my life. I had no room for anything else other than football and family.

Jessica blessed herself. Then she hung her head and walked off the altar.

My legs moved, but my brain was still on neutral. I wrapped my arms around Jessica. "Thank you."

She hugged me back with every ounce she had and bawled into my chest.

I rubbed her back. "Leigh will always be with us."

She flashed cloudy dark eyes at me. "I loved her so much."

I was a second away from bawling with her until she ran back to her seat.

Five minutes later, the service ended. People I didn't even know lined up to pay their respects by saying a prayer in front of the coffins.

I sat there, watching, while Kari and Franklin stood off to the side near me, shaking hands with people. Some tried to talk to me, but all I could do was nod. I was numb from head to toe with Jessica's words on repeat, and I knew that in about an hour, we were about to bury my family.

The lilac scent gave Haven away before her soft hand landed on mine. "Ryker."

Heaven.

Her voice was like an angel's.

She closed her hand over mine. "I'm so sorry for your loss."

I turned slightly, lifting my gaze to hers. Those fucking emerald eyes were mesmerizing, bewitching, and enchanting. I sighed as though she were the air I needed.

She leaned in and kissed me on the cheek with soft lips then whispered in my ear. "I know how it feels to lose someone. If you ever want to talk, come find me."

My heart settled a beat until a large, looming man stood over us.

His green eyes narrowed at me. "Son," Senator Hale said. "Please accept my condolences."

Don't make a scene. Don't freak out. Don't punch him.

I wanted to do all of the above.

Franklin came over and extended his hand to the senator. "Eugene, thank you for coming."

I didn't know how in the world Franklin could be so pathetically nice.

As Franklin and Eugene started talking, I tuned them out. I was becoming an expert on tuning shit out, which was good at the moment.

Franklin might have been a seasoned pro at masking his anger, but I wasn't, and even though the incident that had happened at James Enterprises had taken place well over a year ago, it felt like the senator had just ripped open the scar.

"Is there anything I can do for you?" Haven asked.

Only four days ago, she was calling me a jerk in front of a room full of women. Regardless, I had so many comebacks on the tip of my tongue, but I swallowed them. I might have been a dickwad, a jerk, and an asshole, but church wasn't the right place to show that side of me. There would be plenty of time to have fun with the senator's daughter.

I cleared my throat. "Just make sure you're at the fundraising meeting on Thursday." My voice was loud on purpose.

She tensed, pursing her pink lips as I caught a glimpse of the senator whipping his attention our way.

I pushed to my feet. "Senator Hale, thank you for coming."

The large man turned to me with a fake grin plastered on his freckled face.

I draped an arm around Haven's tight shoulders. "I want to also thank you for allowing your daughter to be part of our fundraising efforts for the football team."

He narrowed his eyes, his fury lasering in on her. "Fundraising?"

She lowered her gaze, trying to get away from me.

Inwardly, I grinned like the asshole I was. Man, this woman had a way of changing my mood. I pulled her to me. "All proceeds go to support the Chelsea House for Battered Women."

He schooled his features as he regarded his daughter. "What's involved in the fundraiser?"

"We're auctioning off your daughter," I said. That probably wasn't the kind of attention he wanted for his election.

Haven gasped and managed to get away from me then practically ran out of the church.

Franklin shook his head at me, silently telling me to shut up.

"Son," Senator Hale said. "It would do you best to stick to football."

"First, I'm not your son." *Thank God.* "And it would do you best to stay out of my father's business." I gritted my back teeth.

"I've never been in your father's business," he said. "And from my understanding, his company violated a discharge permit. If I recall, the matter was settled in the appropriate manner."

"So you're going on record that you had nothing to do with making sure the water board took its time in handling the company's case?" I asked while Franklin's nostrils flared.

The senator mashed his lips into a thin line. "I don't work for the water board. But it's my duty to the people of this state to make sure we have a clean environment. Companies such as your father's threaten the livelihood of this state."

My eyes rolled without any effort. Typical of him to avoid the question. "Keeping the oil refineries operating is key to your success too. Isn't it? You've touted how important it is to the Texas economy. After all, the refineries employ thousands of citizens as do the chemical companies, which, by the way, keep the refineries operating."

"Again, stick to football," Senator Hale said. "After all, the loss yesterday isn't a way to start the season."

Asshole.

The loss was hard to swallow, nonetheless.

Franklin touched my arm. "Ryker, can you see if your aunt needs anything?" That was his way of saying, *shut up and leave.*

I silently swore as I walked away, although I didn't check on my aunt. Instead, I headed for fresh air.

"Oh, and Ryker," Senator Hale said to my back. "My daughter is off-limits."

We'll see about that.

10

HAVEN

I sat in the back pew under an eave, where I couldn't be seen unless someone was really looking my way. I'd wanted to leave the church, but I wanted to make sure Ryker and my father didn't get into a brawl.

If it weren't for that, I would have hightailed it out of there and driven as far away from Lakemont as I could. The idea of attending an out-of-state university suddenly became appealing. It wasn't too late either. The semester didn't start until tomorrow.

But I wasn't a quitter, and I wouldn't give my father that satisfaction.

I moved both my knees up and down as I listened to Ryker and my father. Their voices carried through the mainly empty church.

People had left after paying their respects. I suspected that most of them were headed to the cemetery. I'd heard Lucas tell someone that it would only be a few minutes before they carried the caskets out to the four hearses that were parked outside.

I didn't plan on going to the cemetery. Father and I had dinner plans at the ranch. Still, after the interaction between Ryker and Father, our presence at the cemetery definitely wasn't a good idea. Plus, as infuriated as I was that Ryker was using me to get to my father, I would probably deck the jerk.

To think that I'd kissed him on the cheek and offered him a shoulder to cry on.

Stupid me.

I was smarter than that. I knew he wasn't worthy.

Yet there I was, ready to throw myself at him. I knew how death had gripped me by the neck and sunk its claws in so deep that I hadn't been able to breathe when my mother had died. I knew firsthand how the pain stayed for a long time. That shock, denial, and all the emotions that came with death never went away.

The more time that passed, the more I wanted my mom alive. If she were there, then my father might not have been such a bastard. I hated how he lived so carefree and easily, like he'd never known her or loved her, like he had never been married to her. I didn't believe in dragging out the grieving process, but my father never talked about my mom. Arlene was partly to blame, and I couldn't fault her too much. She was his life now, but so was I.

If he loved me, he would want the best for me. But my father was all about himself. All that mattered was politics and sticking it to people he didn't like.

Bastard.

It was clear he didn't like Ryker, and now I knew why. From their conversation, I'd gathered that my father had stuck his nose into the James's family business. I would bet that whatever had transpired had benefited my father or his election. But there were always two sides to every story.

Ryker stormed down the aisle with his shoulders hunched, his face pinched, and his gray eyes swirled with fury. When he got to my row, he stopped and turned as though he could sense me.

Hot rage jumped off him as he slipped into the row and dropped his big body down beside me. He spread his legs in that manly way that guys did when they sat down, and his leg brushed mine.

Immediately, my pulse ramped up.

"Your father is a piece of work," he whispered.

"What did he do?" As irritated as I was with Ryker, my tone was even.

I watched Father talk to the handsome man dressed in an expensive suit. Father smiled and nodded, being as polite as he could. Underneath that grin, though, was nothing but boredom.

"Fucked with my old man's business." Ryker spat the words through clenched teeth.

"I'm sure my father had a good motive." I wasn't taking sides, but when it came to voters and elections, my father wanted to deliver on his promises.

"You would say that," he said.

"I heard something about the environment."

"My old man's company lost millions of dollars, employees, and customers, all because your father stuck his nose where it didn't belong."

"And you know this for sure?" I asked.

"What I know is your old man talks a big game about jobs, the economy, and the environment. But if he keeps submitting bills that hurt the businesses that support the moneymaker, as in oil refineries, he won't win his election."

I didn't get involved in my father's bills or politics. I didn't even help him with elections. Actually, he'd never asked me, and I had never offered. I'd never had the desire.

But I didn't want to talk about my father or politics. Actually, I didn't even want to talk to Ryker, but I did have one question for him. "Why are you using me?"

He looked straight ahead. "Why are you here?" A muscle ticked in his strong jaw. "I'm also curious why your old man is here."

"I asked him to come with me." Arlene had gotten a bug at the last minute. If I were being honest, it was her idea for my father to attend. After all, he donated money to the university, and its star quarterback was grieving.

Or at least I assumed he was. At the moment, Ryker didn't seem to have a grieving bone in his body. He had earlier when he'd emerged from the back of the church, looking strung out and like he was about to cry. He'd certainly shown how distraught he was during the service as friends and loved ones spoke about each of the deceased. The one who had affected him the most, though, was the young lady who had spoken about his sister. The way he'd held her and consoled her had left me shedding tears.

Losing a loved one was hard. Losing four at the same time had to be downright gut-wrenching.

"Why are you even in my life, Haven Hale?" He sounded mortified yet heartbroken.

"That's an odd question," I returned.

"Look," Ryker said. "Forget the fundraiser. I don't need the hassle of your old man on my ass." He rose, and in a flash, he was gone without even a quick look back at me.

My father was scaring away potential suitors.

Bastard.

Yet I didn't know why I was complaining.

He told you to stay away from Ryker. Now Ryker will stay away from you. So you can party, live it up, stay out of the media, and not have to worry about your father on your butt.

Nevertheless, I scratched my head at Ryker's question. Why was I in his life? *Hell if I know.* Maybe my father had a good point about me staying away from Ryker. Because in a freaky kind of way, the quarterback reminded me of my father—bold, aggressive, possessive, and an ass. All those qualities told me Ryker wasn't the right guy. Yet there was one major difference—Ryker had a heart.

Whatever. I didn't need the headache.

Then why do I feel like I've been dumped on the curb?

RYKER

Dark clouds skated by as the threat of rain hung in the air. I took off my tie and jacket then rolled up my sleeves, staring at four coffins, four graves, four souls that had gone to heaven. I still couldn't shed a tear. Not when the preacher had said his final prayers as he blessed each coffin. Not when the football team had carried the caskets from the church to the hearse and then to the gravesite. Not even when my aunt Kari had broken down in a fit of tears, practically throwing herself at the coffins.

The cemetery had emptied out. Lucas was waiting back at the limo. Franklin had taken my aunt home, and all the guests had scattered. I needed a moment to collect my thoughts and say one final goodbye.

But I had no words. My brain was empty. My heart hurt, and I searched for reasons why my family had been taken from me. *Why wasn't I on that plane with them?* It should have been me in one of those coffins rather than my baby brother or sister.

I dropped to my knees, throwing my head in my hands. If I could switch places with them, I would. My brother had had so much ahead of him, as had Leigh.

I pulled on my hair, hoping the pain would seep into me, hoping to feel something other than the numbness coursing through my body or the way my heart was beating out of my chest.

Breathe, man. Get up. Do what your father envisioned for you. Play football. Get married. Have a family. Do the impossible.

I couldn't. I didn't know how. I didn't know if I wanted to do any of those things without my mom telling me that I would make a good husband one day. Or Leigh coaxing me to find a girlfriend. Or my brother Randal talking football and sports and seeing how excited he would get when I won a football game. Or hearing my dad's words, "I'm proud of you, son. The NFL is in your grasp."

Football meant nothing at the moment. Playing wouldn't be the same without my old man or my family.

"Ryker," Lucas called from behind me before he gripped my shoulders. "I got you."

I blinked several times as I lifted my head.

Lucas knelt down. "They will always be watching you, man." His voice cracked. "I miss your pain-in-the-ass brother."

I half smiled. "He loved playing jokes on you. Remember that bearded dragon he put in your bed?" Lucas wasn't a fan of bearded dragons, at least not the one Randall had had.

Lucas laughed. "It got me out of bed."

I chuckled. "Hell, man, you ran home so fast, we couldn't track you."

He swatted at me. "If you ever tell a soul about that, I will deck you."

Silence ensued as a raindrop splattered on one of the caskets.

"So what do I do now?" I asked myself more than Lucas.

"Whatever you want, man. Get laid. Get drunk. Party. Play football. Stick your head in a cold bucket of water. I want to do all those things. I feel your pain as if it were my own, as if my family was taken away from me." A tear slid down his face. "I'm so fucking mad at the world for what happened to them. Your mom was my second mom. Your old man was the dad I never had. It guts me to think I won't see them ever again."

"I haven't gotten past the shock."

Lucas wiped a tear away. "You will."

That was my fear. What would happen when I did?

I stood. "Let's go. We have alcohol with our names on it. Just you and me." I was in the mood for quietness, good company, and a glass of scotch.

Rain started to fall.

I kissed each coffin, my lungs constricting. "I'll see you guys again one day when I make it to heaven."

Heaven.

Haven.

What the fuck!

I went ramrod straight.

"What's wrong?" Lucas asked.

I was afraid to tell him that Haven had popped into my brain. But I shouldn't be. We told each other everything.

"I can't leave. I can't leave them here. I feel like once they're in the ground, I won't be able to function."

"You're not leaving them, man. They'll be in your heart. Always."

I turned and threw my arms around him. "I love you, bro. If you leave me, I'll hunt you down and kill you."

He chuckled, squeezing me tightly. "Ditto."

We stayed like that for a long minute before we broke apart.

Lucas headed for the limo.

I hesitated, took a deep breath, then put one foot in front of the other. With each step, I felt as if I were vanishing into thin air. I felt empty, weak, and so fucking numb that it would be a miracle if I woke up tomorrow.

Lucas jumped into the back seat while the limo driver held open the door, waiting on me.

I looked back. This was it, the end of the road. This moment was a turning point I wasn't ready for. My eyes clouded, but the tears never came.

The clouds opened up, and heavy rain poured down. I swore it was the universe crying for me, or maybe Mom was shedding tears. Or Randall, Jr. Or Leigh. My old man didn't cry, or at least I'd never seen him cry.

A groundskeeper walked over to the gravesites and began lowering the caskets into the ground.

"Ryker," Lucas said. "It's time."

Time for what? I had no idea. I didn't want to leave. For a moment, I debated whether to stay at the cemetery for the night.

"Mr. James, you're going to get soaked," the limo driver said.

I glanced up at the sky, welcoming the rain, not caring how soaked I got.

"Dude," Lucas called again.

Reluctantly, I hopped in. "Let's go to my parents' house." I wanted to stay close to my parents, sister, and brother, and I couldn't do that in the home Lucas and I shared near campus. Besides, I wasn't ready to let go of them yet, even though they weren't there.

Lucas gave the limo driver the address as I leaned my head against the window.

"Isn't Kari having a small gathering?" Lucas asked.

"No. We decided not to." Aunt Kari had been too distraught to plan anything.

I closed my eyes, listening to the swish of the windshield wipers.

"You should take the semester off," Lucas said.

"If I want to play football, I can't."

He looked at me seriously. "Do you want to play?"

I shrugged. "Not sure." I really wasn't. At the moment, football didn't appeal to me.

"Maybe you should consider taking over your dad's company," he said. "Ditch school for a year."

Straightening, I gave him a sidelong glance. "Definitely something to think about. But not likely. My old man set up the trust so that if something did happen to him and my mom, I couldn't take over the company until I'm thirty, or later if I'm playing in the NFL." Dad had wanted me to live my dream.

The limo turned onto the exit for the highway.

Lucas twirled his phone in his hand. "Are you still into the fundraiser?"

I'd forgotten about that. "It's for a great cause." My mom had been helping out at the Chelsea House for Battered Women. That was one of the reasons I'd suggested that charity to the football team.

He swung his light-brown gaze my way. "Do you still want to add a girl to the mix?"

"I was only fucking with Haven."

"I know. I think it would be a nice addition, though. Someone like a senator's daughter might bring in more money. And she's beautiful."

His last line stole the wind out of me. She was fucking unforgettable—her lilac scent and those damn emerald eyes.

"We'll have her old man on our asses," I said.

Lucas grinned. "When has that stopped us from doing something?"

We always did what we wanted. "She won't do it."

"She might if you ask her instead of telling her. I know you have a thing for her."

He knew me well. The last girl I had a thing for was in high school, but Ellie and I had been short-lived. She had stolen my breath away when I'd first met her my freshman year. She'd had blond hair that hung down to her ass, bright-blue eyes that were big and round, and a smile that had sent shockwaves through my body. But my first crush had lasted four weeks. Ellie's father had taken a job in another state, and I never saw her again. After that, I hadn't fallen hard for any girl. Football had become my love.

"I'm not going to lie. She has gotten into my psyche for some odd reason."

He laughed. "You mean she's gotten your dick hard."

"That too. There's something about her."

"Fire. She's an inferno, and right up your alley."

I popped my head back against the seat. "Fire and ice don't match."

"I believe Haven Hale will thaw you out."

Lucas Allen wasn't wrong about much.

12

HAVEN

The last week had been nothing but classes and studying. Vicki had tried to get me to go back to the sorority house with her one night for their recruitment dinner. I'd declined once again. I'd done my roomie duty of attending with her the first time, but she didn't need me to hold her hand. And no amount of coaxing would change my mind about joining a sorority, regardless of the deal I had with my father.

The halls of Woodcreek High School were quiet as I wound my way to Mr. Bridges's government class. I was there to speak on my father's behalf liked he'd asked me to.

My phone rang, the sound echoing through the locker-lined hallway.

Speak of the devil.

"Father, are you checking up on me?"

"I just want to make sure you haven't forgotten about Mr. Bridges."

I rolled my eyes even though he couldn't see me. The week had been quiet, without him breathing down my neck. After the funeral service for Ryker's family, my father and I had exchanged some not-so-nice words. He'd had a fit that I would subject myself to be auctioned off to the highest bidder but only because it would bring bad publicity to his reelection campaign.

I stopped two doors down from the government classroom. "I'm about to go in."

"Have you told the James boy you're not participating in the auction?"

I puffed out my cheeks, staving off the anger that always welled up when I spoke to my father. We'd never had a conversation that didn't end in an argument. In fact, we'd never really talked like a normal father and daughter. If he needed to speak to me, it was mostly to tell me not to do something.

"I'm not going to answer you."

"Haven." His tone was commanding.

"Father."

I hadn't seen Ryker since that day in church. I didn't expect to see him either. I was a freshman, and he was a junior. So we didn't have any classes together. Plus, the campus was big. Vicki had heard that Beverly had tried to contact Ryker with no luck. I chalked that up to Ryker not wanting anything to do with Beverly. She had been at the funeral service. Actually, I thought the entire university had been there, as well as the whole town of Lakemont.

"Let me know how it goes with Mr. Bridges," my father said before the line went dead.

Bastard.

I had the urge to throw my phone at the locker across from me, the locker that I was just noticing had flowers in front of it with pictures and cards taped to it.

The first card I laid eyes on was handmade with glitter and the words, *Leigh, you always made us laugh. We love you and miss you.* It also contained signatures, hearts, and smiley faces.

The next card was similar, as were all the others taped to the locker.

"Ms. Hale," a male voice said as shoes scuffed along the floor.

I pivoted on my heel to find Mr. Bridges walking toward me. He was dressed in his signature bow tie and short-sleeved, button-up shirt. "Sad, isn't it? She was a vibrant and happy young woman."

"I didn't know Leigh James went to Woodcreek High," I said.

"She was a junior and president of her class." Mr. Bridges's bald head shone beneath the fluorescent lights above. "Do you know her older brother, Ryker? He goes to Lakemont University."

"I've met him." If I were being honest, I'd been thinking about him nonstop all week. In particular, I'd been analyzing the question he'd asked about why I was in his life. I certainly didn't know the answer to that one. "Did you go to the funeral?" I didn't recall seeing Mr. Bridges there.

"I couldn't make it. If you happen to run into Ryker, tell him the principal has been trying to get ahold of him."

I nodded even though I wouldn't have any reason to see Ryker. Sure, my father wanted me to tell him I wasn't participating in the fundraiser. But I didn't need to. I'd already told Ryker that, and he'd also told me to forget about it. So that was settled. But I'd failed to mention to my father the words I'd exchanged with Ryker at the church, only because I didn't want to talk about Ryker anymore with him.

I was at the point where I was ready to throw caution to the wind and do something about my sexual needs despite the consequences I could face if my father found out.

So what if I have to move home. Arlene would kick me out after a week of living there anyway. The worst my father could do was stop paying my tuition and expenses. While I wasn't ready for that, I couldn't have him suffocating me or telling me who I could or couldn't see.

"Are you ready to address my class?" Mr. Bridges asked.

A minute later, I was walking into a room of about twenty-five students, most of whom were hurrying to put their phones away.

I smiled, remembering my days at boarding school when the

teachers would confiscate our phones if we got caught with them out during class. I'd had mine taken away a few times. The days of writing notes in class had resurfaced since we couldn't use our phones to text anyone.

Mr. Bridges settled in front of his desk, tucking his hands into his khaki pants pockets. "Straighten up. Ms. Hale is here on behalf of her father, Senator Hale, who couldn't be here today. She'll talk to you this morning about what she does for her father during a campaign."

I stood a few feet away from Mr. Bridges, scanning the room. Two girls in the first and second rows sized me up. It was typical of girls to vet out a new female.

I smoothed a hand down my knee-length skirt. I was dressed in a professional manner and had been taught to dress appropriately for the occasion.

Mr. Bridges waved me over. "You have the floor." Then he went over to the bank of windows that overlooked the grassy area behind the school. Well beyond that, stadium lights stood tall from the football field.

I had no idea what I was going to say. I hadn't thought too much about the topic, and the only thing my father had mentioned was that I should keep my opinions to myself. He'd also told me to talk about how important it was to vote. I couldn't argue with him on that since I agreed with him.

I cleared my throat as I leaned against Mr. Bridges's desk. "Actually, I'm not going to tell you about my role in my father's campaign because I don't help out. For me, school is important."

"So you're not studying politics?" a girl directly in front of me with bright amber eyes asked.

I regarded Mr. Bridges. "I want to be a high school teacher."

"I do too," the girl replied.

I scanned the class, finding droopy eyes and bored faces. I couldn't say I blamed them for being uninterested. I remember how bored I'd been in my high school government class but not because the topic had put me to sleep. I'd already known too much about politics, thanks to dear old dad.

I tried a different tactic. "Instead of me talking, what questions do you have for me that are related to politics? I might not help my dad, but I do know the subject."

"My parents aren't voting for Senator Hale," a boy said from the back of the room.

"Mr. Cleary, ears not mouth," Mr. Bridges said. "Or ask an appropriate question."

A brunette raised her hand. "What's it like growing up with your father in politics?"

Brutal when your father hides you away or doesn't want you to make a spectacle out of him. "I hardly lived at home. I went to a boarding school. But when I was home, my father entertained a lot. So I got to meet lots of politicians around the country." Not that I'd been excited about that. But the girl seemed interested.

Another hand went up from a boy with wavy brown hair that was in need of combing, or maybe unruly was the new fashion trend. "I saw you at the church last Sunday, talking to Leigh's brother, Ryker. Can you get tickets to the football games?"

"Mr. Cleary." Mr. Bridges's tone was deep.

"I'm not going to be president of the country, and I don't care about politics," Mr. Cleary said. "Leigh got us tickets." He lowered his gaze to his desk as though he were remembering her in a loving way.

Mr. Bridges opened his mouth to speak.

"Mr. Cleary," I said.

"My name is Zack."

"Okay, Zack. You may not be president of this country one day, but you should understand who is running for office and vote for those that you believe in." I might not want to go into politics or listen to my father, but I felt it was important to vote.

"So do you vote for your father?" he asked.

I hadn't had the chance to vote in a major election since turning eighteen, and my father had been elected six years ago when I wasn't of age to vote.

"Actually, I will, and not because he's my father, but because I agree with him that we should protect our environment. Look, we live in a state that is home to lots of different industries like the oil industry. Therefore, it's important to keep them running for the economy, but it's equally important to ensure that we have strict laws on emissions, water discharge, and other such things so that we do live in a safe and clean environment."

Mr. Bridges smiled proudly at me. I had no idea what he and my father had discussed. Frankly, I didn't think my father even knew I agreed with some of his policies. Maybe if he gave me the time of day, we could chat about things rather than arguing.

I regarded Zack. "But back to your other question on football tickets. I'll see what I can do." As a student, I had access to purchase tickets easily. I wouldn't mind attending a game anyway. "Any other questions?"

Mr. Bridges joined me at his desk. "As Ms. Hale said, it's important to understand who the politicians are and their policies so, in the end, you can make an informed decision when you reach voting age."

The bell rang.

The students scattered as though the fire alarm had gone off.

Zack came up to me. "Thank you." Then he left, looking like he'd lost his best friend.

"Was he close to Leigh James?" I asked Mr. Bridges.

"He, Jessica Davis, and Leigh were tight."

I remembered a Jessica speaking at the church.

"You did well." He chuckled. "Your dad was worried about what you were going to say. He'll be proud of you."

I doubted that. "I've got to run. I will check on football tickets. I'll make my dad pay for them."

He laughed. "Oh, and if you do see Ryker, let him know about the principal?"

"Sure will," I said on my way out.

Once I was at my car, my phone beeped with a text.

Vicki: *Are you up for going to a party tonight?*

It was Friday. I'd busted my butt all week on homework and studying. It was time to kick back.

Me: *I'm in. Whose party?*

Vicki: *Lucas and Ryker.*

Perfect… or maybe not. The last party at Ryker's had caused trouble for me.

13

RYKER

I held the bottle of scotch in one hand, and the other rested on my bare stomach as I watched a sports channel pick apart all the college football games that had been played that afternoon, with Lakemont being one of them. Damn team didn't win the game. We were now zero wins and two losses. I should have been getting my ass out of bed and in gear to play football, but I couldn't muster up the energy to do anything.

A short brunette reporter stuck the mic at Coach Chapman. "Coach, can you tell us when Ryker James is returning to the game?"

Coach adjusted his ball cap. "I don't have a date yet. Look, it's been a rough road for our star quarterback. So myself, the team, and the university support him if and when he decides to return."

Coach had stopped by midweek to discuss what my plans were or if I would be taking off the season. I didn't have an answer for him, and he couldn't exactly push me to play. After all, if I didn't have my head in the game, then I would be worthless anyway. In fact, my mind hadn't been right since I'd left the cemetery five days ago. After Lucas and I had come back to my parents' house, I'd stayed. I'd curled up in my brother's bed and become a zombie. My aunt Kari kept trying to get me to eat, but I had no hunger for food. The only thing I craved was booze and drowning myself in it—anything to take away the thought of going on with everyday tasks, school, football, parties, and normal shit that people did.

I was lucky I got out of bed to take a piss. I'd only showered once since the funeral, and the way I was going, I would probably die in bed.

A soft knock sounded on the door before Aunt Kari came in. She scrunched her nose, piercing me with daggers. "Before long, your room will have rodents building homes alongside you. This place stinks."

Like I give a shit.

Sinking her bare feet into the carpet as she crossed the room, she flicked strands of her dark hair off her forehead. "At least you had the decency to not stink up the other rooms in the house."

She'd pried me from my brother's bed three days prior. I'd been content to stay in his room and gaze at the *Star Trek* posters he had glued to the ceiling, as well as the pictures of space and planets. He'd been obsessed with anything *Star Trek*. I couldn't blame him. I loved *Star Trek* too.

Aunt Kari opened the blinds, and the afternoon sun came rushing in.

I took a swig of scotch and squinted. "Did you have to?"

She eyed me with a forlorn look before cracking a window. "The room needs venting."

I didn't smell a thing.

She came over to my bed, wiping her hands on the apron wrapped around her waist. "Some of your teammates are here."

I cocked a brow. I hadn't heard anyone come in. Then again, I'd been drowning in my misery for days on end.

"Put on some clothes, splash water on your face, and become part of society again." Her tone reminded me of my mom when she'd been tired of my shit. "Seriously. You're breaking my heart."

I wasn't trying to. I was, however, trying to mend mine.

She grabbed my hand, appraising me with her gray eyes, which reminded me so much of my mom's. "You can't live like this, Ryker. Do you think I'm not hurting? Do you think that I don't cry every night?"

I knocked back more scotch. I'd drunk three-quarters of the bottle, and I wished I could say I was drunk, but I wasn't. The alcohol wasn't doing anything to take away the memories, the pain, or the depression that I couldn't shake.

"What you're doing isn't healthy," she said softly. "You haven't even cried." She swiped the bottle out of my hand. "This crap isn't going to bring them back." Her tone was stern.

I almost snatched it back from her, but I didn't have the energy.

Voices sounded in hall. "Ryker!" Erik shouted. "We're coming for your ass."

With the bottle in her hand, Aunt Kari started for the door. "Maybe they can knock some sense into you." She left, and I heard her say, "He's all yours."

Within seconds, Erik, Lucas, and Ajax sauntered in and surrounded my bed.

Before I could say a word, they lifted me in the air and carried me out of my room.

"What the fuck are you brutes doing?"

Trying to get free wouldn't get me far since the three of them could keep a bear down.

Ajax laughed. "You need a wake-up call."

"This better not be one of your brilliant plans to lock me into some chick's bedroom." Erik and Ajax had done that very thing to me last year. They thought getting me laid before a game would break the bad streak I'd been having on the football field when I'd thrown three interceptions in one game.

"Nah," Lucas said with too much giddiness in his voice. "That would be too kind."

Concern dug into the lining of my stomach, or maybe that was nausea as the furniture in the living room whizzed by. Then my aunt opened the slider to the backyard. Thankfully, I had my boxer briefs on. Otherwise, my aunt would've gotten an eyeful.

Once outside, the guys walked around the pool. Then it hit me. They were going to throw me in. But I didn't care. The pool water had to be about ninety or so degrees. That wouldn't get me fired up.

But when they swung me and I hit the pool water belly-flop-style, I lost my fucking breath as I went under. The water had to be as cold as Antarctica.

I could hear them laughing as I broke the surface, gasping and coughing. If I had been drunk, I wasn't now.

I swam over to the steps of the Olympic-sized pool, dodging large blocks of ice. "I'll kill you guys."

Lucas loomed over me, wearing swim trunks and a T-shirt. "You can't kick my ass, and you know it."

"Maybe not, but I'm willing to give it a try." Then I grinned. "Nice touch with the ice."

Ajax ponied up alongside Lucas. He, too, was wearing swim trunks but no shirt. He swiped a hand over the Celtic cross tattooed on the left side of his chest. "It's time, dude, to get your ass back into the game."

Erik shuffled over, wearing a ball cap backward over his shaggy hair. "We can't keep losing games. Tank is okay as your backup, but he doesn't have your arm."

The three of them sat on the steps and slung their feet in the water.

"Shit," Lucas said. "That *is* cold."

My body didn't feel the chill anymore, and as hot as it was, the ice would be melted in no time.

"Your aunt is going out for the night," Ajax said. "She's given us the thumbs-up to have a few people over. She even bought steaks to grill out."

I could eat, something I'd done very little of the last few days. On the other hand, I wasn't in the mood to have blaring music or a house packed with people.

"Everybody was asking for you last night at the party," Erik said.

I quickly dunked my head under water, and when I came up the three of them smirked like they knew a big secret I didn't. I was sure they did since I hadn't been among the living.

"Haven was looking for you," Lucas said, not losing his cheeky grin.

"I think you guys thawed me out," I said mainly to Lucas since his prediction would be that Haven would thaw me out.

I didn't need her or any gal to bring me out of my funk, but hell if his comment didn't get me thinking about the redhead all of a sudden.

"You know what I think?" Erik asked. "You need to get laid. I swear sticking my dick in a chick always sets me on a better path."

I dragged a hand through my wet hair. "I told you. My dick doesn't work."

"Test it out with Haven," Ajax offered. "See if she can get you fired up."

"It doesn't have to be Haven," Lucas said. "I'm sure Beverly or any of her sorority sisters would help you out."

I was sure Beverly would. Suddenly, her naked body popped into my stupid head. But the vision did nothing for my dick, and that was sad, worrisome, and pathetic. Normally, when I thought of a naked girl or fucking one, I had no problem getting the blood to rush south.

"So you guys are trying to pimp me out?" That was a first.

"Nah, but you'd better get out of your funk before we make you," Erik said teasingly. Or maybe he wasn't teasing. "Seriously, dude. We can't imagine what you're going through. But I bet getting your head back in the game will help."

I sat on the pool step with my body half in and half out of the water, not wanting to think past the next minute. "Hey, where's Vin?"

Erik, Vin, and Ajax hardly went anywhere without each other.

"Family thing," Erik said.

Lucas slapped me on the back. "Come on, bro. Let's kick back. We've had a terrible day after that game earlier, and we need to unleash some pent-up energy. The sun is out. The pool water is perfect, and we're all hungry."

I could eat. I could also kick back with them. Maybe they were right. Maybe I did need to get laid.

"On one condition," I said. "I don't want a house full of drunken jerks."

They all laughed.

"Sure, dude," Ajax said, getting his phone out of his swim trunks. "You always say that."

True. Maybe a party *would* do me good.

14

HAVEN

Vicki and I were sitting by the pool in comfy lounge chairs at a ranch owned by Ryker's parents. I crossed one ankle over the other, sipping a fruity drink that had way too much alcohol in it.

Lucas had texted me earlier to see if Vicki and I were interested in coming out for dinner and drinks. He also knew I'd been wanting to talk to Ryker. I hadn't told Lucas why, only because I wanted to make sure Ryker got the message, and part of me wanted to see the man. Hell, I couldn't get him out of my darn head.

The night before, my roomie and I had gone to the party hosted by Lucas and, at the time, I'd thought, Ryker would've been there. But when I'd arrived, Ryker had been AWOL. According to Lucas, his best bud was recharging his battery.

The quarterback hadn't played in the game that day, which had raised a lot of eyebrows around my dorm. Women were speculating that Ryker was dropping out of school, giving up football, or that he'd gone into hiding.

I wouldn't be surprised if he did any of those things. Mourning the death of loved ones wasn't easy to handle. Still, I didn't think he would give up football, which meant he couldn't drop out of school. Although hiding himself away was doable, and in my mind needed for the grieving process, at least for a short time. I hadn't wanted anything to do with people after my mom died.

A pang of sorrow coursed through me as I eyed the handsome quarterback from across the pool. He hadn't even moved since I'd walked in over an hour ago.

For all I knew, he was staring at me through his dark sunglasses. That thought did perk up my lady parts, even more so as I checked out his tanned upper torso through my own dark sunglasses.

As I envisioned my hands exploring his hills and valleys and, of course, his happy trail, I decided it had been a bad idea to come there.

For one, I didn't trust myself. And two, if my father found out, he might go off the deep end. But I didn't see anyone snapping pictures, and as long as I stayed out of the media, I was golden. Besides, I wasn't about to become a hermit. Part of the college experience was going to parties, and I couldn't help it if Ryker was at one of those parties. Not only that, I wasn't dating the hot-as-sin quarterback, although I was jonesing for maybe a one-night stand with him.

Ryker doesn't want you.

If that were true, then I guessed I didn't have anything to worry about.

Vicki leaned in from her lounge chair. "It's not polite to stare."

"Says the girl who can't keep her eyes off of Lucas." He was at the outdoor kitchen area, which included a bar, grill, small fridge, and an island on one end with barstools.

She snorted. "Touché."

The night before, Vicki had been dying to talk to Lucas, but he had been preoccupied with a girl that Vicki had wanted to make disappear.

I wasn't one of those girls who got jealous, maybe because I hadn't had a steady boyfriend. Sure, I ogled boys. I went out on dates. I had sex. But I'd never found that boy who wowed me or one that stole my breath away. I chalked that up to the all-girl boarding school.

One of the guys over at the kitchen area laughed loudly.

"Ryker, dude, get your ass over here," Ajax said. "We're doing shots."

The girl beside Ryker leaned over, her boobs practically falling out of her swim top as she rubbed his leg with her hand. "Come on. You can do a shot off my chest."

Suddenly, a twinge of something rifled through me, and I wanted to throw Blondie in the pool.

"Yes," Erik shouted. "Get over here, Tab. I'll go first." I'd met Erik the night before along with Ajax and a few of the other football players. Erik reminded me of Julian Edelman from the New England Patriots, only his brown hair hung below his ears.

Ajax twisted his ball cap so the bill was behind him. "I'm next." Ajax sported a military haircut, and where Erik was wide in the chest, Ajax was leaner.

Ryker didn't move as Tab tried to coax him by whispering something in his ear.

Kill the bitch.

I clutched the glass I was holding a little too tightly.

I want nothing to do with Ryker James. He wants nothing to do with you.

So why was I feeling like I wanted to send the blonde packing? Maybe I was a jealous person after all.

When Tab struck out and sauntered over to Erik and Ajax, I sighed.

The rest of the guests scattered around the pool, veranda, and kitchen area watched what was about to unfold.

Tab settled in front of Erik, squeezing her boobs together and at the same time lifting them up to create a way to capture the liquor. "Pour."

"I would never do that," Vicki mumbled as she sipped the fruity drink Lucas had made her.

"You would if you were alone with a guy," I added. "Say... Lucas."

She let out a dreamy sigh. I swore my roomie was going to combust if she didn't get her hands on Lucas soon.

Ajax drizzled the alcohol down Tab's chest as she leaned back slightly. Then like a thirsty dog, Erik lapped up every drop of liquid as he tried to capture one of her nipples in his mouth.

But Tab was quicker than him. She tittered, adjusting her swim top. "If you want this, then you'll have to work harder than that." Then she let Ajax do the same, licking the alcohol off her.

The other guys at the small gathering didn't jump on that train. Some of the girls in the pool shook their heads.

From what I could see, Ryker didn't even look at what his buddies were doing with Tab. I got the feeling he was either still looking at me, or maybe he was sleeping. Either way, he seemed bored out of his mind.

The party was chill compared to the one the previous night. Even the music was tame with a soft beat and low volume.

The Tab scene wore off quickly as she disappeared into the house.

I needed to get back to the dorm and do some studying, but I knew Vicki wouldn't want to leave yet.

"I feel like I'm at a tropical resort," Vicki said. "You wouldn't find a place like this in Maine."

I didn't know anything about Maine except it got cold or stayed cold most of the year in that neck of the country. *No, thank you.* I'd had my fill of that kind of weather going to school in Michigan.

I relaxed into the cushioned lounger, the alcohol beginning to affect me. Maybe Ryker had the best idea. A nap by the pool seemed like something I could get into.

Lazily, I scanned the property. Nice shrubs, colorful flowers, ceramic frogs and turtles, and other planting pots decorated the land-scape around the yard. In the distance, a handful of trees stood tall. Lucas had called the place a ranch, but when I pictured a ranch, I thought of horses and other farm animals. The James's property had lots of land, an expansive one-story home, a small pool house that sat behind Ryker, and an Olympic-sized pool but no horses or animals.

"How's your head?" Vicki asked.

Pushing my sunglasses up on my nose, I rose then slipped my feet into my flip-flops. "Headache is gone finally. I'm going to the bathroom."

Lucas had told me to wear my bathing suit and to dress casually. I had on my swim top, jean shorts, and a sheer cover-up that fell to my waistline.

"I think I'll talk to Lucas," Vicki said.

Just as I motioned to move, Beverly walked out of the house with Tab on her heels. I swung my gaze between the two and realized that they had to be related. I would guess Tab was younger. Both had blond hair, blue eyes, and were similar in size with rounded faces, thick lips, and even the same shaped eyes. I had no doubt they were sisters.

"Is that Beverly's sister?" I asked Vicki.

She shrugged. "Not sure. But I would say yes."

I suddenly felt the need to leave. I didn't need Beverly taking pictures of me and sending them to my father, especially since I was innocent and nowhere near Ryker.

"I'm still curious if she's working for my dad," I muttered, even though my dad had given me the strong impression Beverly was his spy. I was tempted to ask her, but I knew she would deny it. And right now, I didn't care. I had to use the bathroom. "I'll be right back."

Vicki hopped up. "Ryker's head is turning our way."

He was probably looking because Beverly had just come in. Still, I stuck out my chest. I had a small frame, but my boobs weren't small at all. I bordered on a D cup, and frankly, I didn't like that my breasts were big. I'd always thought they didn't match my size-four body.

One of the only compliments I'd gotten from my stepmom, Arlene, was about my breasts. "You should be proud of those," she'd said to me not that long ago.

"So maybe Beverly is here to tell you if you got into the sorority," I said to Vicki.

Vicki had gone through the recruitment process during the week, and she was waiting for word on whether or not she was in. I would be happy for her if she got in, but I would be sad too. I didn't want to lose her as a roommate.

"I doubt that. She doesn't go out of her way to track down potential candidates to give them news. Anyway, I'll be at the bar." Vicki skirted a few chairs until she was sliding onto a stool at the island while Lucas piled meat onto a plate.

Beverly and Tab wound their way around the pool and over to Ryker.

Inwardly, I growled as I trailed Vicki. "Lucas, where's the bathroom?" I asked.

Lucas slid the plate over to the middle of the island. "Pool house."

I hurried in that direction, hoping my bladder wouldn't combust.

The pool house was more like an apartment, with a bathroom, a comfy living space, and what looked to be two more rooms behind two closed doors.

I locked myself in the small bathroom and quickly took care of business. Then I washed my hands and splashed water on my face. I hadn't bothered with makeup because it had seemed pointless to pretty myself up if I were to go swimming. I swiped a hand towel from the rack near the marble counter and patted it over my face.

Wow! I looked like death. Faint dark circles marred the undersides of my eyes. Maybe I should've taken a minute to at least put on concealer. It didn't matter. I had sunglasses on, and I didn't plan on partying until the wee hours of the morning like Vicki and I had done the night before. I had tons of homework to do the next day as well. So I needed all my brain cells. Plus, my father was due home, and I never knew what he would throw my way. Since I'd been living in town, he was in my face more than ever before.

If you go anywhere near Ryker, then prepare for your father's wrath, and let's not forget Beverly is here.

The whites around my green irises were red, and the more sun I got, the more my freckles came out. I really should've thought to mask those spots on my face. That was one of the things I didn't like about myself.

Nevertheless, I fixed my breasts so they weren't spilling out of my bathing suit top then opened the door. When I did, I gasped.

Ryker leaned on the arm of the loveseat with his arms crossed over his bare chest. He was sizing me up like he had plans for me, or maybe I wasn't supposed to be in the pool house.

"Hey," I said. "You scared me."

He sucked in his bottom lip. "I do have that effect on people." His gaze was glued to my breasts.

I snapped my fingers. "I'm up here, big guy."

His gaze didn't move nor did his lips.

I started for the door when what I really wanted was to untie the strings of my bathing suit top and have him suck on my nipples. At that thought, my nipples hardened.

"Why are you here?" His voice was raspy, and his tone was hard.

I came to an abrupt halt and pivoted on my heel. "I was invited. What's your excuse?"

"I live here," he said.

He had a point. "The last I knew, you lived in a house one block from campus."

He placed his sunglasses on top of his head. "Are you my keeper all of a sudden?" His gray eyes were darker than I remembered.

"What do you want, Ryker? You're the one waiting for me outside the bathroom."

"What if I had to use it?"

"Something tells me you don't."

He sized me up, slowly and methodically, as though he were trying to see through my jean shorts and swim top.

I pursed my lips. "You football players are all alike. Aren't you?"

He angled his head. "How's that?"

"You have this look like you want to eat a woman."

One side of his mouth went up. "Eating a woman is fun. Have you tried it?"

I didn't swing that way, but I did recall him asking if I were into threesomes. "What do you want?" I rolled back my shoulders as my gaze ran up and down his happy trail. *Whew.* The remembrance of how he felt in my hand was making me warm and dizzy.

Without thinking, my eyes lowered to his groin.

He groaned. "If you keep salivating for my cock, I just might give it to you."

I raised an eyebrow. "Don't flatter yourself." I turned to walk out.

My lungs were burning for air, and my swimsuit bottoms were soaked. I needed him inside me like stat. One night of unbridled passion with him would surely put out the fire between my legs.

You're lying to yourself. One night with him, and you'll be begging for more.

I laughed out loud as I reached the door.

Before I could even turn the knob, his hot breath was on my neck. "What's so funny?"

"Nothing you would understand." *Liar.*

Then I remembered Vicki had said his nickname among women was Foreplay King.

He sandwiched me in between his rock-hard body and the door, which thankfully didn't have a window. If it did, then Beverly might have seen us and snapped a pic.

His lips grazed my ear. "Try me."

My breathing ramped up as he pressed his crotch into my backside.

Oh my word.

He dragged his large and callused hand down my waist.

I shivered. *Damn body.*

"Well, Heaven, are you going to answer me?" His voice was gravelly as his erection grew.

"It's Haven," I barely said.

His hand came around and went under my sheer top until he was touching my stomach.

Heat, electricity, and mad lust zipped through my body.

He pulled me closer to him. "I think I'll stick with Heaven."

"Whatever floats that boat of yours."

At the moment, I didn't care what he called me as long as I could keep feeling him against me. Oh, I was so screwed.

He nibbled on my ear. "So, do you want me to take you to heaven?"

I giggled. "Is that one of your lines that you use to get women in bed?"

His hand left my stomach, sliding down until he was rubbing my inner thigh close to my throbbing clit, which needed his attention. It had been too long since I'd had sex with a guy. The last time had been at the beginning of my senior year at boarding school, and it wasn't even worth talking about or remembering.

"I don't need a line. All I have to do is this." He found my clit through the fabric of my jean shorts and rubbed.

I moaned.

He continued to rub as his erection poked into me. "Want to come?"

Hell yeah.

But the minute I did would be the minute he would probably throw me away like all his other one-night stands. He wasn't getting to me that easily. One thing my father had taught me was to play hard to get. The harder I played, the harder they fell, and that was idiotic because that saying applied to both sides, and I wasn't ready to fall. I barely knew Ryker.

I jutted out my butt then ducked underneath his arm, breathing like I needed a tank of oxygen.

He laughed. The jerk laughed.

I shook off the incredible sensation of feeling like I was a second away from a climax just looking at the quarterback god.

He continued to laugh.

I snarled.

"Thank you, Heaven. I haven't laughed like that in a long time."

I stuck him with my middle finger. "Glad I could oblige." *Jerk face.*

I really was leaving. but before I did, I remembered a reason that I'd shown up. "I came to tell you that the principal of Woodcreek High has been trying to get ahold of you."

He lost his smile. In fact, he paled. "Why tell you?"

I crossed my arms over my chest.

His eyes immediately went to my breasts.

"I was there on Friday to give a talk to the government class on my father's behalf. Mr. Bridges mentioned it to me."

"Do you always do your father's dirty work?"

"We're not talking about my father." My tone took on a mean streak. "Just call the principal." I inched closer to him, almost flattening my chest against his, hoping I could affect him like he was affecting me. "Oh and stay away from me."

He knitted his thick eyebrows as he glanced down. "You offered an ear if I ever wanted to talk." His tone was even.

I captured my bottom lip in between my teeth. "That was before I knew you were using me to get to my father." I stepped back then pivoted on my heel. "I don't need the hassle."

He belted out a laugh. "You're a piece of work, Haven Hale."

"Just wanted to make sure I pleased you." *What? Where did that line come from?*

He chuckled. "Mark my words, Haven. I will be taking you to heaven. And in case you need clarification, I mean you will be in my bed, between my sheets, with me between your legs."

I tossed an eye roll over my shoulder. "Not in this century." I slammed the door on my way out.

Then I shivered at the thought as the humid air hit my face. He might be right, but I wasn't going to make it easy for him.

15

———

RYKER

The air conditioner blew on me as I sat in my car and stared at the brick facade of Woodcreek High.

Three days had passed since the party at my parents' house—three days of drinking, sleeping, and wallowing in sorrow. I'd thought about what the guys had said. I didn't want to keep disappointing them. They wanted that championship season. Ajax and Erik were sophomores, and Lucas and I were juniors. So all of us had another year at least to win some games. But I was their quarterback. They needed me. I wasn't certain I was ready, or if I could throw a football, or if it were too late to get my head in the game, or if Coach would even play me.

I rested my head against the seat.

If football doesn't work out, you can always take the year off. My parents would be so disappointed in me if I did.

Maybe coming to the high school wasn't such a good idea. Maybe it was too soon to pick up Leigh's belongings.

Go inside, man. Get this over with.

Principal Holland had left a few messages on my voice mail, which I hadn't listened to until Haven had brought up the principal.

Haven. That damn green-eyed redhead had a way of getting inside me. She had gotten me fired up in the pool house, or rather she'd gotten my body singing a tune I hadn't felt in a long time. Maybe she was also one reason I wasn't wallowing in my sorrow. When I was around her, I was finding that I didn't feel like someone had stuck a dagger in my heart. She somehow took away the darkness, which was perplexing since she was related to a man I hated.

Her father's the dick. She isn't. She at least has empathy for what I'm going through.

On top of that, she wasn't the type of girl to roll over for me like all the other ladies I'd taken to bed. She was the first girl to speak her mind and not beg for something from me. Maybe the liquor was eating at my brain. Maybe I was crazy to think that one person could affect me the way she had so far.

But I liked trading barbs with her. I liked that she didn't run from something crass like what I'd said that day in the pool house. I enjoyed a good chase, which had been nonexistent when it came to women, and I had no doubt Haven was about to give me a run for my money.

My phone rang, and Aunt Kari's name lit up my screen. I tapped it to answer.

"Where are you?" she asked. "I went to check your room, and you were gone." Her voice sounded excited rather than worried.

"I decided to brave the new world," I teased.

"Good. I'm glad your friends made an impact the other night."

"I'm at Woodcreek High to pick up some of Leigh's belongings."

"What? Are you sure you're ready to do that?" Her tone dripped with concern. "I can head down and join you."

"Nah. I want to do this alone. I'll talk to you later." I ended the call before she could give me psychological pointers like she'd tried to do the day before. Maybe she was another reason I'd showered, dressed, and shaved. I hated seeing the despair written all over her face. It was as if my mom had been counseling me.

I hopped out of my car and strutted into the school. The halls were deathly quiet as I followed the signs to the admin office. I knew the school well since I'd attended Woodcreek High.

However, instead of heading to the admin office, I decided to take a detour to the library. One of my last conversations with my sister had been about a painting she'd done. Her art teacher had loved it so much, she'd displayed it in the library with other artwork by students.

I hadn't seen Leigh's masterpiece yet. The school had planned an art festival for early September, but with Leigh gone, I wasn't sure if they'd gone through with it.

The halls were dripping in banners that were plastered above lockers, touting the slogan "Go Timberwolves." Memories of my time playing football for the school bombarded me as I strolled down memory lane.

As I approached the library, a memory of Ellie flashed before me. I would never forget that day she'd walked out of the library, flipping her blond hair over her shoulder as we'd locked eyes. I had lost my breath when she'd smiled at me.

But as I grabbed the long handle of the door, my chest constricted, and not because of the memory but because of the apprehension of seeing Leigh's painting.

Maybe Aunt Kari should've joined me, at least to hold my darn hand.

Footsteps resounded down the hall before I could go inside.

"Ryker, is that you?" Principal Holland asked as he walked up. The middle-aged man hadn't changed. He still had a thick crop of dirty-blond hair, which was glued back with gel. He looked sharp in his blue suit, pink shirt, and green tie. The years had been kind to his skin. He only had a few wrinkles around his light-brown eyes.

The principal extended his hand. "I'm so sorry for your loss."

I gave him a handshake. "Thank you. I was checking on the art festival. Did the school ever have it?"

"We postponed it. Let's go inside."

The familiar scent of books wafted around as Ms. Gross looked up from her computer at the main desk. She rose from her chair and ambled toward me. "Ryker James." She gently placed her hand over her heart. "My sincere condolences." Then she gave me a quick hug.

. . .

I SWALLOWED THICKLY. ONE OF THE REASONS I'D SHUNNED THE WORLD was because I couldn't handle seeing sorrow and despair on people's faces.

The graying-haired librarian hooked her arm in mine. "I'm guessing you want to see Leigh's painting." She guided me down the middle aisle. Shelves of books stood on our left, and an open area on our right displayed several pieces of artwork that were either exhibited on the table or on easels that stood on the floor.

Ms. Gross let go of my arm and joined Mr. Holland, who gave me some space. My eyes drifted from a colorful geometric painting that was on the table to a sixteen by twenty canvas that sat on one of the easels beside the table.

My jaw came unhinged. I inched closer to the canvas as my chest constricted more. Leigh had painted me. I'd always known she was talented. I knew she had wanted to study art in college, and I had seen some of her drawings, but this one was fucking amazing. The detail was incredible in how she'd drawn my nose, lips, gray eyes, black hair, and even that cocky smile she'd said I wore all the time coming off the football field.

Hot tears burned my eyes and grew hotter the more I stared at her masterpiece.

"It's beautiful," Ms. Gross said softly behind me. "She loved you, you know. She was so excited for the art festival."

I wanted to punch something. I wanted to turn back time and make things different. I should've been on that plane with them. If I had been, I wouldn't be feeling like I was dying a slow death.

Without turning around, I asked, "Are you still having the art festival?"

"We are, but we haven't come up with a date yet," Mr. Holland said. "We'll definitely let you know."

I wouldn't miss it for anything.

"I have a small box of Leigh's things that she had in her locker,"

Mr. Holland said. "It's not much since school hadn't been in session that long."

I bobbed my head as I continued to stare at Leigh's masterpiece.

Mr. Holland placed his hand lightly on my upper back. "Come on before the bell rings."

I said goodbye to Ms. Gross and walked out of the empty library with Mr. Holland, trying to keep my shit together. If I had stayed any longer in the library, I would've bawled like a baby.

We navigated the halls until we banked around a corner. Fidgeting with his tie, Mr. Holland stabbed a thumb at a locker. "This is Leigh's."

It took me a minute to zero in on what I was looking at. When I did, I lost my breath.

Coming here was definitely the wrong decision.

I was a second away from losing it. Aunt Kari thought I should cry, that crying would expel all the pain and sorrow that was building up inside me. And fuck, I was on the verge of pouring out all the tears I could.

Pictures of Leigh and her friends were taped to the locker with flowers on the floor like a shrine. The sight of it gutted me like a sharp fishing knife to the stomach.

"The students don't want me to take any of this down," Mr. Holland said. "But I'll have to soon."

I pointed at the locker. "Are Leigh's things in here?"

"The box is in my office. Let's head there."

I puffed out my cheeks, running a hand through my hair as sweat beaded up on the nape of my neck.

Get the box and get out.

I swore after I left there, I would be curling up in my bed again.

The admin office came into view, or rather the glass box of hell as Lucas and I had called it when we were in high school.

Mr. Holland had been known to intimidate students when they got into trouble. I knew that firsthand. I'd been frightened the first time I was sent to see him for fighting. I'd been a freshman and had gotten into one brawl with a senior who'd thought he owned the school. I'd won that fight and had also won the respect of my peers. Despite that, the penance I'd received had been well worth Mr. Holland's wrath—a month-long detention and scrubbing graffiti off walls in the boys' bathroom.

"Are you still as mean and tough as you were when I was here?" I asked in a light voice. I needed some other distraction after the last thirty minutes of misery.

Chuckling, he opened the glass door to the admin office. "Let's just say things haven't changed much since you were here."

Thoughts of fights and his strict management skills swept out the door as we walked in, and I laid eyes on none other than the woman who seemed to be showing up everywhere I went.

Haven batted those ball-teasing green eyes of hers at me as she sat prim and proper, dressed in a pair of whitewashed jean shorts and a low-cut T-shirt.

Damn. "Follow the Yellow Brick Road" started in my head. I wanted to lick my way from her toes up her tanned, toned legs, stopping inside her thighs to nibble a tad before I settled my tongue on her clit and took her right to that orgasmic palace at the end of the yellow brick road. Man, the blood was pooling in my groin already as I thought about all the things I could do to her.

"What are you doing here?" I asked in a harsh tone. "Are you stalking me?"

Mr. Holland cleared his throat. "Do you two know each other?"

Haven rose elegantly as though she'd been trained on how to act. I imagined as a senator's daughter, she had. She held out her small hand, showing off her pink-painted nails that matched her lipstick and cheeks. "I'm Haven Hale," she said to Mr. Holland.

Mr. Holland shook her hand. "Robert Holland. Mr. Bridges told me about you." Then the principal addressed me. "I'll get Leigh's box." He ambled around two desks then disappeared into a back office.

The two ladies who worked for Principal Holland stared at Haven and me.

I shoved my hands into my jeans pockets. "What are you doing here?"

"You really need to come up with a new question for me," Haven said.

"It seems you're always in my face. If I recall, you told me to stay away from you. Yet you're following me."

She laughed, light and free. It was a singsong sound that was soothing and made me grin.

"Ryker, you're not the only one who has business here," she said as a matter of fact. "I gave a talk here last week. Remember?"

"That was last week."

The bell rang, and students flooded the hall outside the admin office. Then the door opened, and Zack Cleary ambled in, looking like he'd stuck his head in a wind tunnel.

"Ryker James," Zack said, sounding a bit shocked.

Leigh, Jessica, and Zack had been good friends. It had been ages since I'd seen him. He'd grown out his wavy brown hair, beefed up in the chest and arms, and looked good.

He and I exchanged a manly hug.

When he eased away, tears streamed down his face. "It's awful, man. Losing your sister has gutted me."

Join the fucking club.

Haven went over to Zack and wrapped her arms around him. "It sucks. I know."

I then remembered her telling me she knew how it felt to lose a loved one. Maybe she would be a good listener. *Fuck that.* I didn't want her to listen to me. I wanted her wiggling and screaming my name while I did things to her that I couldn't say out loud. Well, I could, but not in school.

Haven released him. "I got your tickets." She dove into her purse and pulled out two tickets. "Lakemont will be playing at home in two weeks."

"Are those football tickets?" I asked even though I could see the writing. We were playing Regal College at home. "I could've gotten you some, Zack."

"I didn't want to bother you," Zack said. "Thanks, Haven. You're one cool chick. Ryker, when are you going to play again? I know you've got things on your mind, but the team really needs you."

"Soon," I said even though I wasn't sure. I definitely wouldn't be playing in the upcoming game on Saturday. I knew that much. Coach would want me to have at least a week of practice since I hadn't played a game yet that season.

"I know Leigh would want you to play," Zack said. "Anyway, I got to run." He winked at Haven. "If you need a date for the game, call me." Then he bounced out like he'd just won the lottery.

He was right. Leigh would have been on my ass if I didn't play.

Mr. Holland returned with a shoebox in his hands. "Here you go."

I held onto the box like it was the most delicate thing in this world to me. "Thanks. I have to get to a meeting with my coach." My plan was to get my head around my classes, which I hadn't been to since the semester started, talk to Coach Chapman, then get drunk, in that order. Or maybe I would drink once I left the high school. "Please let me know about the art festival."

After Principal Holland and I said our goodbyes, I winked at Haven like Zack had. I thought about repeating Zack's line and telling her to call me if she needed a date, but I didn't date.

So I hustled my ass out of the building and into the hot, humid sun, which was less suffocating than inside the school.

I'd just reached my car when my phone rang.

I answered without looking to see who it was. "What?"

"Gee. Who pissed in your coffee?" Franklin asked.

A redhead with legs, big tits, and a mouth I want to devour. Not to mention, my heart wanted to burst into flames over the loss of my family.

"Kari tells me you got out of bed and that you're back amongst the living. So I'm calling to remind you of your campus civic duty that you were supposed to start last week. I managed to convince the chancellor to cut you some slack. But those ten hours need to start soon."

I'd completely forgotten about that.

"You're to report to the maintenance department on campus on Thursday after your classes. Oh, and I hired a tutor to catch you up on your studies."

I pinched my eyebrows. "Please tell me she doesn't have red hair."

He chuckled. "The dude has brown hair."

Thank fuck.

If he had said her name was Haven Hale, then I didn't stand a chance of passing any of my classes.

16

HAVEN

The sound from the TV droned in the background as I finished up an English paper that was due the next day.

Vicki was over at Delta Sigma Pi, and I was dying to know if she'd been accepted into the sorority. There had been some drama at the sorority house. So Beverly and her team were late in picking the new recruits. I didn't want Vicki to get in, yet I did. I wanted her to be happy, but I didn't want to lose her as a roomie. I'd come to the conclusion that my idea of Vicki and Beverly in cahoots with my father wasn't true on Vicki's part. Vicki was realizing that Beverly wasn't such a nice person after all.

"She's too darn bossy," Vicki had complained. "And she doesn't listen."

Still, the idea of the dorm room all to myself was enticing. I could have dates over and have wild sex without worrying about a roommate. I laughed out loud as my gaze drifted from my spot on the couch to the TV screen across from me. The news was on, and the male reporter was talking about the upcoming election. I grabbed the remote off the small coffee table and turned up the volume.

"Early polls show that Senator Hale is slipping. He's lost several points against his opponent."

I could feel the space between my eyebrows creasing. My father's standing had been good last I knew, but that was several months ago.

The reporter continued. "Ned Lambert has been campaigning hard with his new policy that could cut emissions in Texas by half."

In order to do that, Ned Lambert would have to shut down most of the refineries in the state, and I didn't see that happening, although I didn't know what his plan entailed. What I did know was that my father was probably pacing his office, yelling at his aides, and throwing things at the wall.

The good news was I wasn't the problem—his opponent was. For that, I became giddy. Father Dearest wouldn't be in my face. Then again, he had no reason to be. I'd been a good girl, staying out of trouble and away from Ryker James. After our last encounter at Woodcreek High over a week ago, I'd had no reason to seek out the hunky quarterback.

News around campus was that he'd been hiding in the gym and practicing every morning and every night, getting ready for the home game that upcoming Saturday, which was in three days. The football team's record was dismal with three losses to start the season. The media had been making all kinds of speculations about the game and Ryker's return.

I was sure the stadium would be packed on Saturday. Vicki and I were going. When I'd bought tickets for Zack Cleary, I'd purchased two for Vicki and me right beside him.

The door opened, and Vicki came in with a smile on her face. I tracked her movements as she set down her purse on the small counter where we had a dorm-room-size fridge and hot plate.

I muted the volume on the TV. "Well? What's the verdict?"

She pulled out her clip, and her hair fell to her shoulders. Then she plopped down next to me. "I got in."

I raised my hand to high-five her. "That's great."

She gave my palm a weak tap. "Yeah, but I said no thank you."

"What! Why? You were dying to join a sorority."

Turning to face me, she tucked one leg underneath her and let the other dangle off the couch. "After the meetings, the parties, listening to Beverly, meeting the other women, I don't know. I just didn't feel it. I think for my freshman year, I want to explore. I don't want rules. I had enough of them at home." She picked at something on her bare leg. "I want to hang out with you. We have it made here."

We did. We didn't have to answer to anyone. We could come and go as we pleased. We didn't have chores except that we had agreed to keep things neat in the common room.

"You don't seem happy," I said.

"I am. I'm just…" She trailed off, glancing at the TV.

I waited, watching her bite her lip. "Just?"

"I saw Lucas kissing a girl earlier near Braden Hall."

I didn't know what to say without sounding like her mother or saying something cliché and stereotypical. But some guys liked to play the field. They liked a different girl in their bed, much like Ryker, who was known for sleeping with lots of women.

I gently placed a hand on her leg. "I'm sorry."

She shrugged. "I'll get over it. There are plenty of guys out there. Right?"

Knuckles wrapped on our door, hard.

I popped up and answered it. Once I did, I immediately slammed the door in Ryker's face.

He knocked again. "Open up." He slurred his words.

Vicki's eyes got big as she smiled. "What's he doing here?"

Great question. But I didn't care to find out, so I sat back down.

Ryker knocked again.

"Go away," I shouted.

Girls giggled loudly in the hall.

"I'm saving up money for the fundraiser to buy a date with you," a girl said.

"You know he might get mauled in the hall," Vicki said through a laugh.

"Let him. I don't care."

"You do, and you know it. Remember, big dick."

I snorted. "Stop reminding me." We were as bad as the men. If they were into boobs, we couldn't stop talking about penises. Or at least I couldn't stop thinking about Ryker's dick night after night.

I squeezed my legs together.

He knocked again.

That time, Vicki answered. "Come on in."

"Traitor," I said to her.

She laughed. "Ryker, you've made my night."

He waltzed in like he owned the room. "Wow. We haven't even fucked either."

"It's your lucky night, then," Vicki returned. Then she went over to the fridge and pulled out a soda.

Ryker sat down in Vicki's spot. Actually, he positioned himself almost on top of me.

I flew off the couch. "I told you to stay away from me." I grabbed the can of soda out of Vicki's hand and took a big gulp to rid my throat of the dryness or maybe to cool my heated body.

Ryker was too big for the small living area of our dorm room, and his body was way too big for the love seat we had.

He sat up straighter. "Got any beer?"

"No. And if we did, I wouldn't offer you any. Now leave."

"Ah, Haven," Vicki said. "Don't kick a guy when he's down." She leaned closer and whispered into my ear. "This is the perfect time to take advantage of him. Seriously, he's oozing all kinds of sex appeal right now."

I swallowed thickly. His button-up shirt was open at the top, showing a little chest hair. His sleeves were rolled up on his forearms, showing off his large diver's watch, which glinted in the light, and his ripped jeans hinted at what lay underneath his belt.

He licked his lips. "Can I at least get some water?"

Vicki obliged.

I didn't move. "Are you drunk?" He'd been drinking, but he didn't look wasted like that first night I'd met him and sat on his lap.

He twisted off the cap of the water bottle Vicki had just handed him. "I had a couple of beers." After gulping down half the bottle, he rested his forearms on his thighs as he glanced at the TV. "Your old man is losing his steam." He grinned, no doubt enjoying that piece of news.

I pressed my back into the edge of the counter. "What do you want?"

Vicki took her soda can, which I'd set on the counter.

Ryker raised an eyebrow at me. "Remember our convo in the pool house?"

I hadn't been able to shake his words. He'd been so sure that I would be in his bed with him between my legs.

Yep. "Nope."

He gave me a mischievous grin, almost sending me over the edge. In another minute, I would strip off my pajama shorts and tank for him, not even caring if Vicki watched.

His gaze drifted around the room. "How big is your bed?" He rose. "Which room is yours?"

Vicki choked. "That one over there." She was quick to point it out.

"Traitor," I said again, not sounding at all like I was angry with her.

Ryker walked over and poked his head in. "Mmm. That size will do." Then he went in.

What the heck?

Vicki giggled.

I stomped over to the doorway. "Get out."

The man owned my bed. "Not until we talk."

Suddenly, an image of Ryker and me between my sheets flashed before me.

"I have nothing to say to you."

Vicki waltzed over and nudged me in. "Seriously, you two need to screw and be done with it. I'll head downstairs and make myself busy."

I grabbed her arm. "Oh no, you don't."

"At least hear what he has to say," she said.

That was the problem. I wouldn't be listening to anything except our heavy breathing. Not only that, it didn't thrill me that I would be just another girl on his playboy-style list.

"Yeah, Heaven. Listen to your friend," Ryker whined in a husky voice. "I have a proposition for you. I'm sure you'll want to hear all about it."

I narrowed my eyes at him. "Nope."

Vicki shoved me farther inside. "I'll be downstairs." The door to our dorm room opened then closed.

I hovered near my dresser, staying super close to the door, as my stomach swirled like a tornado and my lady parts screamed for release.

Ryker, on the other hand, smirked. "I do like your roommate." Then his gaze went on a hike, checking me out from my bare toes up to my extremely short pajama bottoms then to my breasts, which were poking out a little too much in my drab tank top.

He leaned back on my bed, propping up on his elbows. "I would like for you to consider doing the fundraiser with the team. Before you say no, hear me out."

If it meant he would leave soon, I was in. So I folded my arms over my chest and waited for him to continue.

"The team thinks that adding a girl to the program would be fun and change things up. Plus, we feel we might be able to raise more if there's a mixture of guys and gals. Our goal this year is to raise twenty thousand dollars to support the Chelsea House for Battered Women."

I could see the team raising that amount with Ryker alone as hungry as women were to get their hands on him.

"Why me?"

"Because you're a senator's daughter. You can bring in at least two thousand dollars."

I laughed hard. "My answer is no." And it had nothing to do with my father at the moment. Sure, Ryker was asking nicely. Sure, Ryker was raising money for a good cause. But the whole senator's daughter excuse was bull crap. He knew my father didn't want me to participate.

He knew it would piss my dad off. He was using me. "Any girl can bring in that amount of money. And let's not forget how many guys are on the football team. That alone should meet your goal. Girls will pay two thousand or more just for you."

"Maybe for me," he said with a cocky smirk. "Only ten from the football team will be up for grabs. We had some guys bow out because of schedules and other shit."

"Have you asked other ladies?"

"We've got nine eager women on the list. We're looking for one more."

"I'm certain you can find one more, but not me."

He got up off the bed so fast, he made me dizzy. "What if I want you?"

The laugh that came out of me was a little choked. "No. You want to get under my father's skin. I will not be a pawn in your game."

He closed the distance between us until I was pinned up against a sliver of wall between the doorjamb and my dresser. "Haven, you're by no means a pawn." He lowered his head until I could feel his alcohol-infused breath breezing over my lips. "You're going to be my queen."

I thought I'd just died and gone to heaven.

"Think about it." He kept his dark-gray eyes on my mouth. "You'll be doing this for charity, but who knows, maybe your participation will help your old man's election." Then he brushed his arm over my chest as he walked out of my room.

When he was gone, I slid down the wall.

The only thing I could do at that moment was address the pulsing need I had in between my legs like I'd done every other night since I'd met him.

17

RYKER

Eleven days had flown by since I'd brought home Leigh's box that Principal Holland had given me. I hadn't opened the box, and I wasn't sure I was ready to. Each day that had passed since the funeral seemed to be getting better albeit slowly, which was why I didn't want to go down memory lane again.

So I'd tried to piece my life back together. I'd talked to Coach Chapman, gotten my ass back into the gym, practiced with the team, did four hours of my campus community service, and met with my advisor and then with my tutor to catch up on my classes. Not one drop of alcohol had entered my system during that time until the night I'd visited Haven in her dorm room. Before I'd gone over, Lucas and I had been sitting in our kitchen, discussing the fundraiser, when I'd gotten a call from the funeral director letting me know the headstones were ready. As soon as I'd hung up, I started drinking, and the last three days hadn't been any different.

I lay on the weight bench in the gym, staring up at the lights. I'd worked out hard for the last two hours, trying to sweat out the alcohol from the night before. I wasn't sure I was ready to play in the home game that day. My stomach was queasy, and my head spun a bit.

The door to the weight room creaked. "Ryker," Lucas called before he loomed over me. "There you are. I got your note. Why didn't you wake me up? I would've come down here with you."

I sat up, shoving my fingers through my sweaty hair. "I needed to be alone."

He went over to the stationary bike across from me. "You look like shit."

Thank you, booze. "I feel like crap."

He angled his head of blond curls. "You sure you can play today?"

I'd busted my ass in practice. My arm was ready, but my head wasn't, and neither was my stomach. "I guess we'll see." I was more afraid my head would get in the way of playing. Home games drew a crowd, and that had always meant that Leigh and my brother, Randal, would be watching me. Plus, the fans were expecting perfection. I wasn't sure I could give them perfection.

Lucas got on the bike, fiddling with the tension before he began pedaling. "Win or lose, man, the game will be good for you."

I grabbed my towel from the floor and wiped the sweat off my face, hoping he was right, hoping the energy and the team would light a fire under me and give me that high I always got on the football field.

Lucas straightened on the bike, holding onto his hips while pedaling away. "Any word from Haven on the fundraiser? I need to get the program printed, update the website, and I need her bio."

"She won't budge." The damn woman was stubborn. At first, I was using her. Actually, playing with her was a better way to put it. But all the guys who were participating agreed with Lucas. Having both sexes involved would make the fundraiser more interesting and give us the potential to bring in more money.

"Why limit it to us guys?" Erik had asked. "I would pay high dollar for a hot blonde."

The rules were that we couldn't bid on anyone if we were participating. Still, there were tons of guys on campus who would support a good cause, especially if a gorgeous woman was up for grabs.

"Maybe you should talk to her," I said.

"We can find another girl," Lucas added, breathing heavily as he continued to pedal. "Although I think she could bring in the most money, not only because she's a senator's daughter, but she does stand out above all the women who are on the list." He sounded sad. "Were you nice to Haven when you asked her?"

My best bud was more disappointed than me that Haven didn't want to be part of the charity event. But Haven was right. We didn't need her. We could raise the twenty thousand dollars with the list of people we had so far. I was sure I could command at least two thousand like Haven had said. And maybe if she weren't in the lineup, she would bid on me. Now there was an idea.

I chuckled. "I was the perfect gentleman."

Lucas stopped pedaling. "You're lying. What did you do?"

I raised my hands. "Truth. I went over there, talked to her, and left without so much as touching her. Look, forget about Haven. We'll raise our goal." The charity was also near and dear to Lucas's heart. He had a cousin who had fallen into a bad situation with a guy.

He harrumphed. "You're probably right. I'm sure you'll bring in a hefty dollar amount."

"As will you, dude," I added.

He didn't react. "I'll talk to Haven, though, and if it's a final no, I'll ask her roommate, Vicki. She's quite hot herself. But we need to finalize the names this weekend. The programs will take at least a week before they're ready, and I still have to get a few more bios."

We had a good month before the fundraiser. So Lucas had time, but I knew him. He had OCD when it came to planning things, which was why he'd been elected to organize our fundraisers every year.

Lucas started in on something else, but I tuned him out, wondering if Haven would bid on me. I knew she wanted me. I would bet my entire trust fund that her panties had been soaked that night I'd had her up against the wall in her dorm room.

Man, I would give my throwing arm just to taste her.

Think of something else, dude, or else your hard-on will be poking out at any second.

That didn't matter. Lucas had seen me with an erection more times than I was sure he cared to. I'd seen him in the same predicament too.

But my mind was still stuck on Haven as Lucas continued talking in the background. Seeing her relaxed in her dorm room with a revealing tank and extremely short pajama bottoms had been a sight to behold. I'd done everything I could to keep my dick from getting hard. I loved how her body reacted to me, though. I loved that she'd been breathing heavy when our bodies were so close. I would have sworn I could feel her tits against my chest.

Lucas snapped his fingers.

I blinked.

"You didn't hear a fucking word I said. Did you?"

I hadn't even heard him come over. "I was thinking."

"Of a redhead."

I shrugged. "So sue me."

Lucas wiped the towel he had in his hands over his face. "You need to get laid, bro."

Fuck yeah, I did. But I didn't want just any girl. My dick was throbbing just thinking about Haven. "Not by her." *You're so full of shit.* "I hate her old man. And she and I would be a disaster. She's stubborn, not a quality I like in my women."

He rolled his neck around before picking up two free weights. "Stubborn is just what you need. If you ask me, you two would be a match made in heaven."

Heaven? He did have to pick that word.

"Can we just concentrate on football right now?" I said more than asked. Otherwise, I would need to jack off before the game.

"Ryker, are you in here?" Coach Chapman raised his voice before he emerged from around the wall that stood in between the weight room and the door. He was dressed in Lakemont colors—a red golf shirt with the Lakemont logo stitched on the chest in gold, a ball cap, and khakis. "The security guard said you were here." He tucked his hands into his pants pockets. "Good to see you here early. How are you feeling?"

Coach Chapman had given me my space even though he wanted me back on the field.

I still had my butt planted on the weight bench. "I'm good."

He regarded me with his blue gaze, studying me hard. "Look, if you're not, I understand."

"He's good, Coach," Lucas said. "If he weren't, he wouldn't play."

In part, Lucas was right. I prayed, though, that once I was out on the field, I would forget everything except football.

Coach nodded, still studying me. "See the trainer. He'll loosen you up." His lips thinned out. "We need a win today, Ryker."

I rose and gave him one of my cocky grins. "We'll win. I'm ready. The team is ready." I had to be confident.

He raised a bushy eyebrow. "You've been through hell. So I'll understand if you're not feeling the game."

I hated seeing the worry on his face. "I've got this."

Hopefully, Lucas was right, and football would be good for me.

18

HAVEN

The football stadium was overflowing with fans of all ages and sizes, but mainly the students of Lakemont University—the marching band, those with painted faces, and everyone decked out in the school colors of rose and gold. The atmosphere was crazy, electric, and exciting.

"Come on. They've got to win," Vicki said at my side, biting her nail.

I was a little nervous as well, more for Ryker than anything. I wasn't a big fan of football. I'd been to an NFL game with my mom and dad many years ago. I didn't remember much of the Cowboys game except that my father had lost five thousand dollars betting against the Cowboys.

Nevertheless, I wanted to see Ryker do well.

"Come on, Ryker," Zack said on the other side of me. "You've got to get this touchdown."

I chewed on my lip, almost holding my breath along with every other fan. We were losing by five points. With one minute to go in the game and the ball on the ten-yard line, Ryker needed to throw a touchdown.

He'd been shaky a good majority of the game. My heart went out to him. I couldn't imagine what had been going through his head on the field, but it was evident he hadn't been concentrating.

"He's rusty," a guy behind me had said.

"Wow," another man had said. "Ryker has never been sacked until today."

I didn't know Ryker's football history, but listening to the fans around me, I'd learned that Ryker James had been number one in passing and touchdowns and had hardly thrown an interception until last year when he'd thrown three in one game.

Still, the entire stadium was pulling for him. I would even bet the rival fans were too. I would imagine that this game wasn't so much about getting a win as it was seeing Ryker do well after what he'd been through.

Lakemont took a time-out, and both teams huddled around their coach.

The fans began chanting Ryker's name.

Both teams jogged out onto the field.

Ryker huddled with his men one last time before getting into position.

The fans jumped to their feet, still chanting Ryker's name. I even joined in.

Vicki took my hand. "He's going to do it."

Before I could even blink, the center snapped the ball to Ryker. He barely had the ball in his hands before he threw it to Lucas, who was in the end zone.

The stadium went quiet.

Lucas jumped up just as a Regal defenseman dove in front of him. The ball hit the tips of the Regal defenseman's fingers before Lucas grabbed the ball and tucked it into him for a touchdown.

The fans went crazy. The decibel level inside the stadium was off the charts. Vicki and I exchanged a hug, as did Zack and me.

"He needed that win so badly," Zack said. "Leigh is flipping out right now." He glanced up at the blue sky.

I'd learned at the start of the game that Zack had been dating Leigh. Mr. Bridges had said Zack and Leigh were tight, but he hadn't mentioned that they were boyfriend and girlfriend.

"She is," I said to him.

The marching band played as reporters gathered down on the field, trying to get to Ryker, who was being mauled by his teammates.

"Haven, thanks again," Zack said. "If you're ever up to it, you can come to one of our football games." He wagged a finger between him and his friend, Chris.

The pimple-faced blond smiled. "Your friend can come too."

Vicki was staring at the field, oblivious to the high schoolers. I had no doubt she was focused on Lucas.

I thanked them for the offer before both of them followed a horde of fans out of the stands.

Vicki nudged me. "Look."

I scanned the field to find a reporter interviewing Ryker and Lucas. Then their voices blared through the jumbotron.

"How does it feel to be back?" the male reporter asked with his microphone in front of Ryker's lips.

"It's been a little surreal, but I'm happy to be playing again," Ryker said. "I credit this win to my teammates. They were the ones who won this game. Our defense was tight, and they had my back out there."

"But you were sacked," the reporter said. "A first for you."

"And a last," Ryker added, then he glanced out at the stadium. "I want to say thank you to you guys." He waved his hand around while he held his helmet in the other. "Thank you for being patient. Thank you for all your well wishes and sympathy messages. I can't tell you how humble I am and what it means to me." Then he looked up at the sky, blessing himself. "This is game is for you, Mom, Dad, Leigh, and Randal."

Tears burned my eyes.

The remaining fans cheered.

Then Lucas leaned down toward the mic. "Cal, if I may. On behalf of the football team, we would like to remind fans that we have a fundraiser coming up. This year, we're doing an auction, and the proceeds will go to benefit the Chelsea House for Battered Women. It will take place at the Marriott Hotel in town four weeks from today. You can find all the information at the Chelsea House website."

"And what are you auctioning off?" Cal asked.

"A night out with your favorite football player or favorite sorority sister or senator's daughter," Lucas replied.

"Sounds like something that could bring in a lot of money for a great cause," Cal added. "You mentioned a senator's daughter?"

Ryker leaned into the mic. "Yes. Haven Hale. So I'm sure the event will be a success."

My blood gelled.

Vicki whipped her head around to look at me. "You said no to him. Why is he announcing your name?"

I was going to kill a quarterback.

My phone went off. I didn't have to look at it to know it was my father. I let the phone ring as I clenched my fists at my sides. And as if Ryker knew I was there, he looked right at me.

It wasn't hard to find Vicki and me. The others around us had left with the exception of a handful of women who were probably waiting for Ryker and Lucas to walk off the field.

A couple of other reporters and their cameramen followed Ryker's line of sight.

I tapped Vicki on the arm. "We should get out of here." A senator's daughter was headline news, especially if the daughter was involved in an auction where she was up for grabs.

Vicki hesitated.

"I'm leaving," I said to her.

She scurried up the steps behind me, and we managed to make it out into the parking lot without any reporters on our tail.

I was about to breathe a sigh of relief when a young lady held out her phone toward me as she pushed off from her car, which was parked in a space close to the stadium's entrance.

"Haven Hale?" the young brunette asked. "I'm Brandi Brock, a reporter for the university newspaper. Is it true that you're part of the lineup for the Chelsea House event?"

Kill Ryker James.

My phone buzzed again. If I didn't answer it, my father would send down his goons to kidnap me.

I held up my hand. "I have to take this." I would rather hear my father yell than answer the reporter, particularly as mad as I was. I didn't want the nice woman to endure my wrath. Not only that, she would probably post in the paper how much of a bitch I could be.

Like father, like daughter.

Vicki and Brandi started talking while I walked a good distance away from them. Cars were trying to get out of the lot while some fans were hanging out on the backs of their trucks, drinking and eating.

"Don't start, Father," I said harshly.

"How many times do I have to tell you that I can't have negative media attention?" His tone was grating.

"How many times do I have to tell you? I'm not part of any fundraiser. Nor am I involved with Ryker James. And before you say anything else, I can't control the man and the words that come out of his mouth."

I swore I wanted to deck both Ryker and my father.

I could hear my father breathing a little heavy. "I'm down in the polls. This isn't going to help me."

Polls, media, and elections were the bane of my existence. Ever since my father went into politics, I'd had to watch how I acted, what I said, and give up on being a normal teenager. I was tired of it all.

"Maybe me helping out a good cause would help you," I said. "If the media sees that I'm doing something good, then it's in your favor. It's not like I'm drunk at a bar or caught with my pants down or making a spectacle out of myself. Besides, I can spin this to your advantage."

"I'm listening," he said in a softer tone.

Wow! That was a first on two things. He was listening, and I was about to help him.

I wasn't sure if I could do the latter. After all, my actions had nothing to do with his policies or the bills he supported, and at the end of the day, what my father could do in the senate and for the state was what mattered. However, any media attention, good or bad, did put my father in the spotlight, which could take away from the message he was trying to get out to voters.

"I'll get back to you." Before he could protest that he wanted to hear my idea, I hung up and walked back to Vicki and Brandi. They seemed to have become fast friends, giggling and talking.

Brandi regarded me with her big brown eyes. "Vicki tells me that you're not in the lineup. How come? It's for a great cause."

Now she was making me feel like a first-class bitch who didn't care about others.

Nevertheless, I pinched my eyebrows for nothing more than to do something while I thought about what I was going to say. Still, I wasn't thrilled to be auctioned off to some guy I didn't know. In my mind, the event was similar to a blind date, but I didn't do blind dates. The last one I'd been on was a disaster.

A girlfriend I'd hung out with my junior year at boarding school had hooked me up with her cousin at a wedding she'd had to go to. Her cousin had turned out to be one of those guys who thought his shit didn't stink. He'd thought that putting me down was giving me a compliment. In the end, I'd understood why he couldn't get a girl even though he hadn't been bad looking.

Brandi stuck her phone at me. "Care to comment?"

I rolled back my shoulders and held out my chin. "The charity event is for a good cause, and my father, Senator Hale, and I feel that we can help out. So I *will* be participating, and my father will also be donating ten thousand dollars to the charity." My father would probably have a baby when he found out the amount I'd committed on his behalf, but I didn't care. If he wanted to show voters a side of him that no one hardly saw, then the time was now. Maybe the charitable donation would help him in the polls.

Vicki's jaw dropped, although the excitement swimming in her eyes said she was more than happy.

I didn't how I felt, but maybe I would walk away with a night out with some hot guy. Maybe Ryker James.

19

RYKER

My house was teeming with people as night set in. Lucas and I had decided to invite a few friends over to our house near campus, including the football team, to celebrate our big win that day.

Not all our teammates could make it, but the tight-knit group of Ajax, Erik, Vin, Lucas, and me were gathered around the kitchen island while other invited guests lounged out by or in the pool.

I was still high from our win. I couldn't believe we'd actually won. I'd had my doubts, especially when I'd walked out onto the field. My nerves had been in my throat, my stomach had been queasy, and my legs had felt like Silly Putty. It had taken me a few plays to get in the groove. Even then, I hadn't been myself. Getting sacked had stymied me, and it had taken all Coach had had to get through to me.

Despite all that, as the game had progressed, I'd started to lose my nerves and the nausea. By the last two minutes in the game, I'd felt normal again, particularly after the win, which was what I'd needed.

When Lucas had said football or the game would be good for me, I'd had my doubts. But I felt like a weight had been lifted off my stomach. Coach Chapman had been pleased but not thrilled. We still had many games to play, and hopefully the next would be easier for me.

Vin handed me a shot while the guys picked up theirs. "Toast."

I pinned a look on Vin, Ajax, Erik, and Lucas, sighing with relief at how they'd had my back on the field, how they would always have my back. Because of that, another weight was lifted.

Vin raised his shot of whiskey. "Here's to Ryker. Man, we know it's been hard for you. We know that this game took all the muscle you had, but you did it."

I held up my hand. "Before we drink, I want to say something. Vin is right. It's been fucking hard as hell for me the last month and a half. Sometimes I don't know if the sun is up or not. Sometimes I don't want to even get out of bed."

A partygoer walked into the kitchen, but Erik shoved him out. "Closed meeting, dude. I'll let you know when you can come in. If you want a drink, the coolers are out on the patio."

I glanced out the sliding glass door that Lucas got up and locked. A muted beat of music pumped out of the speakers we had hanging from the house outside.

"Continue," Erik said, coming back to join us.

"Look, I'm sure I'm going to have more dark moments. So please don't give up on me. Today was refreshing, but tomorrow could be something else." I had no idea how many ups and downs I had to get through before I didn't feel like the world was crashing down around me.

"You need to get laid," Ajax said. "When was the last time?"

I cocked an eyebrow. "I don't need any of you to be my pimps."

Everyone chuckled.

"I swear," Erik said. "A good fuck will help cure you in more ways than you can imagine."

I chuckled, almost teasing that I couldn't get a hard-on to save my life, but that wasn't true anymore, not when Haven was around or I was thinking of her.

"Leave my sex life to me. Now, drink and then get the fuck out of here and enjoy yourself."

We knocked back the shot, then some of the guys shook off the burning alcohol. As for me, the whiskey didn't burn at all. That should've worried me, but I didn't want to analyze anything that night.

The guys scattered.

Lucas slid his phone over to me. "Check it out."

Brandi: *The headline for the paper will read: "Haven Hale will be part of the Chelsea auction in late October." Send me the list of all the names, and I'll add that to my story.*

I shrugged, grabbing the bottle of whiskey. I really wanted that bottle of scotch that Franklin had given me, but that was at my parents' house. "I guess that plug we put in with the reporter on the field did the trick. Now you have your list."

A laugh rumbled out of his chest. "Why do I get the feeling you're disappointed? I thought you wanted her in it."

"Dude, you wanted her to participate more than me. I only started the whole 'add a female' thing because I wanted to fuck with her head and her old man."

"Speaking of her old man, he's donating ten grand to the charity."

I didn't know how to take that one. "I wonder if he's trying to make up for screwing with my old man." I doubted it, but it was a thought.

"Or maybe Haven coaxed him into it," Lucas said.

My stomach did a flip at the mention of her name. *What the fuck?*

"What? You look like you've seen a ghost," Lucas said.

He knew me well. "I'm cool."

Lucas's face twisted. "Bullshit. It's Haven. As soon as her name comes up, you react. It's subtle, but I know you. It's okay to like her."

I didn't like how well he could read me. "Have you met her old man?"

Chuckling, Lucas gripped my shoulder. "Ryker James brooding over a chick."

"Dude, I'm not brooding. Give me a few minutes. I'll come find you guys." I left Lucas before he tried to get me to open up. The day was ending on a good note, and I wanted to leave it like that.

I wound my way through the house, dodging people, with a whiskey bottle in one hand and checking my pockets for my phone with the other. But I came up empty on my phone. I must've left it in my room.

Instead of going down into the basement, I headed upstairs until my gaze drifted like a lazy breeze on a hot summer day to a couple in the living room. The redhead had her back to me, and on first impulse, I ambled in that direction.

I was curious why Haven had agreed to be part of the charity auction all of a sudden. She'd been adamant about not doing the fucking event. But when a tall, lanky dude leaned down and kissed the redhead on the lips, my gut twisted in a weird way.

I froze in my tracks, my brain searching for reasons why a guy kissing Haven would bother me. But analysis went by the wayside when some short and bulky guy bumped into me, causing me to lose my train of thought.

"Sorry, Ryker."

I held up my hand. "No worries." I wasn't about to start a brawl, although I had the urge to punch the dude kissing Haven until the redhead turned around.

It wasn't Haven, but man, the girl could've passed for the senator's daughter. Maybe Haven had a sister I didn't know about. The chick's long red hair matched Haven's in color, as did her curves. But what didn't match were her small tits. Haven's were far from small.

The booze was creeping up on me for sure.

Nevertheless, I continued to my bedroom, dodging people who were sitting on the stairs. As I wound my way down the hall, I found that my door was ajar.

What the fuck?

I always locked my door during a party. Lucas locked his too. I hoofed it down the hall and barreled in as though I were a bouncer ready to throw someone out the window, not caring if a naked girl was waiting for me.

A blonde sat on my bed, fully dressed and searching through…

Motherfucker!

I closed the distance between Tabitha Sims, Beverly's sister, and me. Then I grabbed her by the arm and hauled her up. "What are you doing in my room?" I ripped the picture she was holding out of her hand.

She squealed. "Let me go. You're hurting me."

I eased up on my grip as I deposited her at my door. "I'll ask you again. What are you doing in here?"

She squinted her beady blue eyes. "I came to congratulate you on a great game. So much for that."

I placed the picture of my family back in Leigh's box. I hadn't even opened it, and this stupid woman had the fucking nerve to go through my things. Fury, hot as an out-of-control inferno, blazed through my veins. "You're trespassing. Do you normally go into people's rooms and go through their personal items before you congratulate them?"

She hiked a bare shoulder. She was wearing one of those blouses that slipped down her arm on one side. "I saw the box on your dresser and peeked into it."

This chick shopped at a different mall. Either that, or she was a penny away from crazy town.

I was tired of Tab and Beverly trying to get their claws into me. Granted, the last time Beverly had tried was when I'd woken up after a drunken fest and found her in my bed, although she'd left a few messages on my phone that I hadn't returned. I wasn't going to either.

Tabitha was just like her sister. Both were out to find a husband before they graduated college. Well, I wasn't that guy.

"The next time you decide to go through someone's things when you're not supposed to, I would think twice. The next person might not be so nice." Then I slammed the door in her face and locked the fucker.

I took a swig of whiskey and then another before I set the bottle down on my nightstand. I went to put the lid back on the box but hesitated. Maybe it was a good time to go through Leigh's things. I dropped down on the bed and pulled out more pictures of Leigh and her friends, the one of our family, bookmarks, and her art supplies. But underneath all that, I found an envelope with my name on it.

With shaky hands, I examined the envelope as though it held

secrets I was afraid to see. Holding my breath, I removed the card. Before I could read it, knuckles wrapped on my door, soft and light.

"Go away, Tabitha," I shouted. She'd probably forgotten something, but as I glanced around, I didn't see anything.

Another knock sounded, then the knob turned.

The fury that had waned reared its ugly head. I was going to carry Tabitha out of the house by her flimsy see-through shirt.

I deposited the card back in the box and went to open the door. When I did, my jaw came unhinged. "What do you want?" I asked, sounding like a guy who was about to lose his shit.

Haven craned her neck up at me with a smile that made my stomach do that flip again.

"Please tell me you're here to take care of my libido. Otherwise, you know where the door is."

She rolled her emerald eyes.

"Follow the Yellow Brick Road" popped into my head.

I started to close the door, but the petite woman slipped by me and into my room.

I spun on my heel, ready to unleash something on her, but my tongue wasn't working as she continued to show me her pretty white teeth. Or maybe it was her lips that had me thinking dirty thoughts.

She stuck her hands on her hips, drawing my eye down to her tanned legs, which were on display beneath her shorts. "You mean the last girl who was in here didn't take care of your libido? I find that hard to believe."

I let my gaze roam freely up and down her fantastic body, which was making my dick grow. I was convinced she was my beacon.

I locked us in just in case other women tried to parade through my room, which wasn't far-fetched at the parties Lucas and I had.

She eyed the door. "Are you kidnapping me?"

"Do you want to be kidnapped?"

She sucked in her bottom lip, and my dick jerked.

She whirled around, taking in the normal bedroom furniture in my humble room. Her gaze landed on a painting Leigh had done for me that depicted Lakemont Stadium. Leigh had drawn every detail, right down to the team on the field.

Haven pointed at the painting. "Your sister did that?" I suspected she'd read Leigh's name in the bottom corner.

"What do you want?" I wasn't in the mood to talk about Leigh. My mind was on the card I had yet to read.

Haven abandoned the painting. "I came to tell you that you got your wish. I'm also here for the party."

I leaned against the door. "You mean you came to give me a blow job?"

She snarled. "Why are you so cranky? Is it the booze? Alcoholics tend to get mean."

I belted out a laugh. "Are you my shrink or something?" She might be right. I was probably bordering on becoming a full-fledged alcoholic. "Cranky is my middle name."

She giggled, and if it wasn't a heart-pumping sound, I didn't know what was. I wished I knew why this girl was getting to the places inside me that hadn't been touched in forever.

"Cranky is your middle name? Mmm. I heard it's Foreplay King."

I grinned so wide, I thought the corners of my mouth would reach my ears. "You like foreplay king." I licked my lips. "You're thinking of what I could do to you. Aren't you?" I knew I was.

Her cheeks flushed as she picked up the whiskey bottle. "Not at all." She uncapped it and took a long drink. Once she swallowed, she choked.

I angled my head. "Do you lie a lot?"

After downing another gulp of whiskey, she returned the bottle to the nightstand, wiping her mouth with the back of her hand. "I never lie."

I couldn't lose my grin if she paid me.

She sighed. "I wanted to tell you that I'm going to do your fundraiser."

"I know. I heard. After tomorrow, the whole campus will know.

The question is, does your old man?" I suspected he did since he was donating money, but I wanted to hear it from Haven.

Her nostrils flared. "It was his idea."

I imagined the little nostril gesture was because I'd mentioned her old man.

"Liar. He wouldn't let you." The senator didn't allow things unless they benefited him, and he wasn't thrilled when the fundraiser had come up at the church the other day. "Frankly, I couldn't care less if you do the charity event or not."

She didn't react to anything I'd said, not even a flinch or a raised brow. Then again, she was a politician's daughter. She had probably been taught how to play her cards, and for some reason, that excited the fuck out of me.

I felt a challenge coming on. Would she react if I stripped her naked? Would she react if I devoured every inch of her? Would she react with me inside her?

My cock was jumping up and down, and holy fuck if her mesmerizing emerald orbs didn't lower to my crotch.

Her breathing ramped up as her tits poked out of the low-cut blouse she was wearing.

My cock grew, as did my pulse. I only made the first move when a woman gave me a sign. At that moment, Haven was staring at my groin, and while every vibe in me told me she wanted me, I wanted her to make the first move. But the more she stared, the harder it was not to pounce.

20

HAVEN

I tried to get my heart to calm down as I blatantly stared at Ryker's dick, which was huge and growing in his jeans. I swore the zipper would burst open.

Stupid me for storming into his room like I owned the house, like I lived there. But I'd sought him out to congratulate him and to let him know I would do the stupid charity thing. Or maybe I did want to spar with the quarterback. I was in the mood to do something wild that night. After the reaming I'd gotten from my father about the ten-thousand-dollar donation, I needed to do something to blow off steam.

Now I was trapped, and while excitement seeped into my bones at the idea of Ryker and me naked, a smidge of fear tamped it down. I wasn't afraid of him. I was afraid of me—afraid I would make a fool of myself by ripping his clothes off.

He stared at me with a grin that was all sin as his big body barricaded the door, daring me to leave, daring me to try to get past him.

But my feet were rooted to the carpeted floor as I debated my next move or waited for his.

The heavier his eyelids became, the more heat shot down and

settled in between my legs, and he knew it. The jerk knew it. That grin on his face only got wider.

My chest rose and fell until voices resounded in the hall. If another woman attempted to come in, I might succumb to a catfight.

Ryker pushed off the door like a lion getting ready to pounce.

My pulse flew off the charts.

He took one step then another.

Bang. Bang. Bang. My heart rammed against my ribs, and I licked my dry lips.

He cocked an eyebrow.

Move, Haven. It's now or never. Decide. Stay or go.

My body wouldn't move, and the closer he got, the more my feet sank into the carpet.

He came to a stop with barely any room between us. My only way out was to crawl onto his bed and escape from the other side.

I allowed my gaze to wander over him, drinking in his features—strong jaw, lips that were made for kissing, patrician nose, long lashes that framed gray eyes swirling with sorrow, lust, and mischief.

I got the feeling he was ready to combust, ready to do things to me that I might regret or want more of.

I gnawed on my lip, debating my next move. Then a laugh broke out in my head. The only move I had was to get on his bed, open my legs, and beg for him to do things that would live up to his nickname.

"Problem, Heaven?"

I was beginning to like the name Heaven. I had no doubt he could take me there.

"I need to go," I said in a weak voice. I had nowhere to be, but I couldn't stay there.

He grabbed strands of my hair and twirled them around his finger.

Get out now.

Nothing good could come from a wild night with Ryker, except complete and utter bliss from an experience that would stay with me forever. And that was the problem. One night with him, and I would want more, especially if he lived up to his nickname of Foreplay King.

Then again, his reputation of sleeping around soured me, and I didn't want to be discarded like a dirty condom.

No, thank you.

He inched closer until our bodies were almost touching. Without thinking, I grabbed hold of his belt buckle to anchor myself. Otherwise, I would've fallen back onto the bed, or my knees would've given out.

He angled his head. Those gray eyes grew darker, like the clouds in a summer storm, as he studied me. He let go of my hair and traced his finger down the swell of one breast then the another.

Goose bumps spread out over my entire body as the pulsing need between my legs intensified. Hell, since I'd met the man, I'd become one horny female.

I was tempted to unbutton my shorts and rip off my blouse, but I was a lady and had been taught to act like one. A lady didn't strip naked for a man she didn't know.

Bull. Of course they did in the heat of the moment.

His finger kept tracing my breasts as though he were coloring in the lines.

"I have to go." My tone was breathy.

"So you keep saying." His voice was husky, and oh boy, that elicited more goose bumps. "Do you want me to stop?"

I shook my head ever so slightly as my nipples went from hard to stone.

As if he knew, his finger started in that direction. "You're incredibly sexy."

My head jerked up, and I widened my eyes. "You're drunk."

"Far from it, Heaven."

"Haven."

He lowered his head until his lips were on my ear. "I like calling you Heaven."

I stuck out my breasts. *And I like you touching me.*

"I bet, Heaven, that you're soaked right now."

Asshat. "Maybe you should find out," I said a little too boldly.

"You would like that."

Fucking love it. "Not at all. I don't believe you're the Foreplay King." I was saying stupid shit.

In a flash, his hand went around to my lower back, and he hauled me to him, pressing my body into his enormous dick. Then he was nibbling on my earlobe. "I don't think you can handle me."

"It's you who couldn't handle me, big guy."

Bold much, girl?

His tongue dipped into my ear as he continued to make sure I felt every hard inch of him. "Are you a betting woman, Heaven?"

"I know how to play poker."

He chuckled as he guided my hand until it was seated on his crotch. "Remember how this felt in your hand that night? Well, imagine how it would feel inside you."

I whimpered as I squeezed his erection.

"I will break you," he said as sure as my eyes were droopy with lust.

He would break me in more ways than one. "Stop your bullshit talking and bragging and do something. Or else I'm walking out of here." Or rather stumbling out because my legs were weak and shaky.

He belted out a laugh. "I'm afraid your old man wouldn't like that."

Screw the bastard.

"Do you really want to ruin the moment by bringing my father into this room filled with so much heat between us?"

He flattened his palms against my cheeks, looked me in the eye, and studied me.

I was tempted to fire the first kiss or unbuckle his belt. But I wanted him to make the first move. I'd given him all the signs. Not that I was shy, but if he wanted me, then he needed to show me.

But when he brushed his lips over mine, I lost all thought, and my hands started unbuckling his jeans.

Screw foreplay.

If he didn't get inside me right that instant, I would climax standing there.

That one move was all he needed to rip off my clothes. The good news was that I didn't have much to rip off.

When I was completely naked, he edged back, or maybe stumbled, and his mouth hung open.

The light on his nightstand cast a glow, showing a primitive wildness in his eyes as he drank me in. "No panties? Fuck me." He grabbed his dick.

I pouted. I wanted to be his hand. But if he could play, so could I. I pinched my nipples, not taking my eyes off him.

He watched in lustful fascination, sucking in his bottom lip.

Then I let one of my hands travel down my stomach, slow and sure, keeping my gaze on his.

His breathing increased as he continued to squeeze his dick.

I opened my legs slightly and dipped my fingers into a place I wanted his mouth and tongue.

A look of pain so blissful washed over him. "Play with yourself." His tone was strained and raspy.

So I did, my eyes rolling back in my head as I continued to roll my nipple between my fingers and circle my clit with the other hand. At any second, I would be diving off that cliff, but I didn't want to come yet. I wanted to play with him, not myself.

I removed my hand before I caved. "Your turn."

A grin emerged as he unzipped his pants. "Come here."

I closed the short distance between us.

He tore off his shirt, showing off dips and valleys and that happy trail.

Oh my!

I inhaled a huge breath as I planted my hands on his abs, ready to explore.

His fingers circled my wrists before he guided them down to his zipper. Then he lowered his head and sucked in one nipple while pinching the other.

I squealed then moaned, opening my legs wider.

He dragged his lips over to the other breast and gave that one equal attention.

My hands dove into his thick hair, pulling him to me. "Bite."

He chuckled but bit down on my nipple.

I moaned loudly.

"Fuck, Haven." He bit down on the other nipple.

"Harder," I whispered.

"Say my name."

I pinched my eyebrows as he lifted his head.

"I want to hear my name on your lips."

"Not until you make me come," I fired back.

His lips curled on one side.

"And I want you naked," I said in a pained voice.

He opened his arms. "I'm all yours. Strip me."

I unzipped his jeans and found that he was commando too. That was enough to send my pulse soaring.

He shucked his jeans and stood there naked and godly. He was downright sex on a stick.

I swallowed the dryness in my throat. My gaze was glued to his enormous dick. Before he could move, I dropped to my knees and captured his dick in between my lips.

He tensed.

I swirled my tongue around the tip.

He moaned.

So I sucked harder.

He grunted.

I sucked more.

"Fuck," he almost shouted.

I let go of his dick with a pop. "Say my name."

"You're fucking heaven, Haven."

I rewarded him by playing with his balls then latched on to his erection, sucking and licking, trying to watch every emotion cross his face—pain, pleasure, lust, and euphoria.

I grabbed the backs of his legs for leverage and took him deep.

His body tensed as he groaned and said my name over and over.

Then before I knew what was happening, I was in his arms, and he was throwing me on the bed. The box that was near me bounced, along with my breasts.

I giggled.

He didn't. He placed the box on his nightstand then straddled me, his erection barely touching my stomach. "You're beautiful, bold, and fucking off the charts."

My cheeks flushed. I'd never had a guy tell me as much, at least not in the heat of the moment. I had a feeling Ryker didn't say that to many women he brought to bed, and that made me want him more.

"My turn to play," he said. "Arms over your head, and no touching your body or mine unless I tell you to." He crawled off me, pulled my legs down until my butt was close to the edge of the bed. "Knees up."

I obeyed him like a well-trained puppy. At the moment, I would do anything for him as long as the end game was a climax—a long, drawn-out climax.

"Good girl." He stood erect and played with himself, raking his gaze over my body from head to toe and everywhere in between.

I could feel a snarl forming. While it was a beautiful sight to see him play, he was tormenting me as though he wanted to make me pay for something.

But as much as he wanted to be in control, my body needed a release. So I went to place my fingers on my clit.

He shook his head ever so slowly. "Haven." The warning sent delightful shivers through my body.

Nevertheless, I was intrigued as to what he would do if I disobeyed. I raised my brows, my fingers sliding down my stomach as I spread my legs wider.

He continued to pump himself, trying to reach his own release, all the while piercing me with his eyes as though he were considering what to do with me.

I didn't care if he spanked me. I didn't care if he tied me up. My only goal was to climax.

"R-Ryker," I stuttered.

He smirked. "All I want you to do is watch, beautiful. Feel the pleasurable pain as you watch me." His tongue snaked out as he lowered his gaze to my sex. "Watch what you're doing to me."

"Sixty-nine," I said. "We can come together."

His hand froze. Then in a flash, we were positioned in a perfect sixty-nine with him on top. Before his tongue touched my clit, my lips were around his dick.

I sucked him so darn hard, I swore his groan made the house shake.

Then he dove into me, his tongue capturing my clit, and I bucked off the bed.

I sucked him. He licked me. I licked him. He sucked me. Back and forth we went with moans, groans, and sweet noises.

His head bobbed, as did mine.

Nothing in the world mattered except him and me and making music that I prayed would last forever.

But forever came to an abrupt halt when his tongue dove into me then back up to my clit in quick succession. My body tensed, and my mouth opened wide as lightning flashed behind my eyelids.

He continued to suck through my release. Instead of screaming his name, I clamped down on his erection. When I did, his body tightened, and he pulled out as he came all over my chest.

I relaxed into the bed, trying to catch my breath as my toes tingled.

He crawled off me then adjusted himself until his head was near mine. We lay there, breathing heavy, as the *tick, tick, tick* of the fan blades above us reverberated in the room. Or maybe it was my heart pounding in my ears.

Ryker shoved both hands through his hair. "Holy fuck."

"Something wrong?" If he so much as said yes, I would throat-punch him.

"That was…"

"Unforgettable," I added.

21

———

RYKER

I couldn't get my breathing under control. My body was soaked in sweat, and the ride Haven had just taken me on was… I had no words other than *holy fuck*.

Her breathing was just as labored as mine as we both stared up at the fan. I was still seeing stars, bright, blissful, and so laden with adrenaline, that I didn't think I would come down off this high for at least a month… or maybe a lifetime.

"I need to get cleaned up," she whispered through deep breaths.

I popped up, quick and fast, and grabbed my T-shirt. "Don't move." I didn't want her to leave just yet. I didn't want her to leave ever. I wanted another ride, or a hundred, or a thousand more.

I returned and proceeded to wipe my spunk off her. "Why are you in my life?" I'd asked her that before, and I knew she didn't have the answer, but *fuck*.

I swore she was an angel who'd been sent from heaven to help me because at that moment, another weight was lifted off me. At that moment, my need for air had nothing to do with sex but rather how she was seeping into my psyche, my spirit, and my soul. I sounded crazed and confused, but man, I wasn't making shit up because of the music we'd just made together.

Her naked body glowed in the soft light of the room. "Why do you keep asking me that?"

Once I'd cleaned off her chest, I tossed my shirt in the corner by the window with my other dirty clothes. I was somewhat neat, but I didn't have OCD about keeping everything in its place.

I rested on an elbow and dragged the tips of my fingers down Haven's breasts with my free hand. Her nipples rose to the occasion as she briefly closed her eyes.

"Do you want to spoon?" she asked innocently.

I chuckled. "Heck no. I want to fuck you."

She shivered even more when my hand started to descend down her smooth, silky stomach.

"But first I want to taste you again," I said.

She shivered again. "This is why I'm in your life. So we can have sex. Isn't that why girls enter your room?"

Not you. You're one of a kind. You are the brightest star in the darkest night.

I straddled her, and without so much as a word, her legs fell open for me.

I raised an eyebrow. "Eager much?"

She lifted up on her elbows, sticking out her tongue.

I lifted my brows in a playful warning. "Careful."

"Pfft. I'm not afraid of you."

I dragged my tongue down her chest to her belly button, my gaze never leaving hers. "You should be. I'm the big, bad wolf."

She rolled her eyes, reminding me of rolling green hills beneath a glistening sun. "I need to go."

Laughing, I kissed her belly button. "Sounds like you're trying to convince yourself. I told you I would get you in my bed and between my sheets."

She surveyed my bed. "I'm not between your sheets."

"Maybe not." I slid down farther until my lips were on her pussy. "But I also said I would be between your legs."

I was just about to get comfortable when she scrambled off the bed. *Fuck.*

She started gathering her clothes like the room was on fire.

Snatching her hand, I pulled her to me as I dropped onto the bed. "Come here."

She almost sat on my erection, which was ready to go to round two. Instead, she caught herself, swaying on her feet as fear jumped off her.

My eyebrows dove down. "What just happened?"

She stood in between my legs. Her tits were practically in my face, and hell, my cock was permanently hard.

Pouting, she covered her beautiful breasts with the clothes in her hands as she managed to get away from me. "I had a great time. But we can't do this again."

I usually didn't fuck a girl more than once, although I hadn't fucked Haven. I wanted to badly. I was thirsty for her. I wanted to feel her wrapped around me, squirming, moaning, and riding me like a cowgirl in a horse show.

"I'm listening," I said.

She slipped one leg then the other into her shorts before buttoning them. "We just can't." Her bra went on next.

Her father's words blared in my head. *"My daughter is off limits."*

"It's your old man. Isn't it?"

She whipped her head up as her hands froze on the clasp of her black lace bra.

I'd hit the nail on the head. "Seriously?"

She threw on her shirt. "He'll make my life and yours a living hell."

Grinding my teeth, I got up and found a pair of sweatpants in the pile of dirty clothes. Any urge I had to go another round died a quick death. So much for the high I'd been on. So much for having one night where I could feel something other than pain.

I tied my sweatpants, seething. It was one thing to butt into my dad's business, but to interfere in my personal business... *No fucking way.*

She's a senator's daughter. It would never work out anyway. You hate her old man.

I wasn't planning on marrying the girl. I wasn't even planning on dating her. All I wanted was another hour or two—or hell, the entire night—to screw my brains out.

The guys had been right. I needed to get laid. While I hadn't yet, the oral sex had been off-the-charts amazing, but I wanted more—more of her, more of us, more of that high that had vanished into thin air.

Once she was fully clothed, she inched over to me. That fear she'd had seemed to have waned because now her eyes held pity.

I didn't want her to feel sorry for me. I was Ryker James, bold, strong, and driven. My dad had always told me that I'd been made of steel. I wasn't so sure about that anymore, though.

She flattened her hands against my chest, peering up at me through thick lashes. "I had a good time."

Follow the yellow brick road.

I laughed. "What are you afraid of? That your old man will... what? Surely he wouldn't find out about tonight. There are no cameras in the room."

She dug her nails into me. "There better not be."

I threaded my fingers through her hair. "Dollface, I don't do cameras unless I'm on the field or doing an interview about football. And I might like kink, but I don't get into filming my sexual encounters. So tell me."

"He doesn't want me anywhere near you," she said.

"I know that."

"Is that why you took advantage of me tonight?"

I rumbled with laughter. "Fact number one—you barged into my room. Fact number two—you took advantage of me. Shall I go on?"

Her cheeks flamed. "We can't do this again." She pivoted on her heel.

"Haven, one question."

Hunching her shoulders, she froze.

"If your old man doesn't want you near me, then why did you agree to do the fundraiser?"

"It's for a good cause," she said as she headed for the door.

I padded over to her before she walked out. "Oh, and one more thing."

She turned, her eyes roaming all over me.

Inwardly, I grinned. She didn't want to leave. I would guess it was taking some strong fucking willpower on her part to walk out.

Hell, my own resolve had a crack in it, which was so unlike me. Usually, I had to kick women out of my bed. But I wanted to keep Haven, play with her, and not let her out of my sight.

I caged her against the door. "I have a new nickname for you." I seated my hand in between her legs. "Do you want to hear it?" I began rubbing.

She closed her eyes, lowering her shoulders. "Nope."

I leaned in to whisper in her ear. "Do you want to fuck me?"

She humped my hand. "Nope."

"Are you sure? You don't want my cock inside you? You don't want to experience how wonderful I can make you feel?"

She spewed soft noises.

"Or how about my tongue again?"

She pushed me away, but I didn't move.

"Stop," she said weakly.

I guided her hand to my groin. "He wants you. One more hour. Then you can go."

Her eyes flew open. "Nope."

"I'll make a prediction, then. I had you in my bed, and I'll have you there again. Only the next time, I'm going to fuck your brains out and ruin you for any other guy."

She snarled. "You're an ass."

It was my turn to walk away with a grin the size of Texas.

"What's my new nickname?" she asked.

"The Foreplay Queen."

Giggling, she opened the door. When she did, Beverly breezed in.

Women. Tabitha, Haven, and now Beverly. I was all for women in my room, but I wasn't interested in Beverly or Tabitha.

"Are you here to take pictures of me again?" Haven asked, not moving from the doorway.

Music floated up from below.

Beverly pursed her flaming-red lips. "I didn't take any pictures."

For some odd reason, I believed her. At the moment, she didn't have a phone in her hand either.

She blew past Haven and made herself comfortable on the edge of my bed. "Ryker, we need to talk."

I gripped the doorjamb to the bathroom. "The party is downstairs." The last time she had been in my room, she'd wanted to screw me.

Beverly folded her arms over her breasts. "Alone. That means you can leave, Haven." She flicked her hand, shooing Haven.

My little minx regarded me as though she were asking if I wanted her help. It was probably best Haven didn't stay if she was worried about her old man.

"Wait." Beverly examined Haven then me. "Did you two just fuck?"

Haven laughed, but it sounded somewhat neurotic.

"What do you want?" I asked Beverly.

Beverly eyed the shoebox on my nightstand.

I rushed over to put the cover on the box then shoved it into the top drawer of my dresser. *Nosy fucking family between her and Tabitha.*

"Talk, Beverly, or get out," I said harshly.

"What did you do to my sister?"

I hated nosy people. "I didn't do anything to Tabitha except throw her out of my room, like I might do to you."

"She's saying you hurt her," Beverly said.

Haven reared back. "He's done no such thing. When she left, she was in perfect condition."

Alarm bells went off in my head. It was never good when a woman cried that a guy had hurt her. Even incidents that were innocent could grow like a bad virus.

"She was in my room when I came in." I wanted to give full disclosure, and I didn't want anyone lying about my actions. If Tabitha decided to blow anything out of proportion, my reputation would sink faster than a boulder in quicksand. "She went through my personal things. So I kicked her out."

"I saw him kick her out," Haven said.

"Well, she has a bruise on her arm," Beverly added.

I had gripped her a little too hard. "Do you really want to make this a big thing? Because I have witnesses that can attest to my actions." I hadn't closed the door. Partygoers had been in the hall. So I was sure I had witnesses on my side.

Haven studied Beverly. "You know something? I think you and your sister have some ulterior motives with Ryker, or maybe me."

Beverly fidgeted with a nail. "You're being paranoid."

"No. I'm not," Haven said. "Anywhere Ryker is, you're in his face. Your sister wants something. You want something. And I know you're working for my father."

Beverly rose, a scowl forming on her lips. "If you think Ryker is going to give you a second fuck, you're mistaken. You're a scrawny thing. Not his type."

Haven pushed out her tits. "He didn't seem to mind these babies. I can promise you my breasts are not scrawny."

I held in a laugh. Maybe I would marry Haven Hale. I loved how she made sure no one was going to fuck with her.

Beverly huffed. "Whatever. Look, Ryker, I don't want any trouble. I have a sorority to run." She regarded Haven. "And I'm not working for your father."

"What about your sister?" I asked.

Beverly moved a wad of her hair off her shoulder. "My sister couldn't even tell you who Senator Hale is. She said she was hurt. I didn't believe you would do such a thing, but I had to check."

"Keep your sister out of my room and away from me. She's not welcome here anymore."

Beverly nodded. "I'll see you at the fundraising meeting next week, then." She smoothed a hand down her miniskirt. "I guess I'll see you too." She considered Haven before she left.

"I don't trust her," Haven said when we were alone.

A perfectly good night had turned sour. I was beginning to believe that I should give up women for the time being. Too much drama.

But as I studied Haven, I thought, *No fucking way.* I had a feeling she was well worth any drama, including that caused by her old man.

22

HAVEN

The ballroom at the Marriott was filling up with the contestants participating in the fundraiser. Some were hanging around the bar that was set up adjacent to the door.

"Do you want a drink?" Vicki asked.

She wasn't a contestant, but I'd asked her to tag along. We'd thought we could hit a club for a couple of hours after the meeting. We had class the next day, so we weren't planning on staying out late.

"Just water. I'll grab us seats."

She went to the bar while I headed over to the rows of chairs that were facing the podium. A maintenance employee was setting up the mic while men and women lingered around.

I counted twenty-five people, but I didn't see Ryker or Lucas.

Erik swaggered over to me, holding a beer bottle. His brown eyes were filled with mischief and mayhem. "Hey, pretty lady. I see Ryker convinced you."

I snickered. "He did no such thing."

"He likes you."

"He likes all women."

Erik held back a grin. "True, but you've put a smile back on his ugly mug, and that means something."

I slapped a hand over my heart. "I'm touched."

He stuck out his bottom lip. "You don't believe me."

Vicki interrupted us, handing me a bottled water. "What did I miss?"

Erik casually checked her out. "Have we met?"

Blushing darker than her rosy makeup, she swept a lock of hair behind her ear. "Vicki Moore."

I considered leaving them alone, but I didn't see anyone I knew, and Ryker wasn't present.

Erik pecked the back of Vicki's hand. "Care to get a drink later?"

Vicki looked to me for an answer.

"We can go clubbing another time."

"Dancing?" Erik perked up. "I like to dance."

Vicki and I exchanged a shocked expression. I couldn't wrap my mind around the big and burly football player twirling and swaying his hips on a dance floor.

The two began to talk about dancing and clubs around the campus. I tuned them out as I watched the door for Ryker. Yeah, I was dying to see him. Our sexual escapade was burned in my brain, and so was his dirty talk, which had had me twisted up for days.

As I faintly heard Vicki and Erik, my mind went on a road trip like it had time and again during the last week. I hadn't been able to concentrate. I'd barely listened to my instructors, and I'd struggled to do homework. When it came to sleep, I'd tossed and turned and kicked off the sheets. I felt like I was having withdrawals, like a drug addict not getting her next fix.

As I chewed on a nail, heat pinched my cheeks in anticipation of seeing Ryker. I wondered if he would talk to me or even acknowledge me. *Or maybe he'll be his asshat self.*

Oh my God! I was so screwed.

You were screwed the minute you met him and even more so when you took advantage of him, Foreplay Queen.

My cheeks burned. I'd never been forward with a guy. Ryker

somehow brought out a side of me that was new and exciting. Maybe knowing he was the Foreplay King only made me want to prove to him that he wasn't the only one who could wow a partner in the bedroom. After all, I did like a good challenge. Still, our rapturous, intense, and unforgettable night was something I wanted to do again and again.

He's not that guy. He doesn't do long-term relationships. "One and done." That was Ryker James's motto, at least according to the scuttle around the dorm.

We could never be a couple, not with my father in the picture.

Vicki touched my arm. "Are you okay, Haven? You look pale." She felt my head like my mom had done many times when I was a little girl not feeling well. "No fever."

When I blinked, Erik was near the podium, talking with Ajax and Vin, and more people had shown up.

"I'm fine. Maybe after this, I might go back to the dorm."

"No, you're not. Erik wants to take us to a club. Besides, I know what your problem is—withdrawal from Mr. Big Dick."

The only thing I'd shared with Vicki was confirmation that Ryker's dick was big. In fact, it was huge.

Nevertheless, after a month of living with me, Vicki could read me like a book. But I didn't get the chance to confirm or deny her statement before Beverly Sims glided in with her sister on her heels.

Vicki followed my line of sight.

"Is Tabitha in the lineup?" I murmured.

The sisters could pass as twins, not only because of their physical attributes, but they both wore red miniskirts, black scooped-neck tops, and wedge sandals. The only slight difference in their appearance was that Beverly wore her hair up off her shoulders and Tabitha let her blond waves hang free.

Vicki sipped on her soda. "I checked the website earlier. I didn't see her name."

"Did Tabitha rush for her sister's sorority?" I asked.

"No. Word around the house was that Tab wasn't interested in being under her sister's thumb."

It was clear that Beverly stood up for her younger sister regardless of what the rumor was about Tabitha.

"I still believe Beverly had something to do with taking that pic of Ryker and me that first night I met him."

"Maybe it was her sister," Vicki said. "They both have the same features."

Possibly. I dipped back into my memory bank, trying to recall anything else about the woman other than blue eyes and blond hair. But I'd been in such a hurry to get Ryker a washcloth that nothing else had stuck in my brain.

The door creaked open, and Ryker swaggered in, looking just as delicious in his ripped jeans and Lakemont T-shirt as he did naked.

The air in my lungs evaporated.

"Close your mouth, Haven. It's impolite to drool," Vicki said through a laugh.

I inhaled and shook off the yummy chills that wracked my body.

"You're in so much trouble," she cooed.

In more ways than one.

Tabitha sashayed right up to Ryker before Beverly could stop her.

Most of the thirty or so people in the room stopped talking as though they could sense something big was about to go down.

Ryker tensed his large shoulders, and his biceps flexed at the same time as he held up his hands as though Tabitha were arresting him.

My feet moved quickly, and my brain shut down as I hurried to his rescue. A laugh broke out in my head at the thought that Ryker James needed rescuing.

Lifting up on my tiptoes, I flattened my hands against his hard chest and kissed him on the lips. "Hey, honey." The word "honey" came out a little garbled.

He winced.

Asshat.

But when I stuck my tongue into his mouth, his hands landed on the small of my back, and his body softened as he pulled me to him, taking over the kiss, possessive yet punishing.

I pressed my body to his, losing myself in the moment. I swore I'd died and gone to a world where the birds were chirping, the sun was shining, and water was flowing in the background.

His tongue invaded me, exploring and taking as though I owed him something.

Oh, that's right. I did owe him. He'd wanted more from me last weekend, and I had blown him off.

Stupid me.

I should've hung around longer rather than run out like a scared puppy who had just lost her momma.

"Argh," Tabitha gritted out.

Ryker broke the kiss, pulling my bottom lip with his teeth as if to say he wasn't done with me yet.

I prayed he wasn't.

Nevertheless, I bared my teeth as I whirled around. "I'm sorry. Did you have something to say to my boyfriend?"

Tabitha stuck her hands on her hips. "Ryker doesn't do girlfriends."

Ryker's hand circled my waist until he seated his palm on my stomach. Now my back was pressed to his front. "How would you know? You don't know anything about me."

Tabitha pressed her lips into a thin line. "I know enough."

Beverly flashed us, or maybe just Ryker, an apologetic expression. "Tab, what did I tell you? No trouble."

"Why are you even here?" I asked. "You're not in the lineup."

Beverly's nostrils flared. "My sister is my guest, just as your roomie is yours." Then the two women stomped away.

Ryker directed me to a quiet corner as Lucas's voice blared through the speakers. "Testing, one, two."

Ryker poked me in the chest then gestured to himself. "What's happening here?" He sounded as though I were the dirt beneath his feet.

I stuck my tongue to the roof of my mouth. "What's wrong? You don't kiss?"

His expression was vacant as he studied me.

Suddenly, I felt small, weak, and pissed off. "Well?"

"We're not boyfriend and girlfriend."

I wrung my hands in front of me to keep them busy so I didn't slap him. "Of course not. I was trying to help out a friend."

The blank look on his face morphed into surprise as his eyebrows lifted. "I've never had a girl as a friend." He sounded so boyish.

"Want one?" My heart fluttered at the prospect. Maybe he and I were better as friends.

I'd had a guy friend once in my sophomore year in boarding school. Greer had been a local and attended the public high school in town. Our friendship, though, hadn't lasted long. He'd wanted more than friendship, but I hadn't liked him in the same way.

That would probably happen with Ryker, only I would want something serious with him. So maybe being friends was a bad idea.

"What about your old man?"

"You let me handle my father." Although I was sure that kiss would get back to my father, especially if Beverly was feeding him intel on me.

Lucas called Ryker's name.

"Got to go." Then he swaggered his denim-clad hips up to his best friend.

I was melting into a pile of liquid goo. If I had thought our thirty minutes of bliss the other night was hot, that kiss was hotter.

Still, I had to ask myself the same question. What was happening?

Vicki waved me over.

I put one foot in front of the other and slid into the end chair in the last row. Thank God we weren't in the front. I was beginning to realize I could only take so much of Ryker.

"That was scorching," Vicki whispered. "Everyone was staring."

"Did you notice if anyone snapped pics?"

"I couldn't tell you. I was riveted on you and him."

Great. As Lucas began talking, I started coming up with an excuse for my father. I debated whether I should come clean before anyone else sent him a photo or called him to give him the dirt on me.

"Doesn't Lucas look hot?" Vicki's voice pulled me back to reality.

"What about Erik?"

She shrugged. "I can hang out with Erik and not sleep with him."

"Tell Erik that," I said. "He wants you in bed." I couldn't blame Erik either. Vicki was pretty. She had silky hair, big doe-brown eyes, and a slim but curvy body, and she was tall. Plus, her legs went on forever.

"So? Lucas is with other women."

"Maybe you should ask Lucas to go out," I offered.

"Nah. I might be forward in a lot of situations, but asking a guy out isn't one of them. My mom taught me to let the guy ask the girl out."

"That's ancient advice. You're not ancient."

She giggled. "Let's just have a good time tonight."

I was all for that.

Lucas went through his notes on the fundraiser and gave information on the time to arrive, how to dress, and other mundane tasks that would take place. I knew all about fundraisers since my father's aides had set several up for his campaign.

The crowd was quiet as they listened.

"I still need a bio from Haven." Lucas gazed out at the crowd.

I raised my hand. "I'll get that to you tomorrow." I had one I'd written for my college application, and it didn't need much tweaking.

Lucas nodded. "We're just about sold out of tickets. And before I open the floor to questions, I would like to remind you that as a participant, you're not allowed to bid on anyone."

The ladies in the room booed and pouted.

Vicki clapped. "Ooh, I'm glad I'm not in it. I can try and snag Lucas." She sighed. "On second thought, I don't have that kind of money."

There went my chance of buying a date with Ryker.

"Questions?" Lucas asked.

Tab, who was sitting in the front, waved her hand. "What happens if someone doesn't show at the last minute? Do you have stand-ins?"

She sounded as though she knew someone might not show. "Because I would like to volunteer."

Beverly nudged her then whispered something in her ear.

Lucas glanced at the front row where Ryker was sitting.

The chairs were set up in two sections, separated by an aisle. I had a direct line of sight to Tab and Beverly, who were in the section over from me. But Ryker was in the first row in my section, and big heads and poufy hair blocked my line of sight.

"If someone doesn't show, then we're down one person. That's it. We're not scrambling to find another," Lucas said. "Any other questions?"

"We're ready to drink," someone said.

Lucas held up a stack of flyers. "Make sure you grab one of these. It outlines all the details."

The crowd scattered, each person taking a flyer. Some headed to the bar, while others didn't move, talking to their friends beside them.

Ryker went up to Lucas and said something in his ear. Lucas lifted his head and pinned his gaze on me. Then Ryker and I locked eyes.

Erik came over. "What club, ladies? Ajax and Vin are in."

At the moment, I wasn't into going to a club. I was more interested in finishing the conversation Ryker and I were having before Lucas's speech.

"Excuse me for a minute," I said. If Ryker and Lucas were talking about me, then I wanted to know what they were saying.

I brushed past Tab, who snarled at me. But I didn't stop. If I did, we would be pulling each other's hair out. I settled at the podium with Lucas and Ryker. "What's going on?"

Flicking his blond curls out of his eyes, Lucas chuckled. "I'll leave you two lovebirds alone."

When Lucas melted into the group of people on the floor, Ryker combed a hand through his black hair. It had a bluish hue to it in the bright lights of the room.

I anchored my hands to my hips. "So what did you say to Lucas? I know it was about me."

23

RYKER

This woman was doing crazy fucking things to my head and body. She was standing with her tits out, and they were on full display through her tight shirt—round, full, and needing my attention.

All I could think about was my mouth on her nipples, and I was sure they were puckered tighter than someone sucking on one of those sour gummy candies.

"I told Lucas we should kick you out of the lineup," I said as sure as my dick was growing. Good thing I was behind the podium.

She laughed, wild and free, a sound that sent blood to my groin. "Please do. I'm only in it because, honestly, I was tired of you on my ass."

I feigned a pout. "But you liked me gripping your ass the other night."

Horror flashed in those big emerald eyes as she glanced at the group standing close to us that included the Sims sisters.

Follow the yellow brick road.

I didn't care who was listening.

She inched closer to me. Suddenly, her lilac scent began making me dizzy and horny and itching to do a repeat of the other night.

I swore my libido was on crack. I was a horny bastard but usually not every minute of the day. Hell, I hadn't been able to get Haven out of my head. Jacking off twice a day had been the norm during the past week.

She took a play out of my book and poked me in the chest. "Did you hear what I said?"

I blinked. "I was replaying"—I leaned in close to her ear—"sucking on your tits."

She let out a soft moan. "You're a piece of work."

"How about we get out of here?" I asked.

"Sorry, big guy. I'm not in the mood."

"Your moan and body language say otherwise. Besides, you said you wanted to be my friend."

"Friend. Not fuck buddy."

"Then, friend," I teased, "want to hold my hand while I do something?"

Intrigue flashed in her eyes even though her arched brow said she was skeptical.

Lucas was going to accompany me, but I'd told him I wanted Haven to instead. She wanted to be my friend, and as I had sat through Lucas talking about the event, I'd decided why not. I recalled her telling me that she knew how it felt to lose someone. And she did have a way of calming me, not just in the bedroom. Moreover, that kiss… *Fuck me.* I'd never kissed a girl like that before. Sure, I'd locked lips and swapped spit, but the kiss between us had packed a punch right to my fucking heart.

And how bold of her to rescue me from Tabitha. Normally, if a woman had made a move like Haven had, I wouldn't have kissed her back. No, I would have pushed her away for sure.

I should run as far away as I could from Haven. Yet deep down in the dark pits of my psyche, I didn't want to. I was beginning to realize she was a drug I didn't know I needed and not just in the sex department, and that scared the fuck out of me.

"You went away again, big guy." Her voice was alluring, angelic, and velvety—a bull's-eye to the heart.

I swallowed the dryness in my throat. "Come on. I promise where we're going has nothing to do with sex." The minute I grabbed her hand, something warm traveled up my arm and down into my chest.

She tugged on my big paw, not moving. "I need to tell Vicki."

"Wave to her or send her a text." If we stopped to talk, we would never get out of there, and I might change my mind about taking her with me. Plus, it was still light outside, and I wanted to get there before dark.

Vicki was engrossed in conversation, listening to Erik woo her or some shit. Erik had a way of capturing a chick's attention. He had eyes only for the girl he was talking to, listened intently, and touched her arm or moved her hair behind her ear. Chicks loved that shit, according to Erik.

I'd never seemed to have a problem getting a girl in my bed without doing any of those things.

Of course, Haven, strong-willed and not listening to me, strode over to Vicki, whispered in her ear, then returned. "Now I'm ready."

Erik gave me a nod and a grin, as did Ajax, Vin, and Lucas, who were near Erik and Vicki. My buddies knew where I was going.

The Sims sisters watched Haven and me leave with evil in their eyes. I would also bet every other girl in that room was paying attention.

I didn't give a fuck. *Let them talk.* Hell, I was always part of a rumor or the talk on campus. That came with being the star quarterback. And Haven had her own celebrity status with her old man being a senator. It was almost impossible to do anything without a rumor spreading like the plague for either one of us.

Once we were in my car, she buckled her seat belt. "You haven't been drinking. Have you?"

I fired up the engine. "You tasted me with that kiss. What do you think?" I might be pouring a fifth of liquor down my throat when we were done, although I was praying I wouldn't need any booze with her at my side.

She twirled her hair around in her hand and brought it forward so that it draped down her chest. "Fair enough."

I salivated to be that hand.

Focus on the road, dude.

So I wheeled my old man's Infinity into traffic. He'd loved that car, but mine had been totaled when I'd rammed it into a tree. Yeah, I was still ticking away at my ten hours of campus duty.

"Where are we going?" Haven sounded worried.

"The cemetery."

She tucked her hands underneath her legs and gazed out the passenger's-side window. "My mom is buried there."

Fuck me.

I was a dick, bastard, asshole, and the list went on, but I wasn't one to shove death in someone's face. I pulled off into a gas station. "I wasn't thinking. I'll take you back."

She reached over the leather console and touched my thigh. "Don't. I told you at the church you could talk to me. It's hard to go through one death, let alone four. So if you need me to hold your hand, I'm your friend. I haven't been to my mom's grave in a while. I'm due anyway. You know, two birds, one stone, and all."

"Are you sure?"

She nodded. "I am. But I don't understand why you wanted me to come along."

In part, I didn't either. "Lucas has been my rock. But he needs a break." He'd been by my side every minute of the day. The man was made of steel, but he needed to let loose and not worry about my ass. "I need someone to hold my hand. I like your hand."

She squeezed my thigh. "So that was what you said to Lucas when you both looked at me?"

"Yeah." I probably should've asked her instead of dragging her out of the hotel, although she hadn't protested. But I was finding the woman was making me do crazy things.

I got back on the road. As we made our way through town, passing quaint shops and restaurants, silence followed us, but she kept her hand on me.

I swore if she took it away, I might cry.

Within fifteen minutes, I was flicking on my blinker as I pulled into Lakemont Cemetery and parked not far from where my family was buried. The funeral director had set up the gravestones earlier that day. Since I'd had football practice and then the fundraiser meeting, I couldn't get away. In part, I'd been procrastinating. I hadn't been able to muster up the courage. That was another reason why I hadn't been thinking when I'd dragged Haven out of the hotel.

Dread sat heavy in my stomach and only increased when I got out of the car.

Haven joined me, propping her hip against the car. "I'll give you a minute."

I closed my hand over hers. "No way." I'd brought her there to hold me up.

She didn't object and instead gripped my hand as though she were trying to say, "I got you."

I prayed like hell she did because the moment I laid eyes on the headstones, my pulse banged in my ears like a drummer doing a solo performance.

Mom was buried on one end and Dad on the other, with my brother and sister in between. Each headstone was inscribed with their names, their dates of birth and death, and their epitaphs, which Aunt Kari and I had collaborated on.

As I stared at my mom's stone, I covered my mouth with my free hand.

Mom's epitaph read, *"Flowers are your sunshine."* My mom had loved gardening, and she'd had a thing for colorful flowers.

Then I read Dad's. *"Taking chances is the only way to succeed."*

Randal's was next. *"Your laughter was always infectious."* My brother had laughed all the time at just about anything. If I'd been having a sucky day, he would make me forget why.

I saved Leigh's for last. I knew once I read hers, the tears would come. Hers read, *"You were always the rainbow in the storm."*

I blew out an audible breath.

Haven let go of me and hooked her arm in mine. "It's okay to let it out. No judgment."

I wasn't worried about her judging me. I was worried about having a heart attack.

As I stared at Leigh's headstone, I dropped to my knees. How had my life come to this? Why were they taken from me? I wanted to scream my lungs out or punch the oak tree behind us.

Then Haven began rubbing my back. "Let it go, Ryker," she said in her angelic voice. "I got you."

Fuck if that didn't trigger the waterworks. One tear rolled down my face, then another. I couldn't even think of the last time I'd cried. But the more I thought about Leigh and Randal and my parents, the more the tears started flowing. I inhaled deeply, smelling the myriad of flowers that surrounded the headstones, or maybe it was Haven's lilac scent. Either way, the sweet aroma did nothing to ease the pain or the tears.

"That's it." Haven's voice was just a whisper as she continued to rub my back. The more she did, the more the tears poured out, like a rushing waterfall after a hard rain.

Haven knelt beside me and took my hand. "The hardest thing for me when my mom died was reading her gravestone. Something about seeing the inscription punctured a hole in my heart. I cried like a baby that day, and when I was done, I felt a little less suffocated. I'm not going to give you clichés about healing, and I can't tell you it will get easier. But do those things that will make them proud and happy as they watch down over you."

"Living my dream of playing for the NFL would make my old man happy. Finding love would make my mom and Leigh happy. As for Randal, he would be stoked to see me laugh with him."

"Then do those things." A tear ran down her cheek. "And laugh as much as you can."

I didn't want to be cocky and say playing for the NFL was easy because it wasn't. I hadn't had any scouts talk to me yet, but I still had one year of college to go after this year. As far as finding love or a steady girl… well, that would be like trying to climb Mount Everest.

"I didn't know your family, but reading their epitaphs, I would say they were awesome people, especially your sister."

More tears flowed as I clutched Haven's hand as though she were my lifeline. "Leigh was special." My voice cracked.

She sniffled. "You two were close?"

"Very."

"Tell me something about her."

With my free hand, I wiped my nose. "She was brave and full of life. She worried about me, though. She worried that I would be a single man the rest of my life. She wanted me to find a steady girl. She thought love could tame the beast inside me. Her words exactly."

Haven giggled through another sniffle. "I wish I could've met her."

"She would've liked you."

The trees around us rustled as if Leigh were telling me she agreed.

Suddenly, I was bombarded with memories as though I were on a battlefield. My childhood flashed before me, and I could hear Randal's laugh as if he were right there. I could see my mom's smile as though she were standing behind her gravestone.

I shivered as I listened to my old man tell me to stay focused on football. "Keep your sights on the NFL."

I could even see Leigh smiling at me.

I threw my face in my hands. *Why? Why did the plane crash? What went wrong?* My old man had been flying the private jet. He'd been meticulous about maintenance and repairs. But sadly, I would never know the reason, and even if I did, it wouldn't change the fact that they'd died.

More tears started streaming down until I was laboring for breath.

Haven leaned her head on my arm. "I'm here for you."

I wanted to ask her why she would console a man she hardly knew.

Maybe she was turning out to be someone I could count on, someone I could turn to.

Before I could think, I was sobbing in her arms like a little boy.

She didn't say a word. She didn't have to. Her holding me, rubbing me, crying with me said so much. I knew she had to be mourning her mom, but I also could feel her empathy, sympathy, and so much more.

I shoved my hands into her hair and rested my forehead against hers. "Why are you here, Haven?" I was asking myself more than I was asking her.

She batted her long lashes. "Because I'm your friend."

In that moment, time came to a screeching halt as I captured her lips in mine in a tender, soft, and gentle kiss. Something inside me changed—blooming, twisting, flipping, and flopping—masking the pain I'd been accustomed to since that fatal day.

I slid my tongue into her mouth as she opened for me. One hand cupped her cheek, and the other seated on the back of her neck. My breathing was staccato as I took my time to explore.

She was putty in my hands. Maybe she was allowing me to release my sorrow and my pain. But I knew that was a lie because she was breathing as hard as I was.

She tasted of sunshine and home, and I didn't want to stop. The more I kissed her, the more that stabbing pain eased its hold on me.

I adjusted us so my ass was on the ground and she was straddling me, just like the first night in my media room when I'd known nothing about her and the feeling of her on top of me had been lust, pure and strong.

But now I didn't want to splay her out and have my way with her. I wanted her, no needed her, to make me forget that I was alone on this planet, to make me forget that my family was dead, to make me forget that when daylight came the next day, that I would be okay.

Her hands danced through my hair as she nibbled on my lip, kissed my cheeks, my eyes, then my neck. Her gentleness was suffocating yet freeing. I'd always been rough with women when it came to sex, but this was far from sex.

What was happening between us was intimate and special, and I didn't want it to end.

I let my head fall back. "Kiss me." I needed her mouth on mine. I needed to not stop kissing her because the more our mouths were fused together, the more the pain inside me didn't exist. It had no place to flourish, bloom, and grow.

Her tongue swept inside my mouth as she spewed soft noises.

Tears careened down my face. "You're changing me."

She kissed away every one of my tears. "I got you, big guy. Whatever you need."

I needed a friend, but she was turning into so much more.

24

HAVEN

Six days had passed since Ryker had broken down at the cemetery. That night, I'd learned it was the first time he had cried since he'd lost his family. I hadn't been surprised. Sometimes the shock didn't wear off for weeks, even months. I'd seen that happen to my father. He'd refused to believe that my mom was gone. He'd drunk and moped around, but I didn't see him shed a tear until about three months after we'd buried her. Then one day, I'd found him on the couch, sobbing. I had stayed by his side, consoling him, crying with him, and helping my dad heal.

For me, the process of being there for someone when they were grieving gave me a sense of peace. I couldn't tell Ryker that the pain would ease or that it would get easier, because I still had bad days when I thought of my mom.

Ryker had asked why I was in his life. I now knew the reason. I was there to help him get through this tough time. I was there to give him my shoulder and support. I wasn't a religious person, but I did believe in God and fate, and fate wanted me to help him. To a certain extent, Ryker was helping me.

Before we'd left the cemetery, he'd accompanied me to my mom's grave. We'd both shed tears—lots of them. And when we had driven away, I believed we'd both stitched up a hole in our hearts. I wouldn't say he was out of the woods yet, but processing death was a journey, and I wanted to help him in any way I could.

Ryker and I were walking into Woodcreek High. He'd invited me to join him at an art festival the school was having. A painting Leigh had done was on display, and according to Ryker, he wanted some company or a shoulder to cry on just in case. Lucas was supposed to attend, but something had come up at the last minute. I jumped at the chance to help a friend despite my father's rules.

"I need to send a text," I said as we approached the entrance.

After our first kiss at the Marriott, I'd worried that Tabitha or Beverly would tattle on me to my father. However, all had been quiet. Father had been traveling, and with election day approaching, he was knee deep in getting out to talk to voters.

Ryker studied me, his gray eyes glinting in the late-afternoon sunlight. "Something wrong?"

"Just something I forgot to do. Go. I'll be in shortly." The last thing I wanted to do was bring up my father and ruin Ryker's night. However, as we'd gotten out of the car, I realized that Mr. Bridges might be there. Considering he was friends with my father, I'd decided it was best to nip any potential problems in the bud.

I watched Ryker as he strutted in, his shoulders seemingly tense. He'd been quiet in the car on the way over. I hadn't needed to ask him to know that he was thinking of his sister.

I typed furiously on my phone so I could get inside to hold his hand.

Me: *I'm at an art festival. Ryker is here. So don't be surprised if your spies tell you that.*

I started to pocket my phone since I didn't expect to get a response, but it pinged right away.

Father: *Thanks for the heads up. Tell the quarterback to keep winning games.*

Me: *Are you warming up to him?*

Father: *No. I just want to make sure the money I donate sees a return.*

Unbelievable.

My phone pinged again.

Father: *Haven, remember our deal.*

I was tempted to send the middle finger emoji, but instead, I slipped my phone in my purse.

Bastard.

As I headed in, Zack came out of nowhere and grabbed the handle. Opening the door, he waved me in. "After you, my lady."

The little girl inside me blushed. Zack was a handsome boy with a chiseled jaw and eyes the color of dark chocolate.

Silence followed us toward the library for a beat.

"Were you dating Leigh long?" I asked, turning a corner.

"Since the end of our sophomore year. Are you dating her brother? I saw you get out of the car with him."

I giggled as though I were back in high school. On top of that, all those butterfly feelings I hardly experienced swarmed my belly. "Nah. Just friends."

"No offense," Zack said, "but Ryker doesn't do girls as friends."

"Maybe he's turning over a new leaf." I liked the idea of being friends with Ryker, although I wasn't sure how long our friendship would last considering I wanted to jump his bones. *Friends with benefits could work.*

Zack opened another door for me. "Leigh would like that."

I would too, but thoughts of friends and girlfriends faded as we walked into the library, which was filled with a hum of chatter. Zack went over to a young lady whom I remembered from the funeral service. I believed her name was Jessica if I weren't mistaken. She was tall, curvy, and had long, wavy brown hair and big dark eyes.

I scanned the room, looking for my new friend when Mr. Bridges came up to me. "Haven? What are you doing here?" His baldhead was shiny as ever.

Here we go. I was glad I'd given my father a heads-up. "To support a friend."

"You mean Ryker," he said.

I narrowed my eyes. "Yes." I had no reason to lie.

"Does your dad know?" he asked.

I glared at the nice man. "So you know why my father hates him." It wasn't a question because the resolve in his eyes told me he knew exactly why my father didn't want me with Ryker.

"You may not believe this, but your father wants the best for you."

A not-so-nice laugh erupted from me. "My father wants what's best for him."

"Believe what you will." Mr. Bridges started to leave.

I caught his arm. "Wait. So my father really thinks that Ryker is no good for me because… what? He sleeps around?"

"Your father thinks you can do better." Then he melted into the crowd.

Unbelievable.

Not once in my memory had my father talked to me about boys, men, dating, or anything having to do with love. I'd learned about the birds and the bees at boarding school and in sex education classes. I shouldn't have been shocked, though. My father hadn't told me he loved since way before my mom died.

I shoved Mr. Bridges's words into an imaginary drawer for the moment. I'd almost told Mr. Bridges that my father had nothing to worry about. But maybe my father had a keen sense of what type of men I liked. If I compared my father to Ryker, they had a lot of similarities. They were both powerful in the sense that they could command a room. They were confident, handsome, and strong-willed, although the one difference was compassion. Ryker had that. My father didn't, or if he did, I hadn't seen that side of him since my mom was alive.

Ryker was talking to Principal Holland near where the artwork was displayed. Groups of parents, teachers, and kids were scattered around. Some were talking while some were sipping drinks out of red cups.

As soon as I joined Ryker, he draped an arm around me like we were going steady.

A butterfly flapped its wings inside my stomach.

Principal Holland's eyebrows lifted slightly. "Glad you could join us, Ms. Hale."

"I'm here for a friend." I leaned into the hunky quarterback.

"Good talking to you, Ryker. I'll be sure to call you when we're ready to take down the display." Then the principal moved on to mingle with other families.

"I thought you ditched me," Ryker teased. "It must've been a long text."

I was about to relay my father's message when my jaw went slack.

Ryker tensed, or more like dug his fingers into my arm.

Beverly Sims smiled as though she'd just found the Holy Grail. "I knew I would see Ryker here, but not you." She said the word *you* like it was a swear word.

Confusion clouded my brain as to why she was at a high school art festival until a middle-aged woman glided up, dressed in a flower-patterned sundress. My jaw bounced off the floor.

The beautiful blond woman had the same genes as Beverly, the same blue eyes, and the same seemingly fake smile plastered on her face. "You must be Ryker. I've heard all about your sister's talent. I'm Lorna Sims, the guidance counselor here." Then she swung her attention to me. "Haven, right? Beverly told me about you."

I doubted that. But I knew someone who had probably filled her in about me.

"Are you new here?" Ryker asked. He hadn't let go of me, although he'd lost some of his tension. He'd probably thought Beverly was following us until her mother showed up.

As for me, my muscles were strung so tight that if they snapped, they would fly around the room and sting someone.

"I started at the end of last year," Lorna said.

I wanted to ask where her other daughter was, but my tongue had gone to sleep while my mind scattered, wondering if Lorna Sims knew

I'd seen her and my father together… or more like I'd seen my father's lips stuck to her neck and his body pressed to hers when I'd walked into the kitchen.

I had to hand it to my father. He had balls if he would corner a woman in our house while his wife entertained dinner guests. I couldn't say for sure if my father had screwed Lorna, but I would bet my trust fund and more that he had.

The Sims sisters were out to snag a rich man. I imagined their mom wasn't any different.

"Mom, we should mingle," Beverly said.

Lorna fixated on me. "Are you two dating?"

"We are," I said as my tongue suddenly woke up.

Ryker's chuckle was a little ragged.

Beverly gasped and narrowed her eyes at Ryker. "Since when do you date?" Her tone was mean and dirty.

Ryker clutched me to him like I was his lifeline. Little did he know he was mine, because he was holding me upright. I was a second away from freaking the heck out. But one thing came into focus—Beverly and Tabitha were the moles that my father had hired. I would bet everything I had on that fact.

As polite as he could muster, Ryker said, "It was nice to meet you, Ms. Sims." He ignored Beverly. Then he guided me over to his sister's painting.

I stumbled as I gave the Sims family one last look. Beverly's features were tight and red, and her nostrils flared. I wanted to jump up and down for joy that I'd driven a proverbial knife into her chest.

My happiness died a quick death when I thought of my father. Sure, I knew he had hired someone to watch me. I'd also suspected Beverly or Tabitha of being the spy. Yet confirming that fact made me want to scream. I now wondered if my father wanted me to stay away from Ryker because of the Sims sisters. Maybe he wanted to make sure he kept them happy and not me.

Ryker's breath fanned my earlobe. "That was weird."

Not weird but unbelievable.

"Don't let go of me."

"I got you, dollface."

Normally, I didn't like that nickname. But now that we were friends, "dollface" wasn't so bad, only because "I got you" held more weight and substance than "dollface."

I sighed as Ryker's aftershave wafted around me. It smelled like a cool spring day, and it helped mask the anger that had taken up a home inside me.

"This is Leigh's," he said softly.

I zeroed in on a picture of him, a perfect canvas of Ryker James in a football jersey that had Woodcreek stitched on the front. The detail had been done to perfection, right down to the angle of his jaw. I swallowed hard at how Leigh had captured the happiness in his gray eyes and the cockiness in his expression.

"You seem happy in that painting," I said, holding back a burst of tears for some stupid reason.

Memories of my childhood flooded my brain. I swallowed the sob that was lodged in my throat as I thought of the day my mom had pushed me on a swing at the park.

"Higher," I'd said.

"Baby girl, I don't want you to fall."

"Please, Mom," I cried. "Higher."

When she did, I felt like a bird with wings, flying through the air toward the bright-blue sky. I swore that day that I would touch the sky or at least try. I never did, but Mom and I had had a great time and many more in the park after that day.

I shook my head hard, trying to rid myself of the past and the anger I had in the pit of my stomach at my father, and to a certain extent at the world, for taking my mom away from me.

"High school was a great time." Ryker's voice was soothing and tickled spots inside me. "Want to make some memories of our own?"

I quivered and smiled. "Lead the way."

He closed his hand over mine, and whatever memory he wanted to make, I wouldn't protest.

25

———————

RYKER

Haven was a zombie from the high school to my parents' house. I'd asked her once on the way if she was okay, and she'd nodded and stared out the window the whole time. I suspected that the interaction between her and Beverly was what had Haven in a shell.

I found it odd that everywhere I turned, Beverly was lurking somewhere nearby or in my face—parties, my bedroom, the charity event, and now the art festival. But my brain wasn't interested in deciphering the reasons why.

What I wanted at the moment was to sit my ass on the couch, drink a beer, and maybe get naked with the redhead who was nuzzling her way into my heart—the same woman who had a way of easing my pain.

Stale air choked me as I walked deeper into the house and over to the sliding glass door. The house had been vacant since Aunt Kari returned to England.

Haven kicked off her sandals before sinking her feet into the carpet in the family room.

After opening the slider, I grabbed two beers out of the fridge.

Then I wound my way around the kitchen island and a recliner in the family room until I was handing her a beer.

Grabbing the bottle, she pointed to a picture of my brother and me. We were holding up a fish he'd caught at one of our fishing expeditions. "Nice catch."

Randal had been so excited that day when he'd caught his first bass.

I tapped my bottle against hers. "Cheers."

She chugged the amber liquid down like she was in some sort of contest.

I watched in awe at the way her throat worked and her beautiful features relaxed. I knew that feeling of how booze could seep into the veins and punch the shit out of the cloying feelings that poisoned me.

"Whoa," I said. "Slow down."

She drained the entire bottle then licked her lips. "I needed that."

I took a long pull of my beer. "Care to tell me what's bothering you?"

She plucked my bottle from my hand then set both down on the coffee table. "No talking." She proceeded to unbutton my shirt, sucking in her bottom lip.

My cock jerked. Hell, I had a permanent hard-on when I was around this woman.

When my shirt was open, showing off my abs and that happy trail that women went gaga over, she dragged a long nail down my stomach to the waist of my jeans.

The vision of her mouth around my dick flashed like a neon sign in the frontal lobe of my brain. Blood rushed down in a frenzy to grip my balls. I swore, if she breathed on my dick, I would lose my load in one second flat.

Her small hand flew past my belt and cupped my cock.

I closed my eyes, moaning while I shoved my hands through her thick auburn hair. Then I wrapped it around my hand and tugged her head back gently.

I rained kisses down on her neck as her expert fingers massaged my cock through my jeans, and I saw stars.

"I've been dying to taste you again," she whispered in a breathy tone.

A girl who loved blow jobs only made me harder.

A phone buzzed.

Fuck me.

She proceeded to unbuckle my belt, ignoring the pesky sound.

I knew it wasn't my phone because I wasn't a fan of Johnny Cash. His song "Walk the Line" continued to play.

The phone stopped ringing then started again.

"Someone is trying to get ahold of you."

She fumbled with my zipper. "Not interested in answering right now."

I chuckled. "Let me."

The ringing stopped then started once again.

"Answer the phone," I said in exasperation. I mean, fuck. I couldn't concentrate. I hated distractions when my dick was begging for attention.

She huffed, stomping over to her purse, then plucked the phone out, flaring her nostrils.

My guess was that it was her old man. No one else could get her amped up to the point where she looked like she wanted to throw the phone against the wall. Or maybe she had a boyfriend I didn't know about. If that were the case, then the night was over. I didn't screw other guys' girls.

She typed frantically then shut off the phone before dumping it back into her purse. "Where were we?"

Well, my dick wasn't as hard anymore. Of course, it would only take a little stroking, but the anger on her face wasn't turning me on.

I buckled my belt. "What's going on? Is it Beverly? Your old man? A boyfriend?"

I was an idiot for not continuing where we'd left off or letting her take me to the one place I'd been dying to go—inside her.

"You said you wanted to make memories." Her voice cracked like an egg. "You bragged you wanted to fuck me. So here's your chance." Her attitude was rude, maddening, and irritating.

It was a huge turn-off even though she reminded me of myself.

I laughed.

That only made her snarl. "Something funny?"

I rubbed a thumb over my lip. "You and me. We're a lot alike."

"We're not. I'm fire. You're ice."

I raked my gaze over her sleeveless brown dress that fell to mid-thigh. It accentuated her fine curves and toned body. She sure was fire—hell fire, to be exact. While I was ready to get burned, scorched, and torched, I wanted Haven's mind and body fully on us. Her old man, if that was the reason she was pissed, didn't have a place here.

I clasped her delicate chin with my finger and thumb. "Look at me."

Slowly, her eyes lifted—dark-green orbs with shimmering flecks of gold.

Follow the yellow brick road.

My pulse thrashed around like the wild night I envisioned of her and me in my bed. "You're killing me. But before we make music together, I want to be sure your brain is clear. I don't do half-assed in the bedroom. I want all of you, Haven." I dragged my fingers along her cheek, up to her temple. "Including your attention. Now tell me what's going on."

She stiffened then let out a strained noise. "I caught my father mauling Beverly's mom."

Whoa! I wasn't expecting that type of shit.

She flung herself onto the leather couch. Her purse bounced up and down.

I sat on the edge of the marble coffee table in between her legs. "An affair?"

"Not sure. But I found them in the kitchen one night at the beginning of summer during a dinner party. They were glued to each other while his wife and guests were in the dining room."

The man had some balls. Regardless, I despised cheaters.

"Lorna Sims acted like she didn't know you at the art festival."

"She doesn't. I wasn't part of the dinner. I'd been up in my room. When I went down to get something to drink, I walked in, but when I saw them, I left before they noticed me. But I did confront my father later on. He brushed it off like it was no big deal."

I braced my elbows on my knees. "So she's his mistress?"

She propped her head against the couch. "Don't know. Don't care. Except I firmly believe that her daughters are spying on me."

"Why? I get that your father doesn't want us together. But what does that have to do with the Simses spying on you?"

Her head came forward. "Before school started, I made a deal with him. No sororities and no media attention. If I brought him bad press, he would stop paying my tuition and expenses. But the first night I met you, things changed. I believe either Tabitha or Beverly snapped that pic of you and me on your couch for my father. Because not long after I left your house, he had a photo of me on your lap. I believe the Simses want me gone so they can have you."

"Bullshit." I knew women wanted me, but fuck if they could force me into a relationship. Surely Beverly and Tabitha weren't stupid enough to think I would date either of them.

You saw Beverly's face when Haven said you two were dating. She was in your bed that morning.

Haven exhaled heavily. "I know I'm right. At first, I thought my dad wanted me to stay away from you because of your reputation as a ladies' man. But I'm beginning to believe that he wants to please his mistress. And she wants me out of the picture so her daughters can have full access to you."

A laugh rumbled free even though her idea didn't seem too far-fetched. There were women in college who were looking to snag a man to marry, especially one who had a potential future in the NFL.

"Was that your father on the phone? Did something happen?"

She let out a nervous laugh. "It was him. My guess is Beverly's mom told him we were dating."

"Are we?" I teased. "I mean, we could if you want. I'm all for pissing off your old man."

Her attention was on my bare chest. "You didn't flinch when I told Beverly we were dating. How come?"

My hands slid up her thighs. "Honestly, I thought it was one of your wild stunts, like kissing me in front of a room full of people, or storming into my room and taking advantage of this hot body."

She rolled her eyes. "You're not hot."

My hands glided farther up and under her dress. "Not a little?"

Her eyelids fluttered shut. "Nope."

Her inner thighs were silky as my fingers danced their way to her happy spot until I was feeling her clit. I froze.

Her eyes flew open as she gave me a twisted smile.

"Do you ever wear panties?" *Please don't ever wear them.*

Casually, she shrugged, batting her lashes. "Sometimes."

Innocent and shy were hot features on her.

I scraped my teeth over my bottom lip as I began to rub her clit. Suddenly, I didn't give a fuck if her mind was somewhere else because my cock was screaming to do something right then, especially because of how wet she was.

"Stand up," I commanded.

Her cheeks reddened as she obeyed.

I whipped off her dress and sucked in a ragged breath.

No bra. No panties. Holy fire in hell.

I wasted no time in getting my clothes off and ripping open the condom I'd had in my wallet.

She watched in intense fascination as I rolled the condom over my hard-as-stone cock, which was pointing straight at her.

Fuck foreplay.

I wanted to bury myself so deep inside her and not come out for days.

I sat down on the couch. "Straddle me." I held my cock in my hand as she mounted me.

My heart was in my throat. I knew I wouldn't last but a minute at most. But I didn't give a fuck. I would be hard again in two minutes flat. I was going to screw her five times before the sun came up. I had a mind to jerk off and get the first one over with. That way, I could fuck longer on the second round.

When she sank down, I let out a moan that my neighbors five miles down the road probably heard. She was so tight that I wondered if she was a virgin, and that made me pause.

I shaped her hips. "Is this your first time?"

"No. It's been a while."

I wasn't sure why that made me grin like I'd won the Super Bowl. But when she started moving again, nothing else mattered.

I gripped her ass while she held on to my shoulders, rocking her hips.

"Feels so good," she moaned.

"Heaven. Fucking heaven."

She giggled.

Her tits bounced, and I bent my head slightly and captured a nipple.

Nothing in the world was right, but at that moment, we fit like we belonged together.

Her nails dug into my shoulders as I sucked her nipples, biting, tugging, and licking. "That's it, baby doll. Ride me hard."

She let go of my shoulders and grabbed the back of the couch, pushing her tits in my face as though she were fucking my mouth.

I cupped her breasts, which fit perfectly in my hands.

But I was teetering on the edge, my balls tightening. "I'm not going to last."

I found her clit and started rubbing while she continued to ride me.

Sweat poured off our bodies, slick and slippery. It felt like ages since I'd last fucked a woman, but even then, it hadn't been this intense, powerful, or dare I say, passionate.

All of a sudden, her lips crashed against mine, and her tongue invaded my mouth, taking what she needed as though I were her drug. Hell, she was becoming mine. That much was certain.

I matched her kiss for kiss, tongue for tongue, bite for bite, as we moved and made magic together.

"I can't last," she said as she nibbled on my lip.

"Take me to heaven, then."

She smiled as she rocked harder and faster. I shaped her hips and anchored my hand to hold on.

When she moaned her release, her body shaking, I didn't give her time to come down. I carried her over to the fireplace and eased us down onto the rug. Then I began thrusting in and out.

She sucked on my tongue as I moved in and out, faster and faster. I wanted this to last all damn night, the friction of our sweat-soaked bodies sliding together, but when she clamped down around me, fireworks exploded behind my eyelids.

She smiled up at me, beautiful and sensuous. "Let it go, big guy."

I threw my head back, and with one last hard thrust, I froze while I rode out my orgasm that was out-of-this-world amazing.

She gripped my cock so hard, milking every ounce out of me. And fuck if that wasn't mind-blowing.

Once I had control of my senses, I pulled out, stalked into the kitchen, and quickly cleaned up. Then I grabbed a beer and returned to the beautiful specimen who hadn't moved an inch.

She was angelic and beautiful with her auburn hair fanned out above her, and my heart sputtered.

Holy fuck. What is happening to me?

The fleeting feeling vanished when she lifted up on her elbows with that zombie look she'd had earlier. "Don't say anything to anyone about my dad. No one knows about him and Ms. Sims."

I wasn't a gossiper, and if I did tell anyone, it would be Lucas, who could keep his mouth shut. Nevertheless, I said, "No worries. I'll take it to my grave." While I would like to see her old man sweat bullets, I considered Haven a friend, and I didn't betray my friends.

She awarded me with a brilliant smile. And just like that, my dick started to grow.

Licking her lips, she said in a breathy tone, "I'm ready to go again."

I was ready to go a thousand times more.

26

HAVEN

Vicki and I were on our way back to the dorm after grabbing dinner at the Terrace Cafe on campus. Students strolled by in groups, some wheeled past us on bikes, and others jogged. A warm breeze picked up as the sun dipped lower on the horizon. I loved this time of year when the evenings grew cooler and less humid.

"I shouldn't have eaten that extra helping of pasta," Vicki complained as she held her stomach.

I'd let her take most of mine. I'd hardly been hungry since I'd met Ryker. Or maybe it was because of my father. He'd been calling and texting me for the last week since the art festival at Woodcreek High, and I'd been ghosting him. I was probably more furious with him than he was with me.

I could confront him about Lorna Sims and my suspicions, but he would only deny it or tell me I was paranoid. But I wasn't. The fact that he'd blown up my phone not long after the art festival proved to me that Lorna had filled him in and told him that Ryker and I were dating.

"Walk the Line," my father's special ringtone, blared from my phone.

Vicki laughed. "You should talk to your dad. Otherwise, he might hunt you down." She knew the song all too well now.

"Maybe I should've gone to another school," I muttered. That way, Ryker and I wouldn't have met.

Vicki swatted at me as we approached the dorms. "Nonsense. With election year, you would still be facing the same rules. Well, aside from staying away from Ryker."

Her last statement was the only problem. I had never brought bad press or attention to myself when I'd been in boarding school. So I knew college wouldn't be any different. Sure, I wanted to party and have the ultimate college experience, but I wouldn't make an ass out of myself.

Your actions with Ryker say otherwise.

No, that wasn't true. I hadn't made the news because of Ryker. I hadn't brought bad press to my father's campaign because of Ryker or in general. The Sims family had instigated the pics and the rumors.

Aside from that, I couldn't figure out why my father hated Ryker. Perhaps Mr. Bridges was right when he'd said that my father only wanted what was best for me. Regardless, who I dated was my choice, although I wasn't dating Ryker. The man didn't do relationships.

Johnny Cash's singsong voice alerted me to another text from Father Dearest.

I found a spot under a tree outside our dorm. "I'll meet you inside."

Vicki flashed her brown eyes at me. "Good luck."

Luck wouldn't work with my father.

Me: *I can't talk right now. I'm in the middle of homework.*

I was going to hell for lying.

Father: *Where are you?*

Me: *My dorm room.*

After a minute with no response, I headed inside. I didn't get far before I was bombarded with giggles, whispers, and stares the minute I stepped foot into the lobby of the three-story building.

Several women were hanging out in the lounge area just off to the right, each one of them sizing me up. Or maybe some hot guy was behind me that I hadn't noticed.

A girl with short brown hair peeked over her laptop screen. "So you're dating Ryker James?"

Each of the six women waited for my answer like they were waiting to hear if they'd won a beauty contest.

"Where did you hear that from?" I knew rumors ran rampant on campus, even more so in my dorm. But I didn't think Beverly would spread the rumor unless she wanted to bring attention to me because she knew my father would do something drastic to make sure Ryker stayed away from me.

The hackles on the back of my neck rose.

The brown-haired girl carried her laptop over to me. It was then that I recognized April, whom I'd met at the Delta Sigma Pi party weeks ago.

She tapped a key with her blue-painted nail, and the university website appeared.

The headline read, "Ryker James is officially off the market." The subtitle underneath read, "Ladies all over campus are crying into their pillows."

My gaze drifted lower on the screen, and I gasped. A picture of Ryker and me locking lips was in full color.

Irritation bristled across my skin.

April curled her short brown hair around her ear. "What does that mean for the fundraiser? Surely, he has to participate. He's the reason women are buying tickets left and right."

I brushed off my annoyance and smiled. "I'm not dating him. He's just a friend."

"Doesn't look that way," said a petite blonde who was sandwiched in between two other blondes.

I had no other answer for them. And no matter what I said, a picture was worth a thousand words.

"Don't worry about Ryker. He's still on the market. That much I can promise you. I got to go." I rushed into the stairwell and gripped the bannister, trying not to let out the scream lodged in my throat.

I wanted to hunt down the person who had taken the picture, and I was certain it was one of the Sims sisters. But no matter how much fire I breathed at the person responsible, it wouldn't change the fact that I'd made the news.

So what? A picture of you and Ryker can't hurt your daddy's precious campaign. That was true, but I didn't need the headache of my father in my face night and day.

I puffed out my cheeks and scaled the stairs two at a time until I was walking down an empty hall to my room. But the rage inside me only intensified when I found my father sitting on the couch, dressed in his expensive suit, with a scowl on his face.

I searched for Vicki, more for support than anything.

Father Dearest uncrossed his legs, set his phone down on the coffee table, and raised an eyebrow. "Your roommate isn't here. So you're in your dorm room doing homework." It wasn't a question, and his tone was dripping with disappointment that I'd lied to him.

My face burned and not with anger, but because I would never be the perfect daughter to him. I would always disappoint him.

"Who let you in?"

He angled his head, almost rolling his green eyes. "I'm a senator—"

"Save it, Dad. I've heard the senator speech about how powerful the title is to get what you want." And he always got what he wanted.

He sat forward. "I've seen the picture of you mauling the James boy."

Laughing, I shrugged. "Shouldn't you be campaigning? The election is three weeks away. And you're still down in the polls."

He visibly cringed. "I'll win the election. Polls don't mean squat."

That might have been true, but it didn't mean I couldn't push his buttons like he was pushing mine.

I ducked into my room, threw my purse on the bed, and removed my sandals. If I was going to spar with my father, I wanted to be comfortable. I had a feeling he and I were in for a long one. Then I sat down in a small, comfy chair that Vicki and I had arranged in a corner next to the TV.

Father hadn't moved, but he was reading something on his phone. Then he proceeded to type on his phone.

It figured that he would ignore me.

I tapped my bare foot on the floor. "Why are you here?" I asked to get his attention… or maybe to get him to leave.

His gaze bounced to mine. "I have the town car waiting to take you home."

I gripped the arms of the chair. "I'm not going home. I haven't violated any of your three rules."

He pursed his lips. "You have. You've brought media attention by being in the news. And you're dating the James boy."

Ding. Ding. Ding. There it is.

"How do you know I'm dating Ryker?" I was ready to fly across the room and let my right hook loose. *Save it for the Simses.*

"Isn't that what the picture is telling everyone?" he asked evenly. He had a great way of deflecting, although it wasn't too far-fetched to think that the picture implied we were dating. The girls downstairs had thought the same thing.

"Regardless, who I date isn't going to ruin your campaign. And let's lay our cards out, Father. You're trying to steer him away from me so the Sims sisters have their chance with the future NFL star."

His face pinched. "Who are the Sims sisters?"

"Now who's lying, Dad? Lorna Sims is your mistress." He'd never shared her name with me that day when I confronted him after I'd found them glued to each other. "That will ruin your campaign."

His nostrils flared as his cheeks flamed red. "I told you to be careful with your threats."

"And I told you that I haven't done anything that violates your stupid rules."

"The university paper says otherwise."

"Again, Ryker and me isn't negative press."

He glared at me as his mind spun with his next move.

Bring it, I wanted to shout, but Vicki breezed in. "Senator Hale." Her giddiness did nothing to cut the thick cord of tension hanging in the air. "I've been dying to meet you. I'm a political science major, and I hope to work in DC one day."

I used the distraction to regain my thoughts and let a sigh bleed out.

My father grinned as though she were his daughter and not me. "See, Haven? We still have people who like politics. Maybe you can learn something from your roommate."

The bastard didn't even have the nerve to say her name.

Vicki's giddy attitude died. "I need to talk to our RA about fixing something. I'll be back later."

Smart girl.

But as she left, she choked out, "Ryker?"

My blood gelled.

I couldn't see him since I was sitting in the chair behind the door, but my father could, and fire blazed in his green eyes.

"Not dating him? If you keep lying, Haven, I'll add more rules to your list." Father's tone oozed with scorn. "Why is he here?"

I flew off the chair to find Vicki trying to tug the big, bad quarterback down the hall.

Inwardly, I laughed. Ryker wasn't budging. But he was glaring at my father. That silent laugh died.

Ryker sauntered into the room. His biceps were bulging, his features were hard, and he had a scowl that would frighten a puppy.

Vicki mouthed, "Sorry." Then she left. I couldn't blame her. I wouldn't hang around either, but if I didn't want Ryker and my father to kill each other, then I had to stay.

I flattened my hand on Ryker's chest, trying to guide him out the door. "I'll call you later."

Ryker sidestepped around me and went over to shake my father's hand. "Senator Hale. Nice to see you again." His tone was saturated with sugar.

The air crackled with the calm before the storm, and there was nothing but lightning sparking in Ryker's gray eyes as he waited for my father to shake his hand.

But Father ignored him and pushed to his feet, almost meeting Ryker in height. "I can't say the same." He gathered his phone, buttoned his suit jacket, then regarded me. "Our conversation isn't finished. I expect you to have your things packed. I'll send a car to pick you up this weekend."

I felt as though he'd slapped me in the face. "Dad, if you insist on making a big deal out of the university paper or Ryker and me, then I will have to take matters into my own hands." I had my own gauntlet to throw down. He wasn't getting away with his powerful threats, although I knew when push came to shove, he would win. He had the financial purse to pluck me from the university like I was a pawn in his game.

"Why are you such a dick?" Ryker asked, his voice as hard as the floor beneath his feet.

Father got nose to nose with Ryker. "I don't appreciate you speaking to me that way, son."

"I'm not your son."

Tension as thick as an iceberg floated into the room.

"You're right. You're not. But let's not forget that I support the sports program. I could have you removed from football."

Crap!

Ryker balled his hands into fists, and evil etched into a grin that frightened me. "I bring in money for this university. Let's not forget either that the team has won the last three games since my return. Also, let's not forget that you fucked over my father and his company."

Father and I fighting and threatening one another was one thing, but now that he was threatening Ryker's livelihood, we were playing a whole new game. As much as I wanted to stick it to my father, I couldn't let him ruin Ryker's life. The big guy needed football, especially if he wanted to get drafted into the NFL.

I slid my petite frame in between the two large men, or I tried to and failed. So I grasped my father's arm. "Daddy." My tone sounded like I was ten again. "I'll come home. No need to send a car either. I have mine." I didn't sound convincing. But I didn't want Ryker to do something stupid to get benched or kicked off the team.

The red in my father's cheeks started to fade. "Smart girl." Then he kissed me on the forehead. "I'll expect you no later than Sunday."

So much for college life.

"Senator." Ryker's jaw hardened like steel. "Why not just come clean that you had a hand in slowing down the approval process for James Enterprises to get a certificate from the water board to operate again."

"Would it matter? Would it change how I feel about you or you about me? What's done is done. Now play football and stay away from my daughter."

"I'm not staying away from Haven." Ryker spat venom. "We're friends. Get used to it."

I gritted my teeth, bit my tongue, silently screamed with joy, and held my breath. The top was ready to blow off my father's thick head of hair, but I was elated that Ryker wasn't backing down.

Father's jaw was stone. "As I said, stay away from my daughter."

"Why do you hate me so much?" Ryker asked.

Father guffawed. "You're not good for my daughter."

"Why don't you let her decide?" Ryker volleyed back.

My father didn't care what I wanted. And no matter what I said at that moment, he wasn't going to hear me.

So to ease the tension, I kissed Father on the cheek. "I'll be home this weekend."

He nodded then left without another word.

As soon as the door closed, a sigh rushed out of my lungs.

27

RYKER

I growled my annoyance at the backside of the senator as he carried himself out of the room as though he'd won the war. *Fuck that.* He'd only won the battle with his daughter, which was eating at my gut like a damn piranha.

She'd given in to his demand. She was moving home.

I tamped down my ire only because their feud was none of my business, but hell, I wanted it to be. I wanted to help her and protect her from her bullying old man.

She blinked, and her head twitched at the same time as though she had Tourette Syndrome. I would too if I were related to him.

I roughed my hands through my sweaty hair. I'd been working off my campus community service and had been in the vicinity. So I'd thought I would take a chance and see if Haven wanted to grab a bite for dinner. But I was far from hungry now.

Fucking senator.

"Why do you make deals with him? Why not just tell him to fuck off?"

"He pays for my college." Her voice was small. "It's not like I can afford to live on my own yet."

Okay, I got that. I even understood that it would take a chisel and muscle to get through to her old man. What I didn't get was how he was hanging me over her head like I was the devil's spawn and had come to take her to hell. Maybe she was right. Maybe the senator had his dick so far into Ms. Sims that he would rather please her than his daughter.

At that thought, I fisted my hands. Haven deserved better.

"Live with me." A maniacal laugh screamed in my head. Like I was the better choice. I was a dick too, and a woman in my life, as in a steady woman, wasn't me.

But you've never met a woman like her before.

Haven was the whole package—gutsy, beautiful body, knew how to take me to paradise in the bedroom, and had some magical potion that made me want to get up in the morning.

My pulse was racing like a horse at the Kentucky Derby.

Her eyebrows climbed to her hairline. "Ryker James wants a girl living with him? That would be some headline."

Yeah, dollface. I'm as shocked as you. Lucas would laugh his ass off when he found out that I'd asked Haven to move in with us. But something felt right about her and me living together.

Voices tittered in the hall outside the door, snapping me out of my haze.

I inhaled deeply. "Lucas and I have an extra bedroom."

Haven, who had been frozen in her spot by the coffee table—with her mouth agape, shoulders hunched, and mind working overtime—awarded me with a dazzling smile. "Can I room with you?"

My heart thrashed, thudded, and thumped. And my dick came alive. "We're friends."

"With benefits," she was quick to add with an avid expression.

My gaze licked up and down her delicious and gorgeous body, remembering how we fit so well together.

Silence beat for one second then two.

She busted out laughing. "If you could see the pain on your face. Don't worry. My answer is no."

Little did she know that I wasn't in pain because she would be living with me or sleeping in my room or even sharing my bed. I was suddenly trying to figure out why I was feeling a swarm of butterflies in my stomach, fluttering like someone had disrupted their habitat.

Her laughed died as she wiggled her hips up to me. "I appreciate the offer." She pressed her hands to my abs. "I have to settle my differences with my father before I make any decisions on where I live or what I do."

Man, for some fucked-up reason, it felt like she was breaking up with me or breaking off our friendship. And that made me want to punch the walls.

I cupped her cheek. "I'm serious, Haven. If you need a place to crash, Lucas and I would be stoked to have you. Or if that didn't appeal to you, I can offer my parents' house. My aunt isn't returning until Christmas."

She lifted up on tiptoes and gave me a chaste kiss on the lips.

Oh, hell no.

Before she got away, my hand snaked around to her neck, and I tugged her to me, searching her eyes, which held fear and warmth. I doubted the fear was directed toward me, but I could have been mistaken.

Slowly, I lowered my lips to hers then kissed her as though I were never going to see her again. But with her, I was learning a lot about myself.

She whimpered when our tongues touched.

Warmth spread out in my chest, surrounding my heart. I'd never felt lightheaded and dizzy when kissing a girl.

She crawled up my body and wrapped her legs around my waist. I carried her into her room and eased her onto the bed.

A tear rolled down her cheek as she looked away.

With my hand, I guided her chin until we locked eyes. "Hey, baby doll."

She started crying as if I'd yelled at her.

I squatted between her legs and spread my hands on her thighs. "Talk to me."

"I just…" She sniffled. "I feel like I'm suffocating. He's never let up on me since my mom died."

So many emotions shot through me, but I knocked them down, or else I would seriously pay a visit to her father.

"Then you," she whispered.

Well, fuck. I didn't want to be a burden or the one squeezing the air from her lungs.

She flicked a tear off her face. "You can be such an ass but so sweet at the same time. Why do you care? Why would you ruin your playboy reputation and have a girl move in with you?"

I scrubbed a hand over my stubbled jaw. "We're friends."

"Is that the only reason?"

I straightened to my full height, my fingers flying to my hair, willing that fluttery feeling in the pit of my stomach to quiet down. Hell, crazy shit was trampling through my brain like a herd of elephants on safari.

I liked Haven. Maybe I more than liked her. I wanted her in my life. I wanted to get to know her better.

Fuck all that. I needed this woman like I needed to wake up tomorrow and breathe.

Maybe the university paper was right. Maybe I was off the market.

She held her bottom lip hostage. "You're thinking really hard."

"I need a drink. Got any beer?" I darted out of her room before she could answer and invaded her small fridge to find only water.

As long as it was cold, I didn't care. I couldn't get the cap off fast enough or the cold liquid down my throat.

Tell the truth. Tell her what you're feeling.

Her footsteps gave her away. "Ryker?" Her angelic tone sent a wave of goose bumps along my arms.

Pivoting on my heel, I poured water down my throat, only to spit it out when my gaze rounded on her.

Her ball-squeezing green eyes were riveted on me as if I were some type of lunatic.

I seriously was one nut shy of going to a mental health facility. Maybe then I could get help for my drinking, my mourning, and whatever it was that I was feeling for Haven, which I was afraid to say aloud.

Her chest rose and fell as she stood before me.

"I need to go." I had to get the fuck out of the dorm. I felt like I was standing in one of those tiny houses on that HGTV program. How could anyone live in such a minuscule space was beyond me.

Mom had teased that she wouldn't mind living in one when she and Dad retired. Dad's response had been "not in my lifetime." He'd been a big dude like me, so I could relate.

Haven batted her long lashes, and another tear cascaded down her face. "We need to talk."

No, my lady, we need to fuck. That was the only exercise that was going to dust away the motes in my brain.

She erased the distance between us, and her soft fingers went around my wrists, or tried to anyway. "Come here."

I went with her over to the couch.

"Have a seat," she purred.

I loved that light and airy sound out of her.

She eased her gorgeous butt onto the coffee table and, with her hands, opened my legs, much like I'd done to her when she'd been at my house.

Slide your hands up my thighs. Please. Please. Maybe then I would be able to get my tongue moving.

My wish wasn't granted. But she did place her palms on my knees.

Screw that. I gripped her hips and lifted her until she was straddling me.

She giggled. "You seem to have that move down pat, big guy."

"I like when you call me big guy." I waggled my eyebrows, staring into the glimmering emeralds that I wanted to gaze into for the rest of my life.

Motherfucker.

She touched my cheek then forehead. "You're sweating."

I grabbed her ass. "You're doing things to me that are kind of freaking me the fuck out."

"Like?"

Being in my head. Being in my heart. Being in my fucking soul.

"I came here tonight to ask you to dinner," I said.

"A date?"

I shrugged. "A friend taking another friend out. Besides, we both need to eat."

"We can't date." She said those three words so seriously, and they were a punch to the heart.

I frowned. "Am I not good enough for you?" I was halfway teasing. Maybe she just wanted to be my friend or was only using me for my body. I laughed.

She looked adorable when she puckered her lips and angled her head. "You're a weird guy sometimes. But seriously. We can't date because it would ruin the fundraiser. Women wouldn't bid on you, or guys wouldn't bid on me."

A heavy sigh broke free, but my relief was short-lived. My chest burned at the idea of another guy touching her or even taking her out. I had never been the jealous type. I'd never had a reason to be since I didn't do steady, but with her, I would rip a guy in two if he touched her.

I laughed harder. "You're worried about that?"

She licked her lips. "Maybe."

"Bull."

She was afraid of her old man for all the reasons she'd mentioned before.

The wiggle of the doorknob announced Vicki, who waltzed in. "Oh. I should just go. I saw your father leave, so I thought the coast was clear."

Haven climbed off me. "No. Ryker was just leaving."

I was? It was probably best. I wasn't ready to talk about my feelings or tell her why I cared. The minute I expressed any of my feelings would be the minute my heart would get broken.

And Haven was right about one thing. She had to settle her differences with her old man, because if she didn't, I would for her.

28

HAVEN

I packed a small suitcase with some of my clothes. I wasn't moving home permanently, and if my father thought I was, he was in for a rude awakening. I just hoped he hadn't gone to the admin office to tell them I wouldn't be living in the dorm anymore.

Vicki yawned out in the common room.

It was only seven in the morning on a Saturday. I couldn't believe she was up already. She'd gone out last night and had waltzed in around three a.m.

I only knew that because I'd been awake. I hadn't been able to sleep since my father had paid me a visit on Thursday. But that wasn't the only reason. Ryker had asked me to move in with him. That was all I'd thought about. He cared. He didn't want to admit it, but he did.

I had my own feelings on the tip of my tongue, but I guessed we both weren't ready to talk about how we felt. It didn't matter anyway. No matter how strong my feelings were for him, my father would stand in the way.

Don't let him. I wasn't willing to fight just yet. I had to settle my differences with my father first.

"Knock, knock," Vicki said in a sleepy voice.

I was hunched over my bed with my back to the door as I folded two shirts and set them in the suitcase.

Her bare feet slapped on the tiled floor. "What are you doing?" She clutched my arm until I was facing her.

My heart fell to the floor. I hadn't had the guts to tell her I was moving home. She'd turned down joining a sorority so we could room together.

Her face pinched as she surveyed the clothes on my bed and in my suitcase. "I should rephrase. Where are you going? Does this have something to do with why you've been a hermit and why you haven't talked much?"

Hermit was the right word. I'd barely eaten. I'd hardly spoken, and when I did, it was nothing more than to say I had class, or I would be home late, or I was going to the library.

She'd done her best the other day to get me to talk after my dad and Ryker had left, but I'd only told her that I hadn't been ready to spill the details, especially the part where I'd agreed to move home.

"My father won," I said in a small voice.

She mashed her lips into a thin line. "If politics turns me into a man like him, then I should change my major."

That got a soft laugh out of me. "Not all politicians are like him. Look, it's only until after the election."

"You haven't broken any rules. He's gotten no negative press because of you."

I opened a web browser on my phone and showed her the screen. The university paper was one thing, but the major news outlets were quite another.

She took my phone and paced as she read the headline from one of the big media outlets. "Senator Hale's daughter knows how to work a room."

I resumed folding. "Apparently, the major news outlets got ahold of the picture that was in the university paper of Ryker and me locked in that heated kiss. I believe someone sold that photo to the press." My father had texted that web link to me at four in the morning then ended his text with *Arlene and I will be waiting for you.*

I ground my molars together at the thought. Arlene was in for a treat.

Vicki jabbed a finger at my phone. "This cannot hurt his election."

"It's not just about his election. If he has to explain my actions, then I'm in the wrong. And it's the principle of his rules. I broke them as he sees it."

"At least you and Ryker look like you're in love."

I snorted. "Love and Ryker don't mix, at least when it comes to women he takes to bed."

"Ryker just hasn't found the right woman until now."

I loved her. She was making me feel so much better, although a tiny part of my heart cried. Ryker and I were like oil and water. As much as we tried to mix together, we would always separate or come apart because of the forces we didn't have control over. Case in point: Senator Eugene Hale, Beverly Sims, Tabitha Sims, and their mother.

My downtrodden state of mind morphed into anger, and I itched to give those women a piece of my mind.

Vicki handed my phone back to me. "'Some of the girls on the floor heard the argument Ryker had with your dad. Would he really ruin Ryker's career?"

I bobbed my head. "He has the clout to."

She twisted her blond-and-brown-streaked hair up on her head then secured it with a band she had around her wrist. "So the fundraiser?"

"I'm still planning on being part of it." I would fight my father hard on that one. I didn't see him arguing too hard. After all, I'd already told the university paper that he would donate ten grand. It would look bad on him if he backed out of that donation.

She gave me a bear hug. "I'm sorry you're going through this."

I hugged her back as though she were the only friend I had. "The light in all this is that Ryker wants me to live with him."

She squealed so loud, I swore the building shook. "And you are just now telling me this?" She paced. "Oh, this is great news."

I dropped down onto my mattress. "Not really. My father would disown me for sure."

She stuck her hands on her hips and lifted one eyebrow higher than the other. "Then let him," she said seriously. "Do you want to move in with Ryker?"

I shrugged. "I don't know if either of us are ready for that."

On one hand, I got the feeling that Ryker's offer was made to irritate my father. On the other, I believed he was serious.

"Of course, if you did," Vicki said. "I would be super jealous. That means you would see Lucas all the time."

"If I did, then you would have to visit every day," I teased.

All of a sudden, her mind started working as her big brown eyes glazed over.

I waved a hand in front of her face. "Hello. I'm not moving in with Ryker."

She shook off her daydream. "A guy only asks you to live with him if he has feelings for you. You know that, right?"

I was pretty good at reading people. So I wasn't going to argue the point. But at the moment, I had to take care of family business before I could even think about Ryker James.

29

———

RYKER

The locker room was somber as the guys changed out of their football uniforms. We'd lost the game, or I'd lost the game. My head hadn't been screwed on since I'd left Haven's dorm room three days ago.

Erik ambled up, wiping the sweat off his chest with a towel. "Don't beat yourself up. All of us played like crap."

The low chatter came to an abrupt halt.

Erik waved a hand around. "We did. Admit it. Defense sucked. I played like shit. I didn't protect you like I should have."

Guys nodded, and others verbally agreed with Erik. It was great to hear that I had their support, but I still felt like a loser.

I'd been sacked twice in the game. It wasn't Erik's fault or any of the guys. It was mine. I hadn't released the ball quickly enough. My reflexes seemed to have frozen, my mind was on a hiatus from football, and my arm wasn't working. Even when I had thrown a pass, I hadn't fired it into Lucas's hands, or anyone's for that matter.

I grabbed the ends of my shirt and pulled it over my head. "Listen up. You guys have had my back, and you've been busting your ass every game. I'm the one who hasn't shown up to play, and I'm sorry about that."

"Man," Vin yelled from the other side of the locker room. "You're entitled to a bad day, or a couple."

Ajax, who was stripping down next to Vin, shouted, "Give yourself a break, Ryker. You've had it rough this year."

Everyone chimed in with the same sentiment.

Lucas strutted up, his sweat-soaked hair matted to his head. "It's time to blow off some steam. You've been wound tight for the last couple of days."

I nodded in agreement. I could use a bottle of scotch and a good fuck. But I didn't want to be with any woman other than Haven, and that wasn't going to happen as long as her old man was in the picture.

"Party at our house," Lucas announced.

Shouts of "hell yeah" and "I'm there" erupted from the guys.

I was getting ready to jump in the shower when Coach Chapman blew in like a fucking tornado. "Ryker, in my office in ten," his voice thundered.

The guys around me recoiled.

Lucas slammed his eyes shut briefly.

We knew what Coach wanted—to chew my ass until I had no meat left on my bones.

No one said a word as Coach left a huge wake of tension behind as he flew out of the room.

I didn't waste any time showering and dressing. One thing everyone knew about Coach Chapman was that he should never be kept waiting. I'd already had him swearing like a sailor on the field. I imagined he would be doing the same when he had me alone in his office.

"Good luck," Vin said at my back as I walked out.

"We'll bring flowers to your funeral," Erik teased.

Nine minutes later, I was closing the door behind me in Coach Chapman's office.

He sat behind his desk amid the stacks of folders piled high around him. I could barely see his computer monitor, which he was fixated on.

I stood with my hands cupped in front of me. "I'm sorry." I had no other words. Coach didn't want to hear my excuses on why I'd played like crap.

He groaned as he leaned back in his chair, swiping fat fingers over his bald head. "For what? Losing the game? You didn't lose it—the team did. All of you sucked."

"Why am I here, then?" My grades were good thanks to the help I'd gotten from my tutor. I hadn't missed practice. I'd been working out. I'd even finished my campus community service like a good boy.

He gnawed on the inside of his cheek. "What's going on in your head?"

I flinched. Our relationship had always been professional. I could count on one hand how many times Coach had asked me where my mind was. Of course, one time had been after the recent deaths of my family. But the only other time had been when I'd first joined the team. He'd been worried about my nerves and wanted to know where my head was at.

"I know," he said. "It's going to take time for you to heal. You have been through fucking hell. But you've been doing well for the last three games. All of a sudden, you can't seem to throw a pass."

"Just a bad day." I couldn't seem to catch a break. I wasn't feeling sorry for myself, or maybe I was. I'd found a woman who I wanted to be with. But as it turned out, I couldn't because of her father.

Everyone had been taken away from me—Ellie, the girl who had captured my heart in high school, my family, and now Haven.

He swiveled his monitor around so I could see it. "Have you seen the news?"

I could feel my forehead creasing. I'd skirted the reporters after the game and run into the locker room. I knew once I left the building, there would be reporters waiting, though.

I inched closer and scanned the screen to find a picture of Haven and me locked in that heated kiss at the Marriott well over two weeks ago.

Coach hated bad press, but me kissing a girl wasn't bad press. Sure, it wasn't about football. If we were going to be in front of cameras, Coach wanted it to be because of football and not much else.

"Do you think this is the cause of my poor performance?"

His eyes became pinpricks. "Senator Hale's daughter? Really?"

I cocked my head. "Are you asking or telling?"

His calm tone switched suddenly. "Don't get smart with me."

"It's a fucking kiss. Surely that has nothing to do with football."

He flew forward and slammed his meaty palms on the desk. The sound ricocheted in the messy office. "The problem is the phone call I just got from Senator Hale. You know, the man who donates tons of money to this school. The same one who is the father of the girl you're about to fuck."

No "about to fuck" there. I already had, but that wasn't for public knowledge and never would be. "Coach, calm down. That picture happened over two weeks ago, and there's nothing going on between her and me."

"Calm down, he says." Coach's face was turning ten shades of red.

"My personal life has nothing to do with football."

He stabbed a finger at the screen. "Tell the press that, Ryker." His hard tone softened a tiny bit. "Fuck any other girl other than the senator's daughter."

Anger, hot and sticky, crept up to make me clench my teeth. I was tired of people telling me to stay away from Haven. "I have been the model player, doing everything I'm supposed to do. Two years of busting my ass with one championship in the mix. Two years of giving a hundred and fifty percent of my time and me to this school and team. I haven't had much time to myself."

He opened his mouth, but I held up my hand. It was my turn to let him know how I felt. "With all due respect, Coach, my love life is off limits to you, to the senator, and to anyone who tries to come between me and whoever it is I'm going to date or settle down with." The only people I wanted to care weren't on earth anymore.

His thick, bushy eyebrows twitched. "Are you saying you're dating Haven? And are you saying you have feelings for her?" Concern etched his tone.

I inhaled then exhaled. "What I'm saying is leave her and me alone. There won't be any more pictures of us like that. The only media coverage I'll get other than football stuff is at the fundraiser next weekend, and you'll be there anyway." Even though I had an extremely strong urge to strangle the senator, I didn't want to put Haven in the line of fire with her old man.

I started for the door. If Coach wasn't going to rip me a new one for my performance on the field, then we were done.

"Ryker, I'm on your side. I know how it feels to want someone you can't have. Some advice?"

I hiked a shoulder. "Why not."

"Make sure she wants you as much as you want her. Then fight like a motherfucker."

That got a laugh out of me and nearly made my eyeballs pop out of my head. "Thank you." I meant it sincerely.

After I left Coach's office, I found Lucas perched against my car. "I was worried you wouldn't have a head or an ass when you left his office."

For shits and giggles, I tried to look at my ass. "I think it's still there."

"So talk."

I sidled up next to him. "The senator is sticking his nose where it doesn't belong."

Lucas tucked his hands into his jeans pockets. "Haven is the reason you've been brooding for the last three days." It was a statement, not a question.

I swallowed thickly. "Remember Ellie? Remember how she stole the breath from my lungs?"

"That bad?"

I got my keys out of my pocket. "Worse."

"Do you think Haven feels the same way?"

"Ninety percent of me does. But even so, she's made her decision."

He clapped a hand on my back. "Then maybe it's time to tell her how you feel. Maybe then, she can decide what team she wants to bat for."

"I asked her to move in with us. She said no. So I know how she feels."

He jerked his head toward me, his light-brown eyes glinting in the late-afternoon sun. "You left that part out."

I'd told him everything that had gone down in Haven's dorm room except that. "I didn't think it was relevant because she said no."

"Just because she said no to moving in doesn't mean she doesn't have feelings for you. Fuck her father. Fight. That's who you are. Since when do you give up?"

Since my heart was on the line.

30

HAVEN

Arlene greeted me at the door before I could even open it. I swore she must have been looking out the floor-to-ceiling window in the formal living room in anticipation of my arrival.

"Haven." Her cold and clinical voice matched the atmosphere in the mansion.

There was nothing warm about the house, especially with her in it.

"Arlene," I returned in a snarky tone.

She stuck out her fake boobs and wiped the scowl off her face. "Nice to have you home."

I dropped my suitcase in the foyer and set my purse on top of it. "Not nice to be here."

"Now. Now. We need to get along. Roya is cooking dinner. We eat at six."

I trudged up the spiral staircase, stomping my feet like a child. "Not hungry."

"You will eat with us," she said at my back, talking to me as though she were my mother.

Rage bristled across my skin as I whirled around, holding on to the shiny mahogany bannister. "You don't tell me what to do."

"I beg to differ," she said in a tone as cool as ice. "You're living here. So you will follow *my* rules."

I snickered, albeit sarcastically. "Your rules? You can't tell me what to do. Oh, and I'm not staying long."

One side of her maroon-colored lips turned up as though she knew a secret. "You're right. After this semester, your father is enrolling you in a small quaint college in Washington." Her enjoyment in delivering that news was written all over her heavily made-up face.

I marched down the five steps, scuffing the heels of my sandals on the stairs, hoping to bore deep scratches in the waxed wooden steps. "Hide me away so I don't embarrass him?" I tapped my finger on my lips. "That's not it. He doesn't want me going to the same school as Ryker James."

She flinched ever so slightly.

I'd hit the nail on the head, although that didn't shock me.

I placed one hand on my hip. "So, Arlene, tell me. Why does Father Dearest hate the quarterback so much? I'm guessing you know."

Her blue eyes narrowed to pinpricks. "He's your father. He worries about you."

That was a big, fat lie. "The only thing my father worries about is his reputation. Where is he?" He and I were going to have a serious talk.

He won't talk or tell you the truth.

"He's indisposed. You can talk to him at dinner."

My lips thinned out, debating whether to continue sparring with the woman who made my skin crawl. I brushed past her, bumping her shoulder. "I'll find him, even if he's in the bathroom."

Click. Click. Click.

The sound of her slingback heels echoed as she hurried to catch up with me. "He asked not to be disturbed." The poor thing sounded worried. I couldn't blame her. Anytime anyone interrupted my father, they got their head sliced off. But I wasn't just anyone.

I stopped in the large archway that led to two spacious rooms overlooking the veranda and the backyard. I could usually find my father on the veranda by the pool or in his office, which was located in another wing of the house.

Baxter, Arlene's prized possession, wagged his tail as he jumped down from one of the sofas.

I squatted down to pet the Maltese. "Hey, boy." At least someone in the house greeted me with happiness.

Arlene picked up Baxter. "Haven, why are you so rebellious?"

I straightened and rolled back my shoulders. "I haven't done anything of the sort unless you call liking a guy rebellious. You were a teenager once. What did you do when you liked a boy?" I wasn't mocking her. I was asking her a serious question.

She sighed, smoothing a hand over her blond updo. "Okay. I get it. But Ryker is only going to break your heart. I had a Ryker James when I was growing up. The only thing to come out of falling for a boy like him is heartbreak."

I wondered if she knew about my father's affair. If she did, she was handling it well.

Baxter wiggled in her arms, so she put him down. The dog scrambled back to his spot on the couch.

"I'll be the judge of my love life. Neither you nor my father will have a say in that whenever I fall in love."

"Seems to me you're in love," she said nicely.

"How would you know?"

"Haven, please. Have you examined the picture that's all over the news of you and Ryker locking lips?"

I didn't need to look at the picture again. I'd already studied it over and over again and reminisced about how tingly that kiss had felt.

A smugness blanketed her face. "And the news outlets are raving about how Ryker snagged a senator's daughter."

I wish it were true.

It is true. You just haven't admitted it to yourself.

I spun on my heel and padded through the opulent mansion, passing expensive paintings on the walls, artifacts that my father had brought back from many of his overseas trips, and crystal vases filled with fresh flowers.

When I passed the gourmet kitchen, a spicy aroma floated out. It smelled like the burritos or tamales that Roya was famous for. Maybe dinner wouldn't be so bad after all.

My father's deep baritone voice grew louder as I wound my way down a hall into another wing. Arlene was right. He would probably be livid if I disturbed him. His office wing was off limits to everyone in the house, other than Roya if she was cleaning, his security, and his aides if they were at the house to work.

"Lorna, don't worry about my daughter. She will not be going anywhere near Ryker. I promise. Yes, your daughters have full access to him now."

The air jetted from my lungs as I froze outside his door.

"Listen," he said in a tone that permitted no argument. "When I say I'm going to do something, it gets done. Now I will not discuss this any further. I will send it over."

Bastard.

It was just as I'd suspected. My father was pleasing his mistress and trying to keep Ryker away from me so Tabitha and Beverly had free access to the quarterback.

Adrenaline rushed to every extremity as I tried to get my body to move. I had a good mind to storm in. But that wouldn't accomplish anything other than sparking a yelling match that ended with no outcome.

I was tired of my father's bullshit. I was tired of trying to get him to see me as something other than a problem. For once, I wanted him to be a dad who loved his daughter unconditionally. I wanted him to support me no matter what I did or who I dated.

I wound my way back to where I'd left my suitcase, trying not to scream at the top of my lungs. *Screw staying here. Screw my father, and screw his rules.*

I passed Arlene, who was sitting with Baxter while she read from her iPad. "Tell my father he can shove his rules and deals up his ass."

When I reached the foyer, my suitcase was still there along with my purse. I was surprised Roya hadn't taken them to my room. Maybe Arlene knew I wouldn't be staying long. *Smart lady.* I would give her that.

Hiking my purse on my shoulder, I grabbed my suitcase and didn't look back.

Arlene chased after me. "Where are you going? Your father isn't going to be pleased." She sounded as though she would get scolded too.

I made quick work of throwing my things into the car. "Don't care. Tell him not to look for me because he won't find me." I suspected he would if he sent out his security goons.

Once I was speeding down the long driveway, I screamed at the top of my lungs. Vengeance, rage, jealousy, and so much came out in that scream.

I had no idea where I was going. I couldn't go to the dorm. He would look for me there. I knew one place that could be my sanctuary. So I drove to Ryker's house—the one located right off campus.

Forty minutes later, I was circling the neighborhood, searching for a parking space. Cars lined the street on both sides, and more cars were parked three deep in some driveways. The area was predominately college students who had either purchased or rented the two-story stucco houses, which varied among three designs.

Ryker's stuck out like a sore thumb, only because partygoers were streaming into his house while others spilled out or lounged on the porch.

This was a bad idea. With my luck, one of the Sims sisters, or maybe both, were there. After all, it was a party, and my father had just told their mother that the Ryker empire was open for business.

I found a spot a block down and away from campus. Ryker's house might be the second in line after my dorm, but I had a thirty-minute or more head start.

Once inside, I pushed through groups of people laughing, dancing, and talking over the loud music. The last time I was there, Ryker had been in his room, but something told me to check the kitchen first.

I found Lucas twisting a cap off a bottle of beer. "Haven?" Those tawny-colored eyes bugged out.

Yeah, Ryker had told him about what had happened with my father in my dorm room. Not that I cared. The whole building knew what had happened. I wouldn't be surprised if their fight made the headlines in the university paper.

"Where is he?" I didn't have time to chitchat.

"What are you doing here?" Lucas asked.

"Just tell me where he is." *And please don't tell me he's screwing some chick because I would go postal on the man.*

He flicked his unshaven jaw to the door that led down to the media room. "He's down there last I knew."

A hint of weed floated in the air as my feet sank into the shag carpeting at the bottom of the stairs. It was the same carpet Ryker had puked on the night I'd met him, which seemed liked eons ago.

Music spilled from the speakers while a couple made out on an oversized chair near the TV. When I rounded the large square beam, my gaze landed on Ryker, and my heart stopped.

For the second time within an hour, I lost my breath as the emotions my father elicited from me intensified.

Ryker's head rested on the back of the couch. His eyes were closed, and the faint sound of him snoring tickled my ears. But what had me ready to get arrested was the hunger to send Tabitha Sims to the hospital. She had her head on his chest and one hand on his abs.

I clenched my teeth, my fists, and every muscle in me.

Tabitha batted her blue eyes and stuck out her tongue at me.

Bitch.

I trudged over to the stereo, found the power cord, and yanked on it. The couple who had their tongues down each other's throat broke apart.

Tabitha laughed.

Ryker didn't move or wake up.

His chest was moving, so I knew he wasn't dead. That could change, though.

I kicked his bare foot, which was resting on the coffee table.

The man didn't budge.

"Leave him be," Tabitha cooed. "He's had a hard day."

I busted out with a snort and a growl. She was acting like she and Ryker had a long ongoing relationship. Nevertheless, a part of me felt sorry for her. The other part wanted to pluck her off him by her blond ponytail.

I tapped Ryker on the face.

Tabitha shot up and tried to scratch my face. "Get away from him."

Revulsion and fury pulsed in my veins.

Ryker stirred, and when he opened his eyes, he shot straight up, wobbled, and fell back down to the couch.

Déjà vu hit me as I remembered how he'd acted that first night I'd met him. Nevertheless, I clamped down on my tongue. We weren't dating, so I shouldn't care what chick he had on him. But Tabitha wasn't any chick. She was the daughter of my father's mistress, the girl who wanted to bury her pink-painted nails into Ryker, the same woman who was bringing out a side of me I didn't like. I'd never been one to physically fight, but I had a mean kick thanks to a kickboxing class I'd taken in boarding school.

His eyelids fluttered as he shook off his sleepiness or drunkenness. Or maybe he was high. None of that mattered when he laid eyes on Tabitha. The sight of her seemed to sober him up. "What the fuck are you doing?" He sounded repulsed rather than guilty.

She tried to touch him.

He lifted his hands in the air. "Get off me." His voice was hard and pitted. Then his wild gaze rounded to me, and his jaw came unhinged.

I hugged myself. "Why am I not surprised?" It was more of a question for Tabitha than him.

Ryker pushed to his feet and listed to one side. "Fuck."

Tabitha yanked on his hand and pulled him back down. Ryker went easily, mainly because he was tipsy or trying to shake off sleep.

He tried to stand again. "Tabitha, if you touch me one more time, I'm calling the cops."

Her thin eyebrows furrowed. "I'm calling your father," she said to me, whipping her phone from the back pocket of her shorts before she stomped away.

"Tell him I said hi." At least she was confirming my suspicions.

When Ryker was upright, he roughed two hands through his thick black hair. "What are you doing here?"

"Catching you with other women," I teased.

"No, seriously," he said as if he were stone-cold sober.

My father's ringtone alerted me to a text.

"I have to go," I said. "If my father finds me, you won't ever see me again."

Ryker tensed. "Come on." He started for the stairs.

When we reached the kitchen, Lucas was leaning against the island as though he were waiting for us. "Need help?" he asked.

"Stay with her," Ryker said to Lucas. "I need to get my shoes." Ryker darted out.

"Where did Tabitha go?" I asked Lucas.

He scratched his jaw. "She went into the living room, or maybe she left. Are you in trouble?"

Before I could answer, Ryker was back with shoes on and a T-shirt covering his toned chest instead of the light-blue unbuttoned shirt that he'd been wearing. "If anyone shows up looking for Haven," he said to Lucas, "tell him she was never here. If they ask about me, make up a story." Ryker tugged me along, out a door, and through the garage.

I had no idea where he was taking me, but his hand in mine and his need to protect and help me made me relax for the moment.

31

RYKER

*F*ucking Tabitha. *Fucking senator.* My mind wasn't exactly clear, as the alcohol was doing a number on my equilibrium. But hell if I hadn't sobered up when I'd laid eyes on those big emeralds beaming from Haven. She had an uncanny ability to make me forget how dismal things were for me. The minute I started remembering that Mom, Dad, Randal, and Leigh were no longer there, I thought of Haven.

Even now with her hand tethered to mine, I was able to breathe. I had honestly been in mourning over not seeing her in three days, which was crazy.

"Where are we going?" She sounded more curious than worried.

I gripped her hand like she was my lifeline. In part, she was. She gave me a sense of purpose, like I had a future, like I might make it through the heartache that hurt like a motherfucker every minute of the day.

I was grateful for friends. I was grateful for football. I was beyond grateful that I'd met Haven despite her old man or despite how scared I was to dissect the feelings I had for her.

"You'll see. Hurry. I don't want Tabitha to find us." With my luck, the blonde would be hiding in the bushes, taking pictures of us and then sending them over to Senator Hale.

Haven grunted when I said Tabitha's name, followed by, "Seriously, I can't go on campus."

"I wouldn't throw you to the wolves." I veered down a side street with the lights from campus glowing in the distance. On my way to get my shoes, I'd asked Erik if I could use his place for an hour, or maybe the entire night.

Five minutes later, we were walking into an immaculate home where everything was in its place—two couches, a large-screen TV, a coffee table, a weight bench and workout gear in the dining room, and a kitchen that glinted with shiny stainless-steel appliances.

I flipped on a switch, and the light on an end table illuminated. "Erik, Vin, and Ajax live here."

Haven scanned the floor plan, which was a wide-open space. "Are you sure three men live here? The place is spotless."

"You don't know Ajax. His dad is military. Everything has to be clean."

I crossed the carpeted floor of the family room and headed into the kitchen, then I snatched two bottles of water from the fridge. My throat was parched from all the scotch I'd been drinking since I'd gotten home from the game.

Haven glanced at pictures on the fireplace and on the walls. The guys might have been big brutes, but each of them had a talent when it came to their living space. Ajax was the cleaner. Erik was the designer. He believed a home, even one with three dudes, needed to be homey with pictures and stuff. Vin was the cook, and the guy could whip up some mean sushi rolls.

I set one bottle down on the marble island, which took center stage in the kitchen, and uncapped the other before drinking the entire contents.

Haven finally joined me. It was then I had a chance to really check her out, not that I hadn't noticed the thin fabric of the low-cut T-shirt she was wearing or the shorts that rode up her thighs, stopping midway. I liked that she showed skin, but I was digging how she didn't wear those short shorts that revealed her butt cheeks only because I would kill any man who dared to see underneath her clothes.

"Thirsty?" she asked.

I was thirsty for more than water now that we were alone and the haziness in my brain was dissipating.

She took a swig from her bottle. "So the guys are at your party? I didn't see them."

"They're there. What's going on?" I didn't have to ask. I knew she was there because of something her father had done. Or maybe she'd told him to fuck off, and she'd come to tell me that she would move in with me.

All of a sudden, those butterflies that had died when she declined my offer awakened.

Swallowing water, she rested against the sink across from me. "Could you not feel Tabitha on you?"

I chuckled. "That's what you want to talk about?"

I had other things on my mind than Tabitha, who was turning out to be a stalker in my book. I skirted the island and cocooned Haven between my body and the sink, gripping the edge of the counter on either side of her. I was careful not to touch her yet. If I did, we wouldn't talk.

She craned her neck up, those glistening emerald orbs sucking me in.

Follow the yellow brick road.

I searched her face. "Let's get something straight. I want nothing to do with Tabitha or her sister. I've never slept with either of them. And I might take out a restraining order if I find them anywhere near me again."

She beamed from ear to ear, her chest rising and falling.

That smile had my pulse soaring to new heights.

Tell her how you feel. Listen to Lucas.

I didn't know if I could articulate my feelings into words.

Her phone sang "I Walk the Line." Her damn father. I swore he had a camera on us somewhere nearby.

She tensed as her lips pursed.

I took that moment to press my mouth to hers, soft at first as the sound of her phone faded. Once it did, she opened for me, allowing me to invade her mouth with my tongue. She tasted of the future, home, and sunshine. No matter what happened after tonight, her lilac scent and the taste of her would always be forever embedded in my memory.

Her small hands flattened against my chest. "Your heart is beating crazy fast."

"You have that effect on me. Do you want to tell me what's going on?"

Or can I strip you naked and take my time making you feel like the most beautiful woman in the world.

While I was sure she would let me, we probably should talk before her old man did find her. Knowing him, he could probably track her phone.

"Do me a favor? Shut off your phone for now."

She blinked then jerked. "I'm so stupid." She hurried to turn it off.

I began pacing, thinking of another place in case it was too late.

She sat down on a barstool. "I overheard my father talking to Tabitha's mom on the phone earlier. He confirmed he's keeping me out of the picture to allow the Sims sisters to pursue you."

Motherfucker!

I rubbed my fisted hand. I was ready to punch a wall or maybe the sliding glass door I was near.

My bad fucking day just got a million times worse. By the end of the night, I might be in jail for killing an elected official. "I'm going to talk to your father."

She jumped up and clutched my wrists. "Not a good idea."

"He's already made waves by calling Coach today. He needs to stay out of my personal business like everyone else."

"He called your coach? I'm so sorry." Tears brimmed in her eyes.

"I only agreed to obey him because he threatened you and your football career."

I put my finger on her lips. "Never apologize for your father. His actions are his own. And he can't ruin my career. I mean, he can try, but he won't get far. And wait. What? You obeyed him for me?"

Holy shit! I think I fell harder for her.

She shrugged. "Of course. We're friends."

I cocked an eyebrow, debating whether to ask if friendship drove her to obey her old man or if she had deeper feelings for me. But that weak spot somewhere inside me was afraid she would stick to just friends.

"Thank you for having my back, but, baby doll, you got to stand up to him. You can't let him dictate who you're friends with or what guy you like."

She shied away. "I know."

Slowly, the puzzle pieces were fitting together. "It's all making sense now. Remember that morning you stormed over to my house and tore Beverly a new one? Well, when I woke up that morning, I found her in my bed."

"You didn't invite her?"

"At first, I thought I had. I mean, I barely remembered you when you showed up that morning. But as the alcohol cleared, the events of the night before returned. When I went to bed, I was alone. After Franklin, my lawyer, left, Lucas and I had a cup of coffee then called it a night."

"You barely remembered me, huh?" she teased. "And now?"

I cupped her face and kissed her slowly and sensuously. "Unforgettable."

Her body became mush.

If she thought my heart was beating fast before, she should feel it now because it was going fucking wild. If I kept taking and tasting, we would be naked and not talking.

I pressed my forehead to hers. "Any idea why your father is so determined to please Ms. Sims and her daughters? He doesn't strike me as a man who does things for love."

She sucked in air. "Maybe to keep his affair quiet. After all, he's in the public eye."

A form of bribery. That made sense.

"You're right. I need to confront him, and I need to do it tonight."

"I'll come with you." I couldn't let her face him alone. After all, I was the main reason she was going through hell with her old man.

She lifted up on her tiptoes and kissed me. "Thank you. But I need to do this by myself. And I don't want you to ruin your football career for me."

"I would ruin it and tear down buildings and people for you."

She crashed her mouth against mine and kissed me as though it was our last one ever.

That thought made me want to cry. I knew in that moment and without a doubt in my mind that I was in love with Haven.

32

HAVEN

I ran all the way to my car from Erik's house. After that soul-stealing kiss, I couldn't speak. Even if I did, I wasn't sure what would come out of my mouth. Sometimes actions were better than any words, and I hoped that Ryker had at least gotten the message that I had feelings for him.

My hands shook as I started the engine. I inhaled once then twice, trying to regulate my breathing. Before I got on the road, I texted my father that I was on my way home.

He replied immediately: *I'll be waiting.*

I stuck out my middle finger at my phone then got on the road. My heart was pounding, and dread was setting in.

My phone beeped. That time, it was Ryker: *Text or call me after you talk to your old man. If I have to, I'll come get you. I got you, baby doll.*

Whatever was about to go down, I knew one thing. If Ryker's offer still stood about moving in with him, then I would be packing my bags tonight.

Once on the road, my mind wandered to what Ryker had said. "I would ruin my career and tear down buildings and people for you."

I didn't want to assume anything, but that line sounded like he loved me. Instead of telling him those three little words, I'd kissed him only because my throat had closed up with so much emotion. Also, I was afraid to say "I love you" out loud. I was afraid he might run like the wind the minute I did. After all, his reputation was as a ladies' man.

Traffic was light on the highway. So it didn't take me long to get home. Well, my father's estate wasn't home anymore. Nothing about his place gave me the feeling of home. Come to think of it, I'd really never had a place where I felt like I belonged, at least not since my mom had been alive. But since her death, I'd been a gypsy—boarding school, my father's estate during summers, or traveling with friends and their parents on occasion.

Father was sitting in a rocker on the portico, smoking a cigar, when I pulled up. Arlene was nowhere in sight, which was probably best. I didn't need the hassle of her butting in when I spoke my mind. I was sure she didn't want to hear the questions I had for my father. Not only that, I wasn't a home-wrecker.

I climbed the few steps and sat in the rocker next to him. For a beat, he didn't say a word, and I was waiting for him to start. He could yell all he wanted to, but this was the last time I would endure his wrath. That much, I was certain of.

"How's Ryker?" he asked casually, as though he and I hadn't been in several fights as of late.

"Did you ask Tabitha?" I kept my attitude even and calm. I knew as the conversation escalated, any niceness I had would vanish.

He puffed out a cloud of smoke. "Arlene tells me you left after you came to my office. I take it you overheard my conversation."

I rocked in the chair. "Bits and pieces."

The overpowering hum of the crickets sang around us as a warm breeze hung in the air. The sun had gone down an hour ago, and the only light illuminating my father's hard profile was the glow coming from the long window behind us.

He continued to toke on his cigar, rocking in his chair. "I've made a lot of mistakes in my life, Haven, but you were never one of them."

My head whipped left as if I were watching a horror movie. I had so much to say and nothing to say, which was crazy.

He puffed and rocked. "I sent you to boarding school so you didn't have to put up with public scrutiny as I went into politics. I like you home. I want you to live here and not in a dorm room, and not because of my threats, but because I'm your father and I want us to have a relationship."

I was stymied. "So why use threats? Why couldn't you ask me nicely or explain your feelings? Why treat me like one of your minions? And why all of a sudden do you want to have a relationship?"

He stopped rocking and regarded me. "First, you were dead set on living in the dorms, and I didn't want to take that away from you. I was your age once, and I wanted that college experience too. And you're right. I have been treating you like you work for me. I'm sorry for that. Ever since your mom died, I haven't been one to talk about feelings, but maybe it's time I start." He inhaled. "Believe it or not, Arlene made me realize that if I keep treating you like someone on my campaign, then I would lose you."

Maybe there was hope for Arlene yet. Still, his admission of his feelings was nice, but the bigger issue was Lorna Sims.

"You will lose me, Daddy, if you tell me who I can and cannot date. So the next questions are why do you have two women taking photos of me? Why are you more interested in pleasing them than your own daughter? And why throw Ryker into the mix? He's done nothing to you."

He flicked cigar ash into a tray on the table between us and set his green gaze on me. "Because Lorna Sims is prepared to release information about me that, if it got out, could ruin me."

"Your affair?"

"Partly."

"You mean she has something else on you? What?"

Regret washed over him. "I'm not prepared to discuss the details except to say that Lorna thinks she has something else on me other than the affair, and whether it's true or not, I'll have to deal with public perception. Look, whatever happens between now and the election, I want you to know that I do love you."

My mouth hit the arm of the rocker. It had been years since he'd told me that, and while I was elated that he was sharing how he felt, I was concerned that he was in trouble. Sure, Ryker was right. My father's actions were his own, and he would have to atone for his mistakes, but he was my father, my blood, my family, and I felt I needed to help if I could. The only way I knew how was to live at home for the time being. Maybe he and I could sew the pieces of our relationship back together.

It was my turn to put my cards on the table. "Daddy, I like Ryker a lot. He's a great guy. He has a big heart, and I'm going to tell him how I feel. If he feels the same way, then he'll be around more."

He harrumphed. "I see a lot of me in him."

That wasn't a bad thing, although Ryker didn't strike me as a guy who would cheat. He also had a bigger heart than my dad, although my dad's heart had been ripped out when my mom died. So I should cut him some slack.

"Please tell me what else Lorna thinks she has on you."

"Haven, the less you know, the better." He sounded worried.

"Does Arlene know about your affair?"

He nodded. "She does. My affair with Lorna has been over with for a while now. Aside from the Simses, Arlene, and now you, no one knows about it. I would like to keep it that way."

I wasn't sure marital affairs ever stayed hidden. But my lips were sealed.

"Is your marriage okay?" Not that I cared one way or the other.

"Arlene is a strong woman, and I love her. We're working through things. That's all you need to know. Would you do me one more favor?" he asked nicely. "Can you and Ryker keep a low profile out of the public eye until after the election?"

Irritation crawled up my throat because he wouldn't tell me what else Lorna might have on him.

His big hand landed on mine. "Can you, honey?"

Honey? He hadn't called me that since I was ten. If it weren't for the loud music of the crickets, I would have thought I was on some other planet. Plus, he'd seemed to come to terms with Ryker and me. For sure, I was in an alternate universe.

"You have my word."

The election was coming up in two weeks. During that time, I had classes and studying. Ryker had the same plus football practice and games. However, we did have the fundraiser, which wouldn't be bad press. But even then, we wouldn't be showing any affection in public.

Then my heart stopped beating.

Some woman was going to buy a date with Ryker, and some guy a date with me. I wasn't thrilled about the event, but I'd signed up, and I couldn't disappoint Lucas.

"I do have that charity event next Saturday."

"I know. I suspect one of the Sims sisters will buy a date with Ryker."

I growled under my breath. I really wasn't looking forward to next Saturday.

33

RYKER

I'd been dying to see Haven all fucking week. Since she'd run out of Erik's like someone had been chasing her, I hadn't been able to concentrate. Well, except I'd had most of my head in the football game earlier that day. Thankfully, we'd won, so at least the day had started off well. But now with the charity event upon us, my gut was giving me a bad feeling about that night. I couldn't pinpoint why. Maybe because Haven was an hour late. We still had an hour before the auction kicked off, but all participants were supposed to be at the hotel two hours prior to start time.

I paced the floral carpet in the hall at the Marriott, outside the ballroom where guests who had forked over fifty dollars for a ticket were chatting excitedly.

I wasn't excited in the least. Now that I had finally admitted to myself that I might be in love with a woman I probably couldn't have, I didn't want to be there.

Lucas came out of a room next door to the main ballroom. The other participants were inside, getting ready for the event.

He adjusted his bow tie, looking suave and debonair. "Any word from Haven?"

I shook my head but continued to wear a hole in the carpet. "I sent her a text earlier, but no word."

The only time I had heard from my girl was after she'd talked to her father. She'd been cryptic in her text with only a message that said she'd resolved some of her issues with him, and she'd assured me she was okay. She'd ended by saying, "I'll see you at the charity event."

I'd debated whether to head out to her father's estate, but I'd had too much going on with football and practice.

"You don't think her dad is responsible for her not being here?" Lucas asked.

"I wouldn't put it past him," I muttered.

Maybe he'd locked her in some room until after the election. After all, his poll numbers had dropped big time during the last week for no other reason than his opponent seemed to have a solid backing with voters and some new policy he'd been bragging about in reducing emissions from manufacturers, power plants, and oil refineries.

Taking out my phone from my tux, I settled in front of a window that overlooked a garden.

Me: *Hey, baby doll. Where are you? Everything okay?*

Lucas sidled up to me. "Don't look now, but Tabitha is coming this way."

Motherfucker!

The woman was like a Whac-A-Mole.

"Lucas. Ryker." Her high-pitched voice grated on my nerves.

Lucas, being the nice guy that he was, pivoted on his heel. I didn't move but watched their exchange through the reflection in the window.

She kissed Lucas on the cheek. "You look great in a tux. Maybe I should put my money on you instead of Ryker."

When she said my name, I blanched even though I was stupid to think that she wouldn't be there or bid on me.

She skirted past Lucas and came up to me then hooked her arm around mine. "You smell awesome."

The urge to scream sat heavily in my throat. But I was a gentleman. So I shrugged out of her hold as nicely as I could.

"Ryker," a female voice said.

Thank fuck. Saved by a woman.

My gaze drifted to my savior, who was none other than Vicki.

Lucas lit up with a grin as though he were looking at Vicki for the first time. But Vicki wasn't a stranger, although the way she was dressed was eye-opening. She was rocking an outfit that hugged her curves and showed off just enough cleavage to tease a man.

Tabitha followed me to where Lucas was standing near a fancy table that held a vase of fresh flowers. The sweet aroma floated up my nostrils, almost calming me for a moment. But that feeling vanished when I saw the worry in Vicki's big brown eyes.

She clasped her hands in front of her. "Is Haven here?"

Lucas ran a hand over his hair even though he'd tamed his curls with tons of gel. "What happened?"

Vicki regarded Lucas, Tabitha, then me. "You haven't heard?"

Lucas and I swapped twisted expressions.

Tabitha, on the other hand, had a faint smile on her face as though she knew what Vicki knew.

"It's all over the news," Vicki said in a rush. "Senator Hale has been having an affair."

Holy fuck! What if Haven thought I was the one to leak the news? What if that was the reason she was AWOL?

"That might explain why Haven isn't here," Lucas said.

Tabitha gave us a smug look. "Good luck, gentlemen. Start thinking about where you're going to take me, Ryker." Then she started for the ballroom.

Oh, fuck no. I grasped her cold, clammy hand. "You know something."

She pressed her body to mine. "I don't know what you're talking about."

I gripped the sides of her arms, edging away. "Yes, you do."

She flashed her murky blue eyes up at me. "I suggest you forget about Haven Hale. Because after tonight, you won't want to be associated with the Hales." Then she held her head high and walked into the ballroom.

My legs were locked in place.

"She sounds like something big is about to happen," Vicki said.

My gut knotted. "I have to find Haven."

"We have a lot riding on this event, dude," Lucas said, meaning I was the headline. I was the one who would bring in the money. "Give her a few more minutes."

I hated to disappoint my best friend and a great charity, but Haven came first. "Have you spoken to her this week?" I asked Vicki.

"Yeah. She said she would be here. But maybe she can't get past the reporters. Last I heard, they were at the senator's house." Vicki's eyes drifted past me as Lucas flicked his head.

I looked over my shoulder, and that heartbeat that was only reserved for Haven took off like a horse out of the gate.

Haven sashayed toward us like she didn't have a care in the world. Her auburn hair was piled up in some fancy hairstyle. Her halter dress revealed her toned arms and large breasts. My heart reacted and so did another body part, because that slit in her dress crept up from her ankle to midthigh.

No fucking way was any guy getting his hands on her. I didn't know how I could break the rules, but I had to think of something. However, any thoughts I had disappeared when she gave me a smile that said I was the guy for her—no one else.

Vicki ran up to her. "Oh my God! Are you okay?"

She reared back. "Of course. Why wouldn't I be?"

"The news," Vicki said as a matter of fact.

"My father is dealing with it." She sounded so calm.

Clutching my shoulder, Lucas sighed. "See you inside." Then he strutted up to Haven and Vicki. "Vicki, can I talk to you?"

Vicki cooed or squealed as she and Lucas walked away.

Haven stood ten or twenty feet away, watching me size her up. Or maybe she was doing the same to me.

My mouth was bone dry. My brain wasn't working. And I probably couldn't get my tongue to work either.

She beamed as she drew closer. "Hey, big guy. I love the tux."

And I love you. "I was worried. Are you sure you're okay?"

"Never better."

Her permanent smile said it all, but in that moment, I had to clear the air. "I didn't leak anything to the press."

"I know."

My head jerked. "Do you know who did?"

"Let's not talk about that right now."

It was probably best to wait. Besides, I didn't want to talk anyway. Instead, I wanted to kiss the lights out of her.

But what I wanted had to wait because Lucas returned right then.

"It's time," he said. "I want to address the group now that everyone is here."

I extended my elbow to Haven. "My lady."

She blushed as she took my arm.

No matter what happened from there on out, I was one happy motherfucker.

34

HAVEN

The twenty of us who were in the fundraiser were shuffled into the ballroom amid a packed house and instructed to sit in the front row. I felt like I was in my graduation ceremony at boarding school.

A lady, whom Lucas had introduced as Sandra right before kickoff time, fiddled with papers on the podium. Sandra was head of the Chelsea House for Battered Women and the master of ceremonies for the evening.

I didn't know how I'd gotten the short end of the straw, but I was sitting next to none other than enemy number two—Beverly Sims.

She leaned in. "I didn't think you would make it. Seems your father is in a pickle."

My dad suspected that one of the Simses had leaked the affair to the press because Lorna Sims had been calling him all week, and he'd been ghosting her. He still hadn't told me what else she had on him.

I wasn't sure I wanted to know anymore. I was on the brink of doing something drastic to one of the Sims women, or maybe all three, although a part of me felt sorry for them. It was pathetic watching three women, with no father around, trying to hang on to a rich man's coattails.

"I know you leaked his affair to the press." I wasn't sure, but I wanted to see what type of reaction I could get out of her.

Her hands were clasped in her lap, and her knuckles were almost turning white. "Wait 'til you hear what else we have in store."

Ever so slowly, my head turned in her direction. "So you admit leaking the affair?"

She jutted out her chin. "Your father deserves what's coming to him."

Don't make a scene, Haven. Remember your manners.

As a senator's daughter, I had been taught to keep my mouth shut or, if push came to shove, to divert whatever the topic was that could cause trouble—act normal, polite, confident, and go about my business like nothing had happened.

Sandra, who was dressed in an elegant strapless gown, surveyed the crowd, her dark gaze alight with pleasure.

I wished I was that happy or excited to be there. In part, I was because Ryker was there. I hadn't seen the man since he had whisked me away to Erik's house. Many times during the last week, I'd almost gotten in my car and shown up on his doorstep. But I couldn't risk anyone seeing me or putting Ryker in the spotlight in the event that Tabitha or Beverly was around.

Yet as I sat next to Beverly, tense and a second away from making a scene, I realized I shouldn't have come. My father had advised me to stay home. But I wasn't the type to back out on my commitments. I'd also wanted to confront the Sims sisters after the event. But Beverly was making it hard to do anything other than rip out her blond hair strand by strand.

"No reaction," she whispered, looking straight ahead.

I smiled, realizing that she was trying to get me to make a scene. I wasn't going to stoop to her level.

Sandra cleared her throat. "Ladies and gentlemen, welcome."

"After tonight," Beverly whispered, "Ryker James will not be yours."

"Pathetic," I mumbled.

"I hope you have your checkbooks ready," Sandra continued. "Because we have twenty beautiful and handsome men and women who have graciously offered up dinner with one of you."

Shouts and whistles ensued.

"My name is Sandra, and I'm head of the Chelsea House for Battered Women. I want to thank you for being here. The money we raise tonight will aid us in our efforts to help those women in need. So let the bidding begin."

Sandra waved at the ten football players.

They lined up on the side and at the foot of the makeshift stage. Five players I didn't know were slotted to go first, followed by Ajax, Van, Erik, Lucas, and Ryker. Each of them was dressed in a tuxedo, handsome, grinning, and ready to see which woman in the room won a date with him. Well, except for Ryker. That cocky demeanor he usually exuded wasn't showing that night. Instead, he seemed out of sorts. I knew he had been worried about me. Or maybe he could tell that I was ready to do something drastic with Beverly next to me.

Lucas said something to him.

I glanced behind me to see if I could spot Vicki, but I didn't have to look far. She was right behind me.

She gripped my shoulder. "I'm right here."

I tapped her hand twice, silently saying thank you. Then I turned my attention back to Ryker, who was fixated on me again.

I smiled, releasing some of the pent-up madness I had coursing through my veins. He looked handsome in his tux. His black hair was slicked back, he was clean-shaven, and those gray eyes sparkled only for me.

"What's wrong?" he mouthed.

Everything. When I'd walked around the corner and laid eyes on him, those pesky nerves that had spun a web inside me, quieted. I'd been a mess. The news had broken about thirty minutes before I was scheduled to leave. The reporters had descended on my father's estate, and it had been hard to get around them.

Thankfully, my dad had had two security guards escort me to the Marriott. They'd barreled through the melee without too much trouble.

Despite the reporters, I was worried about my father. The election was in ten days, and the news of the affair wasn't going to help him. Not only that, my father still hadn't told me what else Lorna might have on him, but that worry I'd seen on him during our talk the other night had diminished. Yet Beverly's statement, "Wait 'til you hear what else we have in store," gave me a chill.

Sure, my father was in charge of his own actions and had to atone for his mistakes. But even though we had a strained relationship, I didn't want to see him burn.

Sandra slammed a gavel down on the podium. "Sold to number five."

A lady squealed.

I turned to see the identity of the lucky lady who had purchased a date with the first guy in line.

The brunette who'd won seemed thrilled.

I righted myself in my seat and focused again on Ryker, who was still looking at me.

"Well?" he mouthed.

I shook my head, hoping he would get the message that I was good. Actually, my nerves were singing for another reason. Someone was going to pay for a date with Ryker. Beverly was confident it would be her sister. But whether it was Tabitha or another woman, I wanted to puke as jealousy filled a spot inside me.

I'd forgotten why I'd even agreed to do the event. I really wished that I had stood my ground and not participated.

Thirty minutes and seven thousand dollars later, eight of the ten men had dates with some lucky women.

Next up was Lucas, and the room sizzled with excitement.

I swiveled in my seat to eye Vicki, who had her number-ten paddle ready to wave in the air. Yet if I recalled, she'd told me she didn't have the money to bid on Lucas.

"Let's start the bidding at three hundred," Sandra said loudly into the mic.

"Five hundred," Vicki yelled.

Maybe she'd found money or asked her parents.

"One thousand," a woman yelled.

"Fifteen hundred," a guy shouted.

Lucas's face paled.

Ryker smirked.

"Twenty-five hundred," another woman in the back said.

The room quieted.

I glanced at Vicki.

She shrugged, frowning.

"Last chance," Sandra said. "Okay, sold to number fifteen."

Lucas ambled past Ryker, said something in his ear, then made his way back to his seat in the front row.

The room went deathly silent as Ryker strutted up to the podium, all swagger and confidence.

I dug my nails into my palms.

He glanced at me with the biggest grin, silently saying, "No worries. I only want you." At least that was what I garnered from his expression.

"Here we go," Beverly said. "I can't wait to see the look on your face."

I rolled my eyes. "Why do you think I even care who gets Ryker?"

Her answer was a cocky shrug.

The women in the room went berserk. Some lady nearby tittered. "He's mine."

I actually laughed. The pheromones in the room were off the charts.

I gnawed on my lip as I watched Ryker, who had his gaze on me. I got the feeling he was trying to tell me he was sorry.

It was only one date and dinner and nothing else... I hoped.

"The bidding starts at five hundred dollars," Sandra said.

The ten women who were up next, including me, adjusted in their seats to see the audience.

I found eager eyes and panting smiles on many of the bidders.

The paddles were raised in the air with the bidding zipping up to one thousand dollars in a matter of seconds.

Then Tabitha hopped up from her seat four rows behind us, waving her paddle with the number one on it. "Two thousand dollars."

Another woman with shiny black hair waved her number eighteen. "Twenty-five hundred."

The bidding kept going around the room until the number was as high as four thousand dollars.

Ryker's eyebrows were in his hairline.

Really? I wanted to shout at him. As cocky as he was, he had to know he could get at least that much.

Then a macabre thought brightened my senses, and suddenly I wanted to puke, mainly from jealousy as well as the fact that I might not be able to keep a man like Ryker if those beautiful women, who were throwing out money like it was water, were keen to get their nails into the future NFL star. Maybe Beverly's taunts were not about her sister getting her hands on Ryker. Maybe she was referring to some other beautiful, rich lady who could handle a man like Ryker.

Tabitha raised her paddle. "Forty-five hundred."

The room fell silent, as did my heart. As much as I didn't want any woman going out on a date with Ryker, I sure as hell didn't want Tabitha to win the bid.

The other bidders sat down.

Beverly laughed. "It's for a good cause. You shouldn't look so pale, Haven."

Before I could fire a retort back at Beverly, a voice I knew well said, "Ten thousand dollars."

A collective intake of breath could be heard as the air was sucked out of the room and my lungs.

My gaze rounded to Vicki. She had her paddle in the air with her posture straight, exuding satisfaction and smugness.

I knew my look had to be crazed, shocked, and confused. I stole a look at Ryker. His gray eyes were almost popping out of their sockets.

I didn't know whether to be mad at my friend or if I should jump over the chair and kiss her. But anger was winning out. She had a thing for Ryker like every other woman in the ballroom and on the freaking planet for that matter.

"Bitch," Beverly mumbled.

I sought out Tabitha, who looked dejected as she pouted.

The only one smiling was Vicki. The confusion clouding my brain intensified. Where had she gotten the money? She'd said she didn't have any to even bid on Lucas.

"The lucky lady is number ten," Sandra said, closing the bid on Ryker.

I didn't get a chance to ask Vicki anything or even think before the women were shuffled up to the stage. I was first in line, and I felt like I was in a herd of cows being sent to slaughter. Okay, that was rather harsh and dramatic, but Vicki had just bought a dinner date with my guy.

I was usually a good read of people, but I'd missed the mark on my roommate—correction, ex-roommate.

I didn't hear my name called when Beverly pushed me. I almost stumbled but caught myself.

I growled at her. "Touch me again, and I will make you a bald woman."

Sandra said my name again. "Haven Hale."

As I walked up to Sandra at the podium, two men in black suits hurried up to the stage and snagged me. "Haven, you need to come with us."

Then I was being escorted out of the room by my father's men with no time to say anything to Ryker or anyone else.

RYKER

I bolted out of the stuffy room, which was filled with so many different scents that I had a headache standing on stage. But nothing made my head hurt more than to see Haven carted off like she was some sort of criminal.

I ran as though I were carrying the football down the field, fast and furious, until I was falling flat on my face. Dishes went flying, glasses shattered, and a man started swearing.

I scrambled to my feet, a little disoriented, to find a server picking up dishes that were strewn over the floor.

"I'm so sorry," I said. I should've helped him, but I couldn't lose sight of Haven.

But by the time I skidded to a stop in the lobby, I saw Haven getting into the back seat of a black Escalade with two security guards.

A low and lethal growl erupted from my chest.

I would guess the men were part of the senator's security staff. I would also guess that her old man wanted Haven out of the public eye given the news that had broken. He didn't like media attention, so I suspected he didn't want her to be run through the wringer with questions she could or couldn't answer. For once, I agreed with man.

Lucas huffed as he sidled up to me. "Man, what the fuck is happening?"

I laughed like a crazed man. "No clue. But I'm going to find out."

Vicki jogged up. "You guys need to see this." She flashed her phone in our faces.

Motherfucker!

Lucas's mouth hung open. "The senator is accused of bribery? Wow. When the shit hits the fan, it sure as hell hits hard."

Inside my head, I heard the screeching sound of brakes as the whole debacle with my father and what had happened with his company and the state water board surfaced.

Anger, fury, and rage had me fisting my hands.

Lucas rounded his gaze to me. "Do you think?"

"Fuck yeah, I think."

Vicki glanced at us like we had five heads.

Sorry, pretty lady. I had no time to get into specifics.

"I'm going to the senator's place," I said, trying to convince myself that was the right thing to do when I knew it wasn't, only because I was sure I would put my fist through the senator's nose.

"You probably should wait until you calm down," Lucas counseled.

"Why do I get the feeling you want to kill rather than check on Haven?" Vicki asked in a brittle tone. "Whatever it is that has you all twisted up inside, forget about that. If you have feelings for her, then do something, but don't make a scene. That's the last thing she needs. She's going through hell."

I felt like she'd just sucker-punched me.

"She's right," Lucas said. "The senator will get what's coming if the headline is true."

Maybe, but it sure would feel good to beat his ass.

If you did, then you would lose Haven even before you had the chance to tell her how you feel.

I doubted the senator would let me near her. But I was going to try like a motherfucker, though. I'd lost too many people in my life. I wasn't about to lose Haven.

I fished out my keys. "I'll check in with you later." The statement was more for Lucas than Vicki, although she and I had to set up a day and time for dinner since she had paid ten grand for my sorry ass.

I hoofed it to my car, sped out of the parking garage like I was transporting a bloody victim to the emergency room, and merged into traffic. Of course traffic on a Saturday in downtown Lakemont was hopping.

Groaning, I switched on the radio as I came to a stop at a red light.

The announcer's deep voice filled my car. "Senator Hale is losing steam in the polls. With the election around the corner, this late-breaking news is sure to ruin his reelection to the senate. Our sources tell us that the senator has been paying off state employees in an effort to swing decisions in his favor."

I gripped the steering wheel so hard, my knuckles turned white. I wasn't sure I wouldn't do something stupid when I saw the man.

My phone rang, shutting down the radio.

"Ryker, have you heard?" Franklin asked.

"Shit, yeah. I'm on my way to the senator's house now."

"As your lawyer and friend, I would advise against that. He'll get what's coming to him."

"You're sounding like Lucas now." The light turned green, and I pressed on the gas. "Do we know for sure if the Texas Water Conservation Board is what the news is referring to when they say state employees?"

"Not sure," Franklin replied. "I thought you were supposed to be at the fundraiser."

"I did my part. Now I have something else to do."

"Ryker, don't get involved."

"Too late, man."

"Your father wouldn't want you to ruin your football career."

I sighed heavily. "My dad would do the same thing."

"Maybe. But think before you act." Franklin's tone indicated he was seething and also worried.

"I'm headed there to check on Haven. Nothing more."

"Haven? The man doesn't want you anywhere near his daughter." Franklin was pleading with me.

I merged onto the highway. "Man, I promise I won't do anything stupid."

"You're in love with her. Aren't you?"

I hadn't talked to Franklin in a couple of weeks, although he had sent me a text last week to check on me. At that time, I'd let him know I was fine and busy with football. The only person who knew my true feelings for Haven was Lucas.

"It's time I tell her," I said.

He chuckled. "Nobody like you to make a grand entrance with a grand gesture."

I'd always pushed my way in whenever I wanted something, and I wanted Haven. Nothing, not even her old man, was going to stop me.

"I'll let you know how it goes. Or maybe you'll see me on the news."

"Or maybe I'll be bailing you out of jail."

"Good to know you have my back. Talk soon." I hit the end button and kicked my car into high gear.

After thirty-five minutes going at a speed of seventy-five to eighty miles per hour down the darkened freeway, dodging slow traffic, screaming and shouting at other drivers, and thinking of what would come out of my mouth when I spoke to Haven, I was parking behind a line of news trucks and reporters who had the road practically blocked.

The comment about me making the news might just happen. I pushed through the cameramen and reporters. Some were talking into the cameras, and others were talking on phones.

I was relieved the darkness kept me somewhat shrouded and the media was busy doing their jobs. I hurried up to the gate, where two security men were stationed. Both wore black suits and earpieces in their ears. They looked like carbon copies of each other with buzz cuts and mean expressions.

"I'm here to see the senator," I said to one of them.

"No visitors allowed," he responded.

"Tell the senator Ryker James is here. He'll see me." The senator would probably throw me to the wolves.

My gaze slid past the security guards to the lights twinkling from the house that sat about half a mile down the long driveway. Then I scanned the rest of the property as best I could, given the lack of light. I needed to have a backup plan in case I couldn't get past these two goons.

The security guy narrowed his beady eyes. "I said no visitors."

"Look, man, if you don't want me to start talking to the press"—I stabbed a thumb behind me—"then I suggest you make the call to the senator. I'm sure he'll let me in." Again, I was pulling at straws.

"Are you threatening me?" the security guard asked.

"No threats. Just make the fucking call." I tried to keep my voice low, but I didn't succeed.

A wiry guy with a mic ran up. "Did I hear you say your name is Ryker James?"

I rolled my eyes before addressing the guy. "Who's asking?"

The gate suddenly opened, and the security guard was shoving me in before the reporter could talk to me.

Smart man.

"Why does he get to go in?" the wiry reporter shouted.

"I'm going to rescue my girl," I volleyed back with ease, affection, and giddiness. Yep, it was official. I was in love.

The guard's partner escorted me down to the house, where two more beefy men stood watch outside the front door.

I felt as though I were in some type of political crime drama on TV and was about to be interrogated. But then the front door swung open, and I came face to face with the most beautiful girl in the world.

My heart went haywire, and I knew I had made the right decision to come there.

"It's okay, guys," Haven said in her angelic voice.

One of the guards shoved me in for good measure or to prove to me that he was a badass and would have my head if I messed up.

I snarled at him before entering the house. No sooner had I stepped inside than Haven had her arms around me. "What are you doing here?"

"Saving my girl."

She let go of me. "This isn't a good time."

I checked her from head to toe. No bruises. No signs that she'd been hurt. Every strand of hair was in place. Her big emerald eyes were clear. Above all else, her bewitching smile said she was happy to see me.

I mentally scratched my head. "I heard the news. Is your father here?"

She let out a small laugh. "Everyone's heard of my father's affair."

A tall blonde glided in, angling her head as her blue eyes appraised me. "You must be Ryker James. I'm Arlene Hale, the senator's wife." She pecked me on one cheek then the other. "As Haven said, this isn't a good time."

A small white dog wagged his tail as he trotted in and began sniffing my shoes and legs.

"This is Baxter," Haven said as though she hated the dog.

We hadn't had pets growing up. My dad had been allergic to cats and those dogs that had fur instead of hair. Still, Mom had decided no pets even though my brother and sister and I had hounded her many times to let us have a dog.

I ignored Baxter as he continued to look up at me with his tongue out. "I'm sorry, ma'am, for the intrusion. I saw how Haven was whisked away, and I was worried about her."

"You could've called her." Her tone had an edge.

If I hadn't been driving like a madman or if I'd been thinking clearly, I would've.

"I didn't have my phone on me," Haven said. "Glad you showed up."

Take that, Mrs. Hale.

Arlene's red lips curled at the edges, and it dawned on me that she didn't appear to be a woman scorned—no puffy eyes from crying, her makeup was in perfect condition, and she was as calm as the ocean on a windless day.

"It didn't matter. Phone or not, I had to see that Haven was okay with my own eyes."

"It's good to know that you're a gentleman and the rumors about you are not true, then," Arlene said.

Depends on the rumors.

"Arlene," Haven warned. "Can we have some privacy?"

Arlene picked up her dog. "Come on, Baxter." Then she wound her way around a massive staircase and faded from view.

Haven grabbed my hand. "Let's go out back."

The house was deadly silent as I followed Haven through the expansive rooms of the elegantly decorated home.

A chill danced down my spine. "Why isn't Arlene upset about your father's affair?" I asked as she led me out to a veranda that overlooked a lighted pool and outdoor kitchen.

A young, dark-haired lady came out. "Would you like something to drink, sir?"

"Roya, can you bring some lemonade?" Haven asked.

Roya nodded then left.

I would've asked for scotch, but given where I was and what liquor could do to my psyche, I would settle for lemonade.

After we commandeered two of the six chairs, Haven said, "Arlene knew. Besides, no matter what my father does, Arlene would never leave him. And she is all about keeping up appearances."

"My wife is a strong woman." Senator Hale strutted out, appearing as though he didn't have a care in the world. "Ryker James, what brings you out this way? Or I should ask what makes you barge into my home?" His condescending tone lit a fire inside me.

"Daddy," Haven said. "He's my guest. And we talked about Ryker and me."

I was curious how that conversation had gone and what he knew about Haven and me. But I had a nagging topic to get off my chest now that Senator Hale was looming over me.

I rose from my chair. I wanted to be at eye level when he and I exchanged words. "An apology would be a good place to start." I kept my tone even.

The senator tucked his hands into his suit pockets. "An apology for what?" His green eyes resembled Haven's, but the one emotion missing was compassion. Then again, I didn't expect him to have any for me.

"Is it true you bribed state workers?"

He smirked. "I'm not on trial here. And I highly suggest, as my guest, you tread lightly, son."

Haven might throw me out, but I pushed on. I had to get to the bottom of this once and for all. "You paid off an employee at the Texas Water Development Board to ensure that he would take his time in handling my father's case with James Enterprises."

"Daddy, is that true? This is what Lorna has on you? This is what you wouldn't tell me? This is why you had your men pull me out of the fundraiser?"

I kept my focus glued to the senator as I spoke to Haven. "You haven't heard? It's all over the news about your father bribing state employees."

Haven jumped to her feet. "Father, talk."

Arlene must've been eavesdropping nearby because she rushed out like she was about to save her man. She hooked her arm around her husband's. "Eugene, have a seat. It's time you tell Haven everything."

The senator sighed and found a seat, as did Arlene. I dragged my chair closer to Haven's. I had a feeling I would need that mojo-calming juice she seemed to have.

36

HAVEN

R oya brought out the tray of lemonade, and I couldn't pour a glass fast enough to cool the burn in the back of my throat or the quench the acid that was settling in my stomach.

I didn't know what was worse, the affair or bribery. I stared at my father, who was giving me the vibe that he wasn't worried. In a span of hours, two bombs had dropped on this family, two bombs that I was sure would do damage, at least to his career.

The media would hound me for a while, but as with any rumors, the next one to surface would erase the one before it. I just prayed that the next media frenzy wasn't about my father.

I eyed my dad over the rim of my glass, sweat beading on my neck. "Is there anything else we should know about?"

"No." His tone was as hard as his features.

So that was what Beverly had meant when she'd said, "I can't wait until you hear what else we have in store."

My skin sizzled with fury at my father, the Sims women, and even Arlene, who sat there as though bribery and an affair were no big thing.

"Bribery will ruin your political career," I said. Or it might get him thrown in jail.

Ryker was surprisingly quiet as he watched my father like a hawk. The calm before the storm, I imagined. Maybe that was the reason my father hadn't said a word yet.

I swallowed thickly before taking another sip of the tart beverage, thinking back to the conversation Ryker and I had had at his family's funeral service.

"My old man's company lost millions of dollars, employees, and customers, all because your father stuck his nose where it didn't belong."

I'd dismissed the accusation as nothing more than my father doing his job and developing policies that bettered the state of Texas.

Arlene clutched Father's hand, standing by her man. *Bravo, lady. Bravo. Do you know that he might be in prison next month?*

"Talk, Daddy. Start at the top and with the truth." I swore if the man didn't speak, I would throw the pitcher of lemonade at him.

Ryker's big hands, which knew their way around my body and knew just the right spots to touch, were anchored to the arms of his chair as though he were preparing for a rocket launch into space.

I set down my glass and covered his hand with mine.

He visibly relaxed.

"The bribery accusations are not true," Father began. Then he considered Ryker. "We can't keep contaminating our lakes, rivers, and streams. I get that there are accidents and equipment can break, but believe it or not, we've had some oversight in the system where companies were given the go-ahead to operate only to find that they hadn't been ready. My advice to the man who heads the Texas Water Conservation Board was to take their time when evaluating a case, especially when a company violates the discharge permit."

Arlene poured Father a lemonade.

He brought the glass to his mouth, his gaze never wavering from Ryker's. "I'm not sorry that I want to better this state. I'm not sorry that I want to protect the environment. I'm not sorry that we need to make sure cases, whatever they may be, are handled in the proper manner." I could hear the sincerity in his voice.

Ryker slouched his shoulders and lost the tick in his jaw.

Father took a swig of lemonade. "There was no bribery on my part. Nothing more than counsel."

I cocked my head. "Then why would someone leak that to the press? Is this what Lorna had on you? If so, I'm confused. You seemed worried when we talked the other night."

My father adjusted his body in his chair. "I was because I don't need a lie in the press. Whether rumors are true or not, news like this ruins people and their careers."

"Why should we believe you?" Ryker asked.

Creases lined Father's freckled forehead. "I don't have to prove anything to you."

"Then prove it to me, Daddy. And why would Lorna put her family through something like this? Surely their plot wasn't just about getting me away from Ryker."

Arlene cleared her throat. "Your father has been giving Lorna money to keep her mouth shut about the affair. It just so happens that she overheard a conversation your father had with the head of the Texas Water Conservation Board. He told them if money was an issue, he would see what he could do to increase the budget for overtime to make sure that cases weren't rushed and mistakes weren't made."

"So Lorna took that as bribery," Ryker said.

"Lorna is mad because my husband will not give her what she wants, and that's to leave me for her. So she'll do whatever it takes, even lying. She even went as far as making sure Haven didn't get near you."

Well, that didn't work out too well. "Daddy, you didn't hire her daughters to spy on me?"

"Not at all," Father said. "Look, Haven, I will atone for my affair. But the facts will show I am innocent of the bribery charge."

"So explain to me why you hate me, then," Ryker said. "Why you threatened my football career? Why you don't want me anywhere near your daughter?"

"You're not good enough for her," Father said as a matter of fact. "If you have a daughter one day, you might understand."

"That's not your decision," Ryker said through clenched teeth. "You can keep trying to push me away or use your political status to scare me, but I'm not going anywhere. I might not like you, but I love Haven. And I'll do whatever it takes to make sure no one, and I mean no one, stands in my way."

I choked as my eyes bugged out. "You love me?"

Ryker turned his head slowly, and any signs of anger were replaced with a ginormous smile. He lifted my hand to his lips. "I came here tonight to tell you how I feel. I've never been in love with anyone but you. You have a way of stealing the breath right from my lungs. You have a way of making me see that a future is possible." His warm lips touched my hand, making me tingle. "I'm nuts about you."

Tears rushed out. My throat closed up. My hands were shaking, and my heart was beating so fast, I thought I would pass out. I wasn't sure I could speak. I checked on Father and Arlene but mainly my father. He had his head cocked to one side, dumbfounded. Arlene, on the other hand, was smiling.

Ryker flashed his sultry gray eyes as he continued to keep his lips glued to my hand. I suspected he wasn't letting me go until I said something. I did love him. I did believe he was the man I would marry someday. But I worried whether our relationship could thrive with my father in our lives or the hatred they had for one another.

My eyes drifted to my father again.

"Baby doll," Ryker said in a husky voice, "we don't need your father's approval. If you love me, that's all that matters."

My father knew how I felt about Ryker. But I did want his approval. I did want him to accept Ryker into this family. Ryker's love for me said that he would tolerate my father. But was my father's love for his daughter strong enough to accept Ryker?

Father pushed to his feet and came around until he was standing over me. Then he kissed me on the head. "You have my approval, Haven. I want you to be happy. That's all I ever wanted for you."

I jumped up and hugged the man I remembered from before my mom died. "I love you, Daddy."

He squeezed me to him. "I love you, little one. Always have."

Tears dripped down my cheeks, relishing those three words I'd been waiting for so long.

My father eased away and extended his hand to Ryker, who rose to the occasion.

Father gripped Ryker's hand. "If you so much as treat her badly or break her heart, I won't hesitate to ruin you. Are we clear?"

"Crystal, sir." Ryker's gaze tangled with mine. "I promise you that I will love her, protect her, and cherish her."

I beamed as my stomach fluttered with love, pride, and happiness.

Father released Ryker's hand. "I have to prepare a speech for the press. I suggest both of you lay low for the next couple of days."

Arlene joined us, grasping my father's arm. "I'm happy for the two of you." Her smile seemed genuine, but hurt swam underneath the fake mask she was trying to wear, and it wasn't directed at Ryker and me but at what my father was about to go through and, I would guess, the affair.

I'd always known she was a strong woman, but even the strongest person had to break. As much as Arlene and I didn't get along, I hated that she had to put up with the turmoil my father had created. Sure, she'd known what she was marrying into as the wife of a senator, but cheating wasn't one of them.

Out of nowhere, I hugged her. She stiffened for a second then returned the gesture. We'd had enough hate in this family to last a lifetime. If my father could accept Ryker, it was about time I did the same with Arlene.

"I'm sorry," I said. "For being a bitch to you all these years." I couldn't and wouldn't apologize for my father's actions. That was something he had to do.

"I'm sorry too. A new start?"

I let go of her. "Absolutely."

Father kissed me on the head again. "We'll get through this." Then they excused themselves, leaving Ryker and me standing on the veranda, watching them walk away, hand in hand.

Ryker scooped me up and into his arms then carried me out to a lounge chair by the lighted pool. He went to set me down but wobbled, almost falling into the pool water.

I slid down his hard body, clutching onto him, saving him and me from getting soaking wet. "Are you sure you're *the* Ryker James, playboy, the guy that sleeps around?" I teased.

He burrowed his hands in my hair. "I traded that guy in."

I giggled. "I might love you too."

"Might?"

I gave him a shy look. "I am hopelessly in love with a quarterback."

His eyes darkened, filling up with love and devotion. "And I'm head over heels in love with a senator's daughter."

"But we're oil and water," I said playfully.

"That's perfect," he said. "Because we'll always be trying to mix." He waggled his eyebrows.

As corny as that line was, it was perfect. I didn't want a guy who believed in everything I did or a guy who didn't have a mind of his own. We were both headstrong. We were both determined. Above all else, we loved each other, and that trumped everything.

37

RYKER

I'd been on cloud nine for the last week since I opened my heart to Haven. I was officially off the market, and the university paper made sure every chick on campus knew that too. I didn't care who knew how much I loved Haven Hale. I didn't care that women were devastated over the news.

Lucas and the guys on the team laughed at the way ladies were so distraught, but on the flip side, the guys were stoked for me and for them.

"More women for us," Erik had said.

I only wanted one woman, and I was dying to see her. The week had been riddled with classes and practice and then our away game. But seeing Haven would have to wait.

I nursed a drink at the bar, which stretched the length of the back wall and overlooked the patrons dining at the expensive French establishment, La Provence.

The restaurant was buzzing with chatter, the clinking of utensils hitting plates, and servers rushing around tables.

Vicki had picked the ritzy, elegant, and expensive spot.

"Go big or go home" seemed to be her motto.

The woman had paid ten grand for my ass. Haven had been scratching her head as to how Vicki could've afforded a donation that size, but I didn't bat an eye. Women who were desperate found a way to get what they wanted.

I'd wanted to cancel, but the charity would lose the donation, and I couldn't let that happen. Plus, Haven had encouraged me to stick to the plan. I'd found it odd that she hadn't been angry with her roomie for buying a date with me.

"It's for a good cause," Haven had said.

My phone danced on the wooden bar top next to the scotch I'd barely touched.

I grinned when I saw Haven's name.

Haven: *Is Vicki there yet?*

Me: *No. Maybe you should switch places with her.*

Haven: *I wish, but she paid for your handsome mug.*

Me: *I still can't believe you're taking this in stride.*

At first, Haven had been a little miffed at Vicki for paying an exorbitant amount of money for a man Vicki knew Haven liked. Not only that, I'd learned that Vicki had a soft spot for Lucas.

When I'd approached Lucas, he hadn't thought it was a big deal that Vicki had obtained such a large amount of money to donate to charity.

"But she likes you," I'd said. "And I saw how you looked at her at the fundraiser. You like her."

He'd ignored my last comment and said, "Man, she bid on me but didn't win."

"Dude, she had ten grand to use on you, but she saved it for me," I'd argued.

"Really, Ryker," he'd said. "Are you really trying to figure out why women do what they do? Since when?"

He had a point. So there I was, waiting to get the date with Vicki over with so I could go see my girl. My dick jumped in my suit pants just thinking about what I was going to do to Haven when I got her naked.

But thoughts, erections, love, and anything else that was on my mind completely evaporated when a blonde slid onto the stool next me, and it wasn't just any blonde.

"Ryker, how are you?" Beverly Sims asked.

Where the fuck did she come from? "Are you following me?" My gaze darted around, hoping her sister wasn't anywhere in the vicinity.

Thank fuck I didn't see her. She was crazier than Beverly.

She pursed her red lips. "I'm here with a date." She stabbed a red nail at a table near the long windows on the other side of the restaurant. A dark-haired man sitting by himself waved at us.

I guess she wasn't lying. "What do you want?" I asked.

She toyed with a lone coaster. "I wanted to say I'm sorry."

"Shouldn't you be saying that to Haven?"

"I will." I heard a hint of regret in her voice.

But I wasn't jumping on the "I believed her" train. When she actually apologized to Haven, then I would believe her.

"Why force someone into liking you?" I asked. "You're pretty. You seem to have it together. So why me?"

She pushed out her shoulders. "I like you. My sister loves you. We thought one of us could snag you."

I narrowed my eyes. "You and your sister need help."

She slid off the chair. "You don't have to worry about us. We're moving to California when the semester is over. By the way, where is Haven? Oh, wait. You're here on that fundraising date. Aren't you?"

"Is that the dude that paid for you?" I asked.

"Yes. He's a nice guy. Good luck." Then she wound her way back to her date.

I was about to gulp down my scotch when I spotted Vicki pointing me out to the hostess. She glided over, wearing shorts and a T-shirt— certainly not proper attire for the sixty-dollar-a-plate restaurant.

"Hi," she said. "Sorry I'm late."

I hadn't been looking at the time. I'd been wallowing in sorrow that Haven wasn't my date, but Vicki didn't need to know that. Still, I blatantly swept my gaze over her. "Did you not realize this is a ritzy place?"

She checked herself out. "Oh, yeah. Um…"

The bartender came over. "Miss, would you like a drink?"

Vicki regarded the gray-haired man. "I'm not staying."

I could feel my forehead wrinkling. "What?"

She schooled her features. "Ryker James, I am one girl who is not interested in you. But I know someone who is."

My jaw bounced off the top of the bar when someone tapped me on the shoulder from behind.

I spun in my chair and lost my fucking breath. The greenest eyes on the planet beamed at me. My heart thumped, thudded, and thrashed.

Follow the yellow brick road.

Haven awarded me with a smile that had my cock reacting, my mouth watering, and my heart beating out of my chest.

Never in my life had I felt so emotional over one person before. Her presence did crazy things to my head, my body, and my soul. I wasn't a dramatic guy, but fuck. She was the moon, the stars, the sun, and the whole damn planet.

My hands shook as I reached out to touch her just to be sure she was there. "I didn't see you come in."

"We had her come in through the kitchen," Lucas said.

Lucas?

I whipped my head to the right to find Lucas standing beside Vicki.

"Close your mouth, dude. You're drooling."

I had every right to drool at my girl as I shaped her waist then brought her closer to me. "Hey, dollface."

She drank me in, sucked me in, and pulled me in with her aura. "Hey, big guy."

I had no idea what was happening, but I wasn't complaining. "Are you crashing my date? You know I have to do this for charity."

Haven's tongue darted out to wet her lips. "I am your date."

"I don't understand."

Vicki snickered. "I bid on you to make sure Tabitha didn't win."

Hell yeah.

"My father asked Vicki to make sure she could win whatever the cost," Haven said.

I checked on my best bud. "You knew about this?"

Lucas gave me a cheeky grin. "I was all in."

"So let me get this straight," I said. "The man who hates me asked Vicki to win the bid for me so that Tabitha wouldn't win?"

"That's about right," Lucas replied, keeping the damn smirk front and center. "It was a perfect plan. And here we are."

"Senator Hale paid the ten grand?" I was still trying to shake off the shock. I mean, he'd set up his plan even before I had declared my love for Haven.

"Technically, you should be on a date with my dad," Haven teased.

Teasing or not, Eugene Hale and I would probably kill each other. Still, I had a little more respect for the man now.

"In total, we blew out our goal of twenty grand," Lucas said. "Sandra is pleased. She wants to do the event next season. Not you, of course." He was quick to add that last sentence.

Who knew what next year would bring, though? Sure, I was off the market, and Haven was the only girl for me. But Lucas could be tied at the hip to some woman, and so could the others on the football team. But it was premature to think that far ahead.

I leaned in to give Haven a kiss when Vicki gasped.

"What is she doing here?" Vicki asked in disgust.

Haven visibly tensed when she saw Beverly.

Beverly raised her hands. "Don't make a scene."

It wasn't Haven she had to worry about but a feisty Vicki, who slid in between her friend and Beverly. "I suggest you leave."

"I wanted to say something. Then you'll never see me again," Beverly said.

Haven nudged Vicki, who moved out of the way.

Beverly addressed Haven. "I just wanted to apologize for every-thing. I can't help what my mom has done, but my intentions were never to bring you into our mess. My sister was the one who took the picture that night of you on Ryker's lap. She sent it to my mom, who decided to use the pic to squeeze a little more out of your father and to make sure you didn't ruin our plan to get Ryker. It was either Tabitha or me. We didn't care which one of us succeeded in snaring Ryker, but when I started to see how he looked at you, I knew we didn't stand a chance. I can't say the same for Tabitha. She was going to do whatever she could to get you out of the picture." Beverly sighed. "Tabitha went to the press about the affair."

"Pathetic," Vicki said under her breath.

"And the bribery charge?" Haven asked.

The senator had been doing his best to clean up the shit storm. He'd come clean about the affair, and the head of the Texas Water Conservation Board had stepped up and made a statement confirming what Haven's father had told us—there had been no bribery on the senator's part.

Beverly puffed out her cheeks. "My mom twisted the truth. She was angry with your father and wanted to make him pay."

Beverly's date sidled up to her, wrapping his arm around her waist. "We should go." The man, who I would guess to be in his late twenties, flashed a perfectly white smile at us.

Meanwhile, Vicki and Haven were ready to attack Beverly.

"You should go," I parroted.

We didn't need to rehash what had happened.

Beverly sighed as her date quickly guided her toward the exit.

Smart man.

Haven let out a soft growl. "Unbelievable. I hope I never see her or her sister or her mother again."

I explained to them the conversation I'd had with Beverly before they'd shown up and that the family was moving to California. The Sims sisters, politics, and Haven's old man were quickly forgotten, especially when Lucas and Vicki finally left us alone.

I buried my nose in Haven's neck, inhaling her lilac scent that drove me batshit crazy. "So what would you like to do on our date?"

She placed her lips on my ear. "Taste you."

Fuck.

I didn't hesitate to pay my bar tab.

38

HAVEN

The pool water was tepid but refreshing, especially after hearing Beverly's admission at the restaurant earlier that night. I prayed I didn't see her or anyone in her family ever again.

My father had the same wish, as did Arlene. He had been battling the press day in and day out. But no matter how much he explained himself, I didn't think he was going to get reelected. His low standings in the polls had more to do with his opponent's policies than my father's indiscretions.

I ducked under then came up, swiping my hand over my face and hair.

Ryker strutted out of his parents' house with nothing but a towel wrapped around his waist, carrying a shoebox.

I angled my head as I rested my arms on the edge of the pool and my chin on my hands, admiring the man I loved. His abs were chiseled, that V of his was mouthwatering, and every part of him was perfect. And he was all mine.

"What's that?" I vaguely remembered a shoebox in his bedroom at his campus house the night we'd had sex for the first time.

He sat down on the edge of a lounge chair across from me. "This is

Leigh's, her things that Principal Holland gave me." He sighed. "I've been meaning to look at one thing that's inside. Truth be told, I've been afraid to."

"Wasn't that box at your other house?"

He took off the cover. "After Tabitha dove into it then her sister got nosy, I decided to bring it here. It belongs in Leigh's room anyway." He removed an envelope and stared at it.

I climbed out of the pool, squeezing the water out of my hair. Then I grabbed a towel from a chair, wrapped it around my naked body, and went over to him.

He handed me what felt like a card. "You open it."

I gave it back to him. "This is something you have to do. It's addressed to you."

With shaky fingers, he pulled out the card then read silently.

I stood over him, waiting for him to react or say something, but all he did was set the card down, throw off his towel, and dive into the pool. He stayed under the water a little too long in my book.

Whatever was on that card had to be heavy. I couldn't help but read it.

Happy Birthday to the hero in my life. You've always been there for me, and I want you to know I'm always here for you. My wish is for you to find that special girl by your next birthday. With all my love, Leigh.

Ryker finally surfaced, shaking the water off his head, then strutted out of the pool, naked, determined, and somewhat angered.

He swaggered up, his dick semi-hard, plucked the card from me, placed it on the table, then lifted me in his arms.

"When was your birthday?" My boobs bounced freely as he carried me into the house.

I thought we were going to his bedroom. Instead, I found myself on the cool leather couch in the family room. Once Ryker was seated beside me, I straddled him.

His hands cupped my breasts as his erection grew between us. His eyes brewed with love, lust, and something else I couldn't quite figure out.

His chest was rising and falling, but his concentration was far away.

I started to probe him again, but I decided to let him work through whatever was bothering him. So I let him have his way with me as he brushed a thumb over my lip then dragged a finger down my neck until he was pinching one nipple then the other.

I sucked in a breath as I rocked my hips, wanting that blissful friction of his dick against my clit.

He tunneled his fingers into my wet hair, pulling me in until our lips were locked. His kiss was possessive, brutal in his delivery, yet soft in his execution. He tasted, took, moaned, and groaned like he needed me more than he needed anything ever in his life.

Emotion clogged my throat. I was so in love, I swore it was hard to breathe at times. I rocked faster against him, lust twisting low in my belly, love swirling around my heart. The mixture was explosive as I gripped the velvet flesh of his dick and guided him inside me.

I groaned loudly, as did he, not moving but watching him watch me. The look on his face was intense, raw, powerful, and blissfully painful. I'd never experienced such emotion before, not with anyone ever.

Tears filled his eyes. "I've found love." His voice was raspy. "Leigh and my mom would be so fucking happy right now. But Leigh was wrong about one thing. Love doesn't tame the beast inside me. It only makes him wild and hungry."

I didn't know if I should be scared or not, but his next move was all beast. He picked me up, and before I could process anything, we were on the floor in front of the fireplace, rolling around, me on top of him, him on top of me, kissing, nipping, sucking, and ending in our original position from the very first time.

"That's it, baby. Suck me hard."

"I love it when you talk dirty," I barely said as I licked the tip of his cock before taking in all of him.

He flattened his tongue against my clit and licked and lapped until I was writhing. My body splintered as the orgasm surged, swirled, and consumed me until I was screaming his name.

He sucked hard one last time before adjusting himself and driving into me before I had a chance to take a breath.

He pumped hard and fast, making my breasts bounce. He crashed his mouth against mine. "I love you, Haven Hale. I fucking love you."

I wrapped my legs around his waist as he grabbed my ass with one hand and anchored the other on the floor. He thrust into me once then twice before his eyes were rolling back in his head.

"You feel so fucking good."

I squeezed around him, holding him in my grasp as I watched him ride out his release.

Beautiful was the only way to describe him. Under all that cocksure bravado and coolness lay a man who had more compassion and love in his heart than any other man I knew, and he was mine.

EPILOGUE

RYKER

Seven weeks had passed since I'd read that card from Leigh. I'd been ready to bawl my eyes out that night, but instead, I'd turned my attention to Haven and made love to her at least five times that night. Since then, we'd been inseparable. In fact, we were now living together at my parents' house.

At first, her old man hadn't been stoked about the idea, but Haven had convinced him that by living off campus, she would have more privacy and hence less media around or gossipy women in the dorm. Vicki was bummed, but she understood.

I sauntered into the kitchen to find Lucas popping a bottle of champagne. "The house is packed."

The party was in full swing.

Coach Chapman was talking to Haven's father. Yep, the man had accepted our invitation to join our celebration. We'd won our bowl game the week before. The season had been tense, but the team had given two hundred percent to get us into the bowl game. Senator Hale was just as stoked as Coach was. After all, Eugene Hale had donated quite a bit of money to the university. More than that, he and I had warmed up to each other. We weren't close or anything, but it was nice that Haven and her dad weren't fighting and that he and I weren't tearing off each other's heads.

Speaking of the senator, he'd lost the election back in November. The preliminary polls had attested to the senator's decline with voters long before his indiscretions became public, but election day had ended with the senator and his opponent in a close race. The fresh ideas and policies that his opponent had campaigned on had won out in the end. Although I would guess the senator's mistakes had played a role as well.

Lucas poured champagne in those fancy flute glasses. "We've come a long way since…" He stopped pouring. "Never mind."

I stood across the island from him. "Say it. I'm not going to go apeshit."

He regarded me with sad brown eyes. "That's okay. You don't need to be reminded."

"Dude, I think about them every day, and it hurts like hell. But one of the reasons I moved back home was so I could feel close to them. Living here with all the memories is helping." The house I'd grown up in gave me peace and comfort, and it also helped that Haven was by my side.

"I know they're looking down and are proud," Lucas said.

Haven sashayed into the kitchen, wearing a tight dress that hugged and accentuated her fantastic bod, which I was sad to see covered.

She kissed me on the cheek. "There's the birthday boy."

That gave me another reason to party. Haven had wanted to do something special long before now, but I'd said no. I'd felt weird since my family wasn't around anymore. Mom had always made a big deal about birthdays, and honestly, after reading Leigh's card, I just couldn't bring myself to be happy about turning twenty-two.

But when Lucas and I had decided to throw a party to celebrate our bowl championship, Haven thought it would be good to at least have a cake. I could do a cake. I just didn't want a birthday to overshadow our huge win.

I had my fingers on a glass when Franklin waltzed in, looking relaxed in jeans and a buttoned-up shirt, a stark contrast to his expensive lawyer suits. On his arm was my aunt Kari, who was prettier than I remembered. Maybe Franklin had something to do with her glow or rosy cheeks. Regardless, her dark hair was pulled up in a messy bun, and her gray eyes were clear and bright—a big difference from when she'd been in town for the funeral.

Franklin and I exchanged a hug before I wrapped my aunt Kari in my arms. "I'm so happy you guys are here."

Aunt Kari kissed me then started talking to Haven as both moseyed over to the dining room table, which held tons of food.

Franklin poured himself some scotch. "Take a walk with me." He sounded serious, like something bad had happened.

We found a quiet spot out back on the other side of the pool, away from my guests who were hanging out on the patio.

"What's going on?"

He regarded me with panic in his dark eyes. "I'm getting married to your aunt."

A heavy sigh jetted from me. "Man, I thought you had bad news. Congrats. But why do you look pale?"

"I guess I've been nervous to tell you. She's your family, and I didn't know how you would take it."

I clapped him on the back. "I'm excited for you and her. My mom would be too, man."

Franklin finally smiled, releasing any tension he'd had when he came in. "You're right. Kari said the same thing. So will you be my best man?"

"Fuck yeah."

It seemed as though we were moving on with our lives, and while we needed to, my heart still hurt, although it wasn't as painful as time went on.

"What about you?" Franklin asked, sipping his scotch. "Do you plan on popping the question?"

"One day at a time, man. There are days my motto is 'one hour at a time.' But there is no doubt that Haven and I will marry. Probably when she graduates." She was only a freshman. I was a junior. We both had to finish college.

Franklin flicked his head at my girl, who was walking toward us. "She's a great lady, and she loves you."

Haven snuggled up to me. "I hear congrats are in order, Franklin." Her voice was light and happy.

"Thank you," Franklin said. "I should go find my bride-to-be." He headed into the house.

I lifted Haven's left hand up to my lips. "You will be my bride one day."

She snickered. "I know. But I'm in no rush. I'm yours forever, Ryker James, with or without a piece of paper that says we're married."

I briefly looked up at the dark sky, thanking my guardian angel for bringing Haven and me together. I believed my mom and Leigh had had something to do with guiding my fate, and for that, the hole in my heart closed a little bit more.

I would never get over losing them, but with Haven at my side, I knew without a doubt that I was going to be okay.

———

Thank you for reading and reviewing **Unforgettable**. There's more books coming in this sports romance world.

In the meantime, if you would like more sports romance check out **Crazy for You** here or you can type the following URL in your browser: https://books2read.com/crazyforyouskyler

ABOUT THE AUTHOR

Bestselling author **S.B. Alexander** is an independent author with over 30 titles to date. She writes paranormal, new adult, and sweet romances that feature hot heroes stealing hearts.

S.B. or Susan as she likes to be called is a navy veteran, former high school teacher, and former corporate sales executive. She's a lover of sports, especially baseball, although nowadays you can find her on the golf course, swinging for that hole-in-one.

Her motto: "Life is too short to waste. So live every moment like it's your last."

You can connect with S.B. Alexander in the following ways:
Reader Group: http://sbalexander.com/sbareaderroom
Author Book Store: https://sbalexanderbooks.com
Author Website: https://sbalexander.com
Newsletter: https://sbalexander.com/newsletter
Email: susan@sbalexander.com

facebook.com/sbalexander.authorpage
x.com/sbalex_author
instagram.com/sbalexanderauthor
bookbub.com/authors/s-b-alexander
pinterest.com/sbalexander0046
tiktok.com/@susanbalexander